PRAISE FOR DENISE HUNTER

"A poignant romance that's perfect for fans of emotional love stories that capture your heart from the very first page. With her signature style, Denise Hunter whisks readers into a world where broken hearts are mended, lives are changed, and love really does conquer all!"

—NEW YORK TIMES BESTSELLING AUTHOR
COURTNEY WALSH, ON *MULBERRY HOLLOW*

"Hunter delivers a touching story of how family dynamics and personal priorities shift when love takes precedence. Hunter's fans will love this."

—PUBLISHERS WEEKLY ON *RIVERBEND GAP*

"Denise Hunter has never failed to pen a novel that whispers messages of hope and brings a smile to my face. *Bookshop by the Sea* is no different! With a warmhearted community, a small beachside town, a second-chance romance worth rooting for, and cozy bookshop vibes, this is a story you'll want to snuggle into like a warm blanket."

—MELISSA FERGUSON, AUTHOR OF *THE CUL-DE-SAC WAR*

"Sophie and Aiden had me hooked from page one, and I was holding my breath until the very end. Denise nails second-chance romance in *Bookshop by the Sea*. I adored this story! Five giant stars!"

—JENNY HALE, *USA TODAY* BESTSELLING AUTHOR

"*Autumn Skies* is the perfect roundup to the Bluebell Inn series. The tension and attraction between Grace and Wyatt is done so well, and the mystery kept me wondering what was going to happen next. Prepare to be swept away to the beautiful Blue Ridge Mountains in a flurry of turning pages."

—NANCY NAIGLE, *USA TODAY* BESTSELLING
AUTHOR OF *CHRISTMAS ANGELS*

"*Sweetbriar Cottage* is a wonderful story, full of emotional tension and evocative prose. You'll feel involved in these characters' lives and carried along by their story as tension ratchets up to a climactic and satisfying conclusion. Terrific read. I thoroughly enjoyed it."

 —FRANCINE RIVERS, *NEW YORK TIMES* BESTSELLING AUTHOR

"*Falling Like Snowflakes* is charming and fun with a twist of mystery and intrigue. A story that's sure to endure as a classic reader favorite."

 —RACHEL HAUCK, *NEW YORK TIMES* BESTSELLING AUTHOR OF *THE FIFTH AVENUE STORY SOCIETY*

"*Barefoot Summer* is a satisfying tale of hope, healing, and a love that's meant to be."

 —LISA WINGATE, #1 *NEW YORK TIMES* BESTSELLING AUTHOR OF *BEFORE WE WERE YOURS*

MULBERRY

Hollow

ALSO BY DENISE HUNTER

The Riverbend Romance Novels
Riverbend Gap
Mulberry Hollow
Harvest Moon (available
September 2022)

The Bluebell Inn Novels
Lake Season
Carolina Breeze
Autumn Skies

The Blue Ridge Novels
Blue Ridge Sunrise
Honeysuckle Dreams
On Magnolia Lane

The Summer Harbor Novels
Falling Like Snowflakes
The Goodbye Bride
Just a Kiss

**The Chapel Springs
Romance Series**
Barefoot Summer
A December Bride (novella)

Dancing with Fireflies
The Wishing Season
Married 'til Monday

The Big Sky Romance Series
A Cowboy's Touch
The Accidental Bride
The Trouble with Cowboys

Nantucket Love Stories
Surrender Bay
The Convenient Groom
Seaside Letters
Driftwood Lane

Stand-Alone Novels
Bookshop by the Sea
Summer by the Tides
Sweetbriar Cottage
Sweetwater Gap

Novellas included in
This Time Around, *Smitten,*
Secretly Smitten, and
Smitten Book Club

MULBERRY
Hollow

A RIVERBEND ROMANCE

DENISE HUNTER

THOMAS NELSON
Since 1798

Mulberry Hollow

Published in Nashville, Tennessee, by Thomas Nelson. Thomas Nelson is a
registered trademark of HarperCollins Christian Publishing, Inc.

Thomas Nelson titles may be purchased in bulk for educational, business,
fundraising, or sales promotional use. For information, please email
SpecialMarkets@ThomasNelson.com.

Publisher's Note: This novel is a work of fiction. Names, characters, places, and
incidents are either products of the author's imagination or used fictitiously.
All characters are fictional, and any similarity to people living or dead is purely
coincidental.

Library of Congress Cataloging-in-Publication Data

Names: Hunter, Denise, 1968- author.
Title: Mulberry Hollow / Denise Hunter.
Description: Nashville, Tennessee : Thomas Nelson, [2022] | Series: A
Riverbend romance ; [2] | Summary: "From the bestselling author of The
Convenient Groom (now a beloved Hallmark Original movie) comes the
second romance in her latest series!"-- Provided by publisher.
Identifiers: LCCN 2021051562 (print) | LCCN 2021051563 (ebook) | ISBN
9780785240532 (trade paper) | ISBN 9780785240549 (epub) | ISBN
9780785240556 (downloadable audio)
Subjects: LCGFT: Novels.
Classification: LCC PS3608.U5925 M85 2022 (print) | LCC PS3608.U5925
(ebook) | DDC 813/.6--dc23/eng/20211021
LC record available at https://lccn.loc.gov/2021051562
LC ebook record available at https://lccn.loc.gov/2021051563

Printed in the United States of America
22 23 24 25 26   LSC   10 9 8 7 6 5 4 3 2 1

One

Two glaring realizations flashed through Wes Garrett's mind as he blinked against the morning sunlight: he was alone in the camping shelter, and he was soaked to the skin. A few other insights struck—his head throbbed, his muscles ached, and despite the July heat, chills racked his body.

He groaned and rolled over, pushing off the sleeping bag. He labored to draw a full breath. He should just go back to sleep. Why was this happening now, with only a couple of weeks of his two-month hike remaining?

He thought of Lillian, awaiting him in Albany, New York. Thought of his best friend Landon and their plan to complete the Appalachian Trail after their return to the US. Thought of Landon's last moments before he died in the Colombian dirt—in Wes's place.

So could he lie here in the shelter and give in to the oblivion of sleep? No. He would push through for his friend. He'd overcome much worse than this.

Resolved, he sat up, the floorboards of the raised shelter creaking beneath him. His head spun from the motion, and he blinked against the salty sting of sweat in his eyes, recalling the coughing man he'd slept next to a few nights ago. *Thanks a lot, buddy.*

The sunlight glinted through the trees in the clearing. Had to be going on ten at least. He hadn't once slept past six on the trail. The three hikers he'd shared the shelter with were long gone, the only evidence of their existence a ghostly curl of smoke rising from the firepit.

He was on his own.

He swallowed against a dry, sore throat and reached for his water. He had to get moving. He'd feel better once he had some food and coffee in his system. He'd make it at least as far as the next town, then reassess. Thoughts of a shower, a real mattress, and a home-cooked meal pushed him to his feet.

But twenty minutes later all his optimism faded and grim reality settled in. Getting dressed and fed had bled him of his energy, and Riverbend Gap was still fourteen rigorous miles away.

———

Avery Robinson had spent her entire adulthood dreading her thirtieth birthday—and it had finally arrived. She winced as her family, gathered around the picnic table, belted out the "Happy Birthday" song. Terrific family, stellar people, but singers they were not.

Avery's stepmom, Lisa, blonde hair pulled back from her pretty face, set the cake (really, a brownie) in front of Avery.

Thirty candles flickered in the July breeze, lighting up the night like a bonfire.

Her oldest stepbrother, Gavin, hit a note well out of his range, making her snort. Her other stepbrother, Cooper, gave him an aggrieved look. Cooper was the only reason the song was half recognizable. His fiancée, Katie—also Avery's best friend since college—leaned forward, her long, honey-colored hair swinging over her shoulder as the song (thank God) came to a close.

"Gosh, guys." Avery grimaced. "Thanks a lot."

Dad's eyes crinkled in that Kiefer Sutherland way. "Make a wish, sweetheart."

"She'll probably waste it on a doctor for the clinic," Cooper said.

"Wish for a man," Katie blurted. "But be specific. Good sense of humor. Good looks, gainfully employed . . ."

"Willing to put up with a workaholic," Cooper added.

"Who has a mountain of books on her nightstand."

Lisa gave her sons a mock scowl. "All right, boys, be nice. It's her birthday."

"The only man I want is one who holds a medical degree and who's willing to live in a tiny mountain town. And accepts carriage-house accommodations as partial salary," Avery added offhandedly.

"Have you seen your carriage house?" Cooper raised an eyebrow.

"Have you seen this town?" Gavin added.

"Hey . . . ," the rest of the family chorused.

"Anyone would be lucky to live here, doctor or no," Lisa said.

Gavin pushed his black hair off his forehead, exposing

bright-blue eyes. "Which is why she's had so many responses to her ads."

"Hmm, let's see . . ." Cooper squinted his brown eyes. "Six-figure salary and fancy penthouse or shoebox with faulty plumbing."

"The plumbing works just fine, thank you very much."

"Honey," Dad said, "if having another doc will reduce your hours, you go ahead and wish for one."

"Absolutely." Lisa rubbed her shoulder. "You're wearing yourself out, and you really don't need that."

It was as close as anyone had come to mentioning the significance of her thirtieth birthday. Avery stared at her blazing brownie-cake, giving her wish further consideration while the family weighed in on Avery's workload. She didn't really believe in wishes, but as Gavin had so kindly reminded them, her ads—and numerous prayers—didn't seem to be working.

She'd planned to wait until next year to hire another doctor for her clinic, until she'd had time and money to renovate the carriage house. But the long hours were getting to her—and then there was that fateful night back in April.

Her gaze drifted to her dad, sitting catty-corner to her and fully engaged in the conversation. His color was good tonight, and he seemed in high spirits. They'd come so close to losing him—and it was all her fault. That helpless panic she'd experienced as a child had rushed back, making her chest hollow and achy. Only this time she was an adult, a doctor. She should've been here for him.

"All right, everybody, the candles are melting." Lisa's words jolted Avery from the terrible memory. "Make a wish, sweetheart."

Avery dredged up a smile as she eyed the candles. It was her birthday wish, and daggonit, she did need another doctor. Her family was correct about one thing: she couldn't continue at her current pace. She drew in a lungful of oxygen and blew out all thirty candles in one long breath.

Gravel popped under the Jeep tires as Avery backed from her parents' long drive. The smile she'd forced all evening had melted away the second she slipped from the house. Her dad had wilted as the evening wore on. He tried to hide it, but there was no fooling Avery.

The two stents had seemed to do the trick, and his cardiologist was optimistic the problem had been resolved (she'd all but harassed the man for details on several occasions). But hearts and their arteries could be tricky.

She drew in a deep breath and released it, counting to ten. He would be fine. She would never again leave him—or the rest of the community—vulnerable by leaving town. Not until she had another doctor in place. Maybe she'd win one of those grants she was applying for so she could actually offer a living wage.

Minutes later she drove through town, deserted since they rolled up the sidewalk by eight o'clock. She passed the church and headed toward the campground, which Gavin managed, and finally entered the heavily wooded side of town known as Mulberry Hollow. The road curved and twisted alongside the river, and the full moon cast a ghostly glow over the treetops. On the other side of the river, the Appalachian Mountains rose to rounded peaks, silhouetted against the evening sky.

To some, this town was a place from which to escape.

Goodness knew most of her schoolmates had felt that way. But to Avery, Riverbend, nestled in its guardian mountains, was a safe haven from the rest of the world. She'd known she wanted to grow old here even before she'd realized she wanted to be a doctor. The people were friendly and quick to lend a hand. And the Robinson roots were deep here—five generations deep. She came from farmers and entrepreneurs, all devoted to this small mountain town. She was proud to carry on the family legacy.

She drove past the old Craftsman-style homes set close to the road and, in recent years, converted into businesses that mostly served hikers and nature lovers. A bait-and-tackle store, an outfitters shop, a rafting company.

Her clinic was just past the last of these. The sign by the street, lit from both directions, swung in the breeze. *Riverbend Medical Clinic*. The hours and phone numbers were listed, including an emergency number. Those calls had her desperate for another doctor. Sure, she had help: Katie, her nurse, and Sharise, her nurse practitioner. But Sharise was a single mother of two, so the responsibility of off-hour care fell on Avery.

She slowed and pulled in to the gravel parking lot, formerly the house's front yard. Her apartment upstairs was as dark as the porch. When she left the light on, someone inevitably showed up at midnight with a hangnail, thinking it was an all-night clinic despite the posted hours.

Her headlights swept across the clinic. It was one of the larger homes on the street, but the mountain beyond it dwarfed the brick structure. She shut off the Jeep's engine, then grabbed the gifts and leftover brownies, which Lisa had condensed down to one Over-the-Hill gift bag (compliments of Cooper). Avery looked forward to indulging in another brownie—it was her birthday, after all. She'd enjoy it as she resumed her Jane Austen literary marathon—she was currently halfway through *Emma*.

As she stepped from the vehicle, her gaze flickered up to her darkened apartment where her cat, Boots, was almost certainly nesting in the living room window, awaiting her return. The night smelled of wood fires and gardenias. Avery took in the flowers Lisa and Katie had planted in the spring, but it was too dark to appreciate their beauty.

She'd added a private entry in the back but headed instead toward the clinic door, the most direct route. She took the porch steps and was withdrawing her key from her purse when her foot connected with something solid.

The shadowed lump gave a low, male moan.

Two

"Hello?" Avery leaned over the man and gave him a gentle shake. "Sir?"

When he didn't respond, she stepped over him, unlocked the door, and turned on the porch light. She was back at his side in seconds. Was he drunk?

He lay curled on his side, head propped on a backpack. He wore hiking shorts and a gray tee. Dark-blond hair fell in waves over his face, most of which was covered by an overgrown beard and mustache. All of the above—plus the earthy smell emanating from him—pegged him as a thru-hiker. She estimated him to be in his upper thirties, though the facial hair made it hard to ascertain his age.

No obvious injuries. His face was flushed but he wasn't sweating. She touched his forehead. Midgrade fever.

The man stirred. His eyes squinted open, glazed but fixed

on her, a startling pop of cornflower blue against his bronzed skin.

"Sir, do you have an injury?"

His Adam's apple bobbed. "Sick."

"All right. Well, let's get you inside where I can examine you. Do you think you can stand?"

With what appeared to be Herculean effort, he pushed to a sitting position.

"That's it." Avery grabbed his upper arm—and what an arm it was. Sculpted and hard beneath her palm. It took three tugs to get him to his feet and then she saw why; he topped her by at least six inches. At five feet seven she wasn't exactly petite.

He wavered on his feet.

"Steady there." She gave him a moment to get his bearings, then opened the door. "Are you all right to walk? I'm Dr. Robinson, by the way, and I'll be seeing to your care tonight."

"My pack . . ." His voice held a ragged edge.

"It'll be fine here on the porch for now. Let's get you settled in a room." She led him on a slow walk toward exam room one. "Can you tell me what's going on?"

"Fever. Fatigue. Sore throat."

"Any tick or mosquito bites?"

"Not that I know of."

"Rash?"

"Don't think so."

"Have you been around anyone who's sick?"

"Few days ago at a shelter. Guy was coughing a lot."

Maybe a nasty virus, but she'd save the diagnosis until she'd properly examined him. "When did all this come on?"

"This morning."

They were almost halfway to the room. She got the feeling he wasn't used to requiring help and didn't like feeling needy, so she changed the subject. "Where are you staying while you're in town?"

"I—I don't know."

Because he was confused? Or because he hadn't made plans yet? She assisted him through the exam room doorway. "You don't know?"

"Just got here."

"Where did you spend last night?"

"Laurel Knob."

She slid him a sidelong look. "That's almost fifteen miles away, and I didn't see a car in the lot."

He said nothing as he dropped onto the bed, sagged down, and closed his eyes. His breaths were labored, and he shook with chills.

Avery took his blood pressure. Laurel Knob was north of town, which meant he'd climbed over two thousand feet of rugged terrain before descending into the valley on a humid day that reached into the midnineties. Challenging even for a healthy adult.

His blood pressure was on the low side, and his heart rate was high, from dehydration, exertion, or both. She clipped the oximeter on his finger and waited for a reading. Normal.

She finished the exam, asking questions when they arose. By the time she checked his lungs, he was hardly responding to her questions.

"Mr.—sir, can you wake up for me?"

His lashes fluttered open and his sleepy gaze fixed on her.

"You never told me your name."

He wet his lips. "Wes Garrett."

"Okay, Wes. Well, you might have a pretty good upper-respiratory infection going on. But the more worrisome issue is that you're dehydrated. I'm going to call over to Mission Hospital and have them send an ambulance. You'll need an—"

"No."

"I understand your reluctance, but your medical needs are beyond the scope of the clinic. You need an IV, perhaps some diagnostic tests, and overnight care."

———

That wasn't going to happen. Wes shook his head, the motion making it pound. "Can't."

Probably just a little virus. Granted it had literally knocked him to his knees today—more than once if he was honest. And he couldn't begin to explain the relief he'd felt upon reaching the clinic. After the hot trek over the mountain, the rest felt divine, and the cool concrete porch was as welcoming as a luxury mattress.

"You're severely dehydrated, Wes. You need IV fluids."

His gaze locked on the doctor's face. Ivory skin, smattering of freckles across her nose. Delicate brows arched over green eyes that would've stolen the show if not for that mane of brown hair.

She didn't look much like a doctor in her white sleeveless top. Didn't smell like one either; he drew in a fragrance that hinted of sunshine and coconuts. Then he realized she must be smelling him too.

Time to go. He pushed up to a sit, the movement taking ridiculous effort. He blinked against his throbbing headache and pushed off the table.

The doctor placed her hands on his shoulders, holding him in place. "Whoa, whoa, where are you going? Did you hear what I said? You're dehydrated—and you need an X-ray of those lungs and possibly other diagnostic tests to rule out something more serious."

"I'll be fine. I'll drink some water and rest a couple days." As he got to his feet the room spun. His vision went dark around the edges, coming down to ragged pinpoints of light.

Come on, Garrett. Fight it back.

She put both hands on his arms and easily pushed him back down to the table. "What's your problem with the hospital?"

He waited for the spinning to stop, then locked his eyes on hers. "No insurance."

"They'll treat you there anyway. It's a terrific hospital. They'll take good care of you."

But they'd still bill him, and he had no way of paying for it. He didn't take on debt if he could help it; it was a matter of honor. He licked his lips. So thirsty. "Don't think so. Can you recommend a place nearby with a shower and bed?"

"Mr. . . . Wes. I highly recommend you rethink your plans. You really do need fluids and—"

He pushed to a stand, the wave of dizziness not taking him by surprise this time. "I appreciate the diagnosis, Doc. We can settle up and I'll be out of your hair."

He started toward the door, his legs wobbling as if he were on stilts. His head spun and his heart thrashed against his rib cage. He powered through, exiting the room. He had exactly

$127 in his bag. Probably shouldn't have bothered with the clinic because that would likely cost everything he had, and he still had to pay for a—

"Wait. Wait." The doctor stepped in front of him. "Do you have friends or family in town?"

"No." He braced a hand against the wall.

She pursed her lips. "Fine. You can stay here. I'll set up an IV. I don't usually do that, but I'll make an exception this time."

"Not necessary. I'll be fine."

She narrowed her eyes on him, her full lips going tight at the corners. "Actually, you won't be. You're feverish but not sweating. You have a rapid pulse and you're light-headed. And then there's that headache you haven't mentioned. All signs your body's in desperate need of fluids, Wes, and you need them now. If you try walking to the nearest motel—which, by the way, is over a mile away—you'll pass out on the side of the road, and when someone finds you in the morning, they'll be calling that ambulance for you."

"I don't have—"

"Insurance, I know. We'll work something out." She grabbed his elbow. "This way. I have a hospital bed in room four where you'll be comfortable."

He was too weak to fight. And he hated to admit it, but she was probably right about passing out. Even now the room was spinning, and putting one foot in front of the other was a challenge. He followed her down the hall, his hiking boots feeling as if they were weighted with sand.

An overnight stay in a medical clinic that obviously wasn't staffed for nighttime emergencies—this would cost a fortune he wouldn't be able to pay back anytime soon. Visions of his childhood swam in his head. The creditor messages, the eviction notices, the middle-of-the-night departures his dad tried to sell as a grand adventure.

He pushed away the memories and focused on walking. He entered the room and spotted the bed. Almost there. Just a few more steps and he could finally sink into oblivion.

Three

Avery had been dozing on and off, but concern for her patient once again had her sitting up. She blinked against the glow of the hall light. Her Fitbit read 3:17 a.m., about seven minutes past the last time she'd checked. As she stood the air conditioner kicked on, and she folded her arms against the cold blast of air.

For the third time that night she padded from the office, down the hall, and pushed open the door to room four. Her patient didn't even stir as light flooded the room. She neared the bed and noted the slow rise and fall of his chest. The beads of sweat on his forehead verified the IV was doing its job. In the morning she would send him on his way.

The thought brought a little pang. Even though her sleep had been restless, it was kind of nice having someone here. The building and her apartment were so quiet at night. She was alone a lot—which was not the same thing as lonely. She was not lonely. She had her work and her family and friends.

Well, *friend*. Katie was really the only person outside her family to whom she was close. But she had many acquaintances and neighbors, people who cared, and that was the same thing, wasn't it?

She checked the IV site and lowered the rate of infusion.

Wes gave a low moan. The blanket she'd covered him with was pushed to the side and hanging over the rail. He wore the hospital gown he'd insisted on donning himself last night. But he hadn't secured the neckline, and it had slipped down, exposing well-defined shoulders.

She hoped he had the good sense to rest up until the illness passed, but these thru-hikers were a driven lot. He wouldn't be the first to push through illness or injury for some arbitrary deadline and end up worse for the wear.

She placed the back of her hand on his forehead. Hot to the touch. He was shivering a bit so she adjusted the blankets over him.

"Time is it?" he croaked.

"After three. How are you feeling?"

"Better."

She took that with a grain of salt since he seemed intent on downplaying his symptoms, and his fever was still high enough to cause myriad unpleasant symptoms.

"You didn't have to stay." His eyes fluttered shut, calling attention to long lashes she would've traded her best brownie recipe for.

She'd explained this last night but did so again. "My apartment's upstairs so I crashed in my office. Just give a holler if you need anything."

"I'm fine . . ." The sentence trailed off and his breaths lengthened once again.

He was weak as a baby and clearly in the throes of this virus. Maybe he wouldn't be moving on so quickly. Today was Sunday and the clinic was closed. There was no reason to rush him out the door. Besides, it was Fourth of July weekend, and finding an available bed would take a miracle.

Avery awoke to a loud crash. She bolted upright in bed and blinked against the daylight. Not bed. Sofa. She'd finally fallen into a sound sleep, and now it was . . . seven thirty.

Another sound came from down the hall, and she remembered her patient. She pushed back the blanket, sprang to her feet, and rushed down the hall, following the sounds of muttering.

Wes was sitting up in bed, the IV out, the pole tipped over onto the floor.

"What are you doing?"

"Sorry 'bout that."

"Lie back down and let me get your vitals."

"I'm fine. I've taken up enough of your time."

She gave him her best doctorly expression. "It will only take a minute. Lie down please."

He held her gaze for five full seconds before his jaw ticked, his thick beard twitching. With seemingly great effort he swung his legs back into the bed and sank down, his eyes falling shut. The minimal movements had left him winded, and fever still flushed his cheeks.

Avery took his vitals. His blood pressure and oxygen levels were in the normal ranges, but his heart rate was rapid, though that was probably from exertion. She withdrew the thermometer from his mouth. "You're properly hydrated and your vitals look good with the exception of your temperature: 101.8. You must be feeling pretty crummy."

"If you could just recommend a place nearby with a bed and a shower, I'd be much obliged."

"Tell you what. You take it easy for a minute, and I'll go make a few calls."

"Don't have to do that." But Wes was already drifting off again. Just as well. The man needed rest.

Wes's eyes snapped open and fell on the doctor as she swept into the room. He must've been asleep awhile—sunlight now flooded the room. Plus the doctor's hair was done up in a ponytail, and she'd changed into a collared shirt and white lab coat.

With great effort he pushed himself to a sitting position. His head throbbed and every muscle in his body screamed. But his skin felt clammy, like maybe his fever had broken.

"Seems like you had a nice nap."

He rubbed a hand over his face, getting a palm full of bristly hair. "Time is it?"

"A little after ten. I'm afraid I have some bad news—I wasn't able to find accommodations for you. Tomorrow is the Fourth of July so this weekend is a busy one around here."

"You mentioned a campground before . . ."

"The cabins are full but there was a cancellation for a

campsite. However, the hard ground is no place to recover from an illness."

"I'll be fine. I have a tent."

The doctor regarded him with an enigmatic expression. "It's up to you, of course. But you're welcome to hang around here awhile. We're closed Sundays so it'll be quiet."

He was already shaking his head. He'd already be paying for this medical detour for months—and just when he'd almost cleared his dad's debt. "Thanks for the offer but as I said before, I don't have insurance. And I don't want to be a bother." This was probably the doctor's only day off.

"I'm sure we can work something out."

"Is that code for me making payments for the rest of my wage-earning days?"

One side of her lips lifted. "No, it's code for we'll work something out. Financing in a small town can get a little creative. Let's just say I have a year's supply of freshly grown vegetables at my disposal. The door to my apartment? Trade. And how do you think I came by my adorable kitty?"

"Gee, I'm fresh out of veggies, doors, and kitties."

"You *are* feeling better. Like I said, we can work something out."

"How much am I in for so far? Ballpark estimate."

She cocked her head, holding eye contact for a beat before she quoted a rate that made his body break out in a sweat again.

"But I'll cut you a deal for today since you're off the IV and will require minimal medical care." The rate she named was equivalent to a stay in a hotel—the kind Doc might stay at.

He had marketable skills, but he didn't exactly have a job waiting for him in Albany. And there was Lillian to consider.

He didn't like the idea of starting their lives together digging out of debt.

But if he was honest he wasn't sure he could make it all the way to the campground, and he couldn't in good conscience thumb a ride when he was contagious.

"So what do you say?" The doctor stared at him, those green eyes holding something he couldn't quite decipher. "Stick around for another night?"

The fatigue made every movement feel as if he were swimming in molasses. He regarded her for a moment. "Any chance you have a shower around here?"

"We do. And I can grab some food from the deli if you feel up to eating. You must be starving."

His stomach gave a hard, empty twist. He couldn't remember the last thing he'd eaten. "All right. One more night."

Four

Avery's fingers flew across the keyboard. Applying for grants was a long, tedious process, but she was becoming quite adept. If just one of these came through, maybe she'd have a prayer of finding a decent doctor.

The only sound in the clinic was the patter of water from the shower across the hall. She was unreasonably glad Wes had decided to stay. It was only because of his tenuous health. This way she wouldn't worry about him trying to recover on the ground in the sweltering heat. It was better for her peace of mind, that was all.

The water had been running awhile—she hoped he was all right in there. But it had probably been weeks since he'd had the luxury of a warm shower, and there were built-in bars and a seat where he could rest. Having been vomited on more than once, she was quite familiar with the shower.

Her phone pinged with an incoming text. Earlier, she'd let her family know she wouldn't be at church so they didn't worry. They probably wanted to know if she could join them for lunch.

The message was from Cooper. Where are you?

At work, she responded.

A minute later a loud knock on the clinic door made her jump. She stood, her chair scuttling out behind her, and headed for the entrance.

When she opened the door, her brother's prominent brows drew tight over his deep-set brown eyes. At six two Cooper towered over her, and in his sheriff's uniform he cut a formidable figure.

"Why are you here?" he asked.

"Isn't that my line?"

"You said there was an emergency last night that kept you up late."

"There was." This was where she should probably add that her patient was still here. But she didn't keep patients around after the emergencies passed. And she certainly didn't offer them a shower and a bed in which to recover. Speaking of which, she could faintly hear the rush of water from here.

"You gonna let me in or what?"

She reluctantly stepped aside and closed the door but didn't move from the foyer.

Cooper tilted his head and a lock of dark-brown hair fell over his forehead. "So really, what are you doing in here? This is your day off."

She rolled her eyes. "I'm writing a grant."

"You work too much. You should take better care of yourself."

"Pot, meet kettle."

He scowled, no doubt wanting to add that their circumstances were entirely different, but her arched brow dared him to say it. It worked.

"Which brings us back to, why are *you* here?" she asked.

"Are you at all interested in Rick Rodriguez?"

Avery blinked. "That was blunt and awkward, even for you."

"He was asking about you again this morning. He's single, gainfully employed, and I'm told he's a nice-enough-looking guy."

"He's a flirt."

"No doubt. But surely you can tell he likes you. He's been interested for months."

Avery sharpened her gaze on him. "Katie sent you, didn't she?"

He rubbed the back of his neck.

Busted. Katie might be Cooper's girl, but her best friend knew Avery pretty well. "What is this, sixth grade? I don't need help getting a date, and I'm sure Rick doesn't either."

"Katie thought you might want to double-date with us. You know, just to make things easier or whatever. Besides, you won't give him your number, and I'm tired of hearing the guy pine after you at the office."

In the distance the shower shut off. Avery glanced down the hall. Wes would be coming out soon, and she really didn't care to explain why she'd kept him around another night. She wasn't even sure she knew the answer.

"So whaddaya say?"

She could say that dating was a waste of time because she was never going to get married. But she wasn't ready to go there just yet. "As I've said before—many times—I'm focusing on my work right now."

"Your clinic is up and running—and doing quite well from what I understand. Maybe it's time to invest in a social life. You're not getting any younger, you know."

She narrowed her eyes. "Really?"

"Just saying. Come on, he's a nice guy. One date. What would it hurt?"

A sound came from the back, and Cooper's attention focused down the hall.

Avery stiffened.

The air conditioner kicked on.

He must've attributed the noise to its machinations because his attention returned to her.

But Wes would be exiting the bathroom any moment, hopefully wearing more than a towel—did he even have clean clothes? Her decision to let him stay had been unprofessional; she realized that now.

"Just say yes. One date. If the two of you don't click, I'll never mention him again."

She shifted toward the door. She had to get Coop out of here. "Fine, one date."

His eyebrows hitched. "Really?"

"I just said so, didn't I?" She opened the door.

Cooper's face relaxed as he crossed the threshold. "That's great. I'll have Rick give you a call and we'll set something up."

"Fine, fine." She started to close the door. "Wait, don't give him my number . . . Cooper!"

But he was already down the steps and acting as if he didn't hear a word.

Avery thanked the teenage boy who worked at the Grab 'n' Go Deli and closed the clinic door. The building was quiet, the air cool on her skin. The scent of fresh bread emanating from the food bag made her stomach growl. She set it on the counter and went to check on her patient. He'd become feverish again after breakfast and had been sleeping ever since. But now it was going on six, and he should eat a little something.

Wes had pushed off the covers again, revealing the shorts and black T-shirt he'd changed into after his shower. His hair had dried into enviable dark-blond waves. As grizzly as he appeared with that face full of whiskers, he seemed like a nice man. Not irritable, despite his discomfort. Stoic. Two empty water bottles sat on the bedside table.

He stirred and that blue gaze locked on her. "Time is it?"

"Almost six. You've been asleep awhile. How are you feeling?"

"Better."

She took his temperature. It had been more than six hours since she'd given him ibuprofen. When the thermometer beeped she read the display. "Your fever has broken again. Are you hungry? The deli delivered some food."

He wet his lips. "Your deli delivers?"

"If you know the right people. You must be feeling a little cooped up. Want to eat on the back deck? It's a mild evening."

"Sure." With some effort he swung his legs over the bed, sitting up. "Your clinic has a deck?"

She smiled. "Shh, don't tell anyone. Oh, here's your cell phone. It's the same as mine so I took the liberty of charging it in case you needed to reach out to someone."

"Thanks." He stashed the phone in his pocket.

She grabbed the food and led him through her office and out the French doors.

Once on the deck he dropped into one of the padded chairs, his breathing labored.

She settled in the seat next to him, pulled the carton of soup and club sandwich from the bag, and set them on the table between them, along with plastic cutlery and two bottled waters.

They ate in silence, the tweeting birds and nattering squirrels filling the evening, along with the constant babbling of the river at the back of the property. She'd always enjoyed the hushed sounds of nature. Even though the houses were close together, the businesses were deserted after closing hours. On this stretch of road she was the only one who actually lived above her shop.

Wes cleared his throat. "I'm a little embarrassed to ask at this point but . . ."

"What is it?"

"I didn't catch your name last night."

"You were a little out of it. It's Avery Robinson."

"Nice to meet you, Dr. Robinson."

"Just Avery, please. We're not much on formalities around here."

"Is this your clinic then? You mentioned an apartment upstairs."

"Mine and the bank's." She'd paid her medical school debts with her mom's life insurance and used what was left for a down payment on the clinic.

"You run it on your own?"

"Oh no. I have a nurse and a nurse practitioner, plus office help. I could sure use another doctor, but that'll probably take some time." In the meantime she'd continue working seventy-hour weeks.

Wes started on his sandwich, nodding as he chewed. "This is good."

"That's my brother's favorite. I'm partial to the chicken salad, but I thought that might be a bit much for your stomach."

"He your only sibling?"

"No, I've got two older brothers."

"Two boys and a girl—all-American family, huh?"

She snorted. "Not quite. My dad was married before, to my mom. But she passed away. Then he met Lisa and fell in love—Cooper and Gavin were part of the package."

"Blended family. Sounds tricky."

"There were rough patches for sure. I created my fair share of them. But it all turned out okay. How about you? Siblings?"

"Only child." There was a pause as he seemed to contemplate his next bite. "I'm sorry about your loss. My mom passed away when I was a child too."

Avery's heart squeezed, partially in memory of her own pain and partially in empathy for his. "I'm sorry. That's a rough thing for a child to endure. What is it you do, Wes, when you're not hiking the Appalachian Trail?"

He held up a finger while he finished chewing. "I've spent the past several years in South America, working for Emergency Shelter International. Before that, I did a little of this and a little of that."

Avery smiled to herself at his vague answer. "Where are you from?"

"The Midwest mostly. Moved around a lot growing up. I settled in Indianapolis for a while."

"Is that where you're headed once you finish the trail?"

He started to say something, then hesitated.

Awkwardness settled between them. She was used to professional exchanges with patients, superficial chats with neighbors. But otherwise, her social skills were a bit rusty. "Sorry, you don't have to answer my questions. I guess I'm not used to having company."

"That's all right. I'm planning to settle in Albany once I finish the hike."

"Haven't had enough cold winters?"

They shared a smile. At least she thought he smiled. His eyes crinkled at the corners and his mustache twitched a little. His eyes were really striking, a beautiful color that reminded her of the bluebells growing at the back of the property behind the carriage house.

"Who's over the hill?" he asked.

"What?"

He wadded up the sandwich wrap, the crinkle loud in the quiet evening. "The bag you were carrying earlier."

"Oh." She laughed. "That would be me. The big three-oh and my brother's idea of a joke."

"Yesterday was your birthday—and you spent the evening taking care of me."

"Part of the job. Besides, I was all partied out anyway."

His gaze swept over her. As quick as the assessment was, a ripple of chills swept down her arms.

"You don't look like you're on your last legs," he said in that smoky voice of his.

"You flatter me, sir." Her cheeks went warm. How lame was her life if she considered that a compliment. And it would be helpful if she conversed in modern English. "Sorry. I guess I've been reading too much Jane Austen."

The buzz from the clinic's doorbell sounded above the whisper of the river. She welcomed the interruption, likely not an emergency as people called the posted number.

"Doesn't anyone text anymore?" she muttered as she stood, then addressed Wes. "Be right back."

Five

Wes watched Avery go. She'd shed the lab coat, exposing a light-green top, and donned a pair of faded jeans. Her ponytail swung behind her. And then she was gone around the corner of the building.

She was an interesting woman. Obviously smart and confident about her work but also a little awkward. He thought of the way her cheeks flushed prettily when she was uncomfortable and the way her hair seemed brown under fluorescent lights and reddish in the sunlight. Did she have a significant other who appreciated those things? *Knock it off, Garrett.* As far as he was concerned, he was unofficially off the market.

Speaking of which, he needed to call Lillian and let her know he'd been delayed. She wouldn't be annoyed. Even though he'd never met her in person, he knew her well from the letters they'd exchanged after Landon's death. He'd known her well even before that since his buddy used to read his sister's letters to Wes. Landon probably felt sorry for him because he didn't get regular letters from anyone.

Even though they'd been written to her brother, Wes looked forward to Lillian's letters and pictures. In return for his friend's kindness, Wes would tease Landon about Lillian's attractiveness. It was true. With curly brown hair, olive skin, and doe eyes, she was a natural beauty. But he got a kick out of laying it on thick just to get under Landon's skin.

Landon would scowl. "Don't even think about it, scrub."

But that afternoon, when Landon lay helpless, his life seeping into the dirt, his words displayed the depth of his trust. "Take care of Lillian. Promise me."

Wes swallowed against the lump in his throat. His agreement had been automatic. Of course he would look after her. He and Landon were as close as brothers and, letter by letter, he'd grown to care for Lillian too. All along he'd planned to settle in Albany after he and Landon finished out their contracts. He would keep to his plans and take care of Lillian.

But after exchanging many letters with her in the months since Landon's passing, he'd found his commitment level growing. Wondered if he shouldn't do more than check up on her and take her out to dinner on occasion.

It wasn't until he'd called her from the States that his thinking had begun to shift. During that phone call she sounded so lost in grief. She was also worried about her day-care business as one of her moms—with three children—had just decided to quit her job and stay home with them. He didn't want Lillian worrying about finances.

He was thirty-three and ready to settle down and start a

family. Why not do that together? They loved each other. He had yet to approach Lillian about a potential future together—that could wait until he arrived in Albany. But the moment he had that thought, he could almost feel Landon's approval from beyond the grave. As often as his friend had claimed Lillian was too good for Wes, there was obviously nobody he'd trusted with her more.

He took a swig of water and checked the time. He had no idea what Lillian would be doing on a Sunday evening, but she wouldn't be working. He hadn't spoken with her since he called from Erwin, Tennessee, six days ago. She was still dealing with a lot of sadness over her brother's passing.

He tapped her number and she answered on the second ring with her soft-spoken voice. "Well, hello there. You must've reached civilization again."

"I have indeed. How are you doing?"

"Oh, you know. Pretty good. I try to stay busy—sometimes it keeps me ahead of the waves."

He heard what she hadn't said. "And sometimes it doesn't?" He knew this well as he'd been going through it himself.

"These things take time. So where are you now? I'll bet you're glad for a shower and mattress."

"For sure. I'm in a little town called Riverbend Gap in North Carolina. The trail runs right down Main Street."

"Your voice sounds funny."

"Well, that's the thing. I seem to have a little virus going on. I'm afraid I've been held up a little bit."

"Are you okay?"

"Sure, sure. Just need a little rest, and I'll be on my way again."

"Is there anything you need? Anything I can send you? A batch of my homemade chicken noodle soup maybe?"

He chuckled. She was such a caretaker. "I'm aiming to be on my way before it'd ever get here. But thank you for the offer."

"All right then. I hate that you were delayed. You were making such good time too."

How many days would this virus set him back? He was feeling better for the moment, but the fever came and went at will.

Lillian cleared her throat. "In case I haven't told you, Wes, I think it's really amazing that you're doing this for Landon. He always did hate leaving things unfinished."

Landon had been hiking the Appalachian Trail in sections. He started shortly after graduating from college, at Mount Katahdin in Maine, the northern end of the trail. During vacations he added to the hike and made it as far south as Harrisburg, Pennsylvania.

Then Landon had gotten hired by Emergency Shelter International. He and Wes had met in Colombia and formed an immediate bond. When Landon told him about his progress on the trail, Wes committed to completing it with him when they finished their contract. He loved the outdoors, and the idea of being completely self-sustaining held great appeal. They'd talked often about their plans. Wes never dreamed he'd be returning to the States and completing the hike alone.

"Wes? You okay?"

"I'm fine. The hike's been good for me—the time alone out in nature. I've had a lot of time to think."

"What have you been thinking about?"

He wasn't sure he wanted to get into that over the phone. "Oh, you know, the past, the future, things like that."

Her quiet laugh sounded over the line. "Now that's a vague answer if I ever heard one."

"We'll have plenty of time to talk when I get there. Did you place that ad for your day care?"

"I did, but I haven't gotten any calls yet. It's strange only having two children here. And they're six and ten, so come fall they'll be in school. I really need some little ones. Besides, I miss those baby cuddles."

"I'm sure you'll find some new kids to love on soon."

"I hope so. I sure miss those kiddos. I get too attached, I know. Landon was always telling me that, but it's impossible not to."

"You have a big heart."

"Sometimes it's hard to believe we've never even met in person. I feel like I know you so well."

His lips relaxed into a smile. "I feel the same."

"I've been keeping my eyes open for an apartment for you, and I have one that sounds interesting. I'll text you the details and you can look it up."

"I don't want you worrying about me. You have enough on your plate."

"I don't mind. Listen, you sound tired. I'll let you go so you can get some rest."

"I'll call you when I'm ready to hit the trail again."

"Don't rush it. You don't want to have a setback."

"I'll be careful." They said their good-byes and he disconnected.

He hated that she was having financial troubles and wished

he could provide immediate help. But if she'd been too independent to accept assistance from her brother, she wouldn't accept it from him. Besides, he wasn't exactly in the financial position to offer help at the moment anyway.

He thought of the bill he owed the clinic and winced. He sure hated the thought of that debt hanging over his head. Logically, he knew there was no crime in having to make payments. But emotionally it dragged him right back to his vagabond childhood. He would never be like his dad.

Wes took another slug of water, forcing himself to drink more than he really wanted. He couldn't afford—literally—to get dehydrated again. The thought of that bill made his head throb again. Or maybe he was just more cognizant of it now that there were no distractions.

He swept his eyes across the well-kept backyard. Flowers and bushes lined the stained deck. A red bird feeder hung from a blooming tree. A flagstone path wound through a manicured lawn and back to an old brick carriage house that probably dated back to when the house was built.

But wherein the house had been updated with new windows and roof shingles, the outbuilding was still languishing somewhere in the mid-twentieth century. The white paint on the gridded windows peeled, and the double doors had faded to a dirty gray, the hardware rusting. The old shingles on the roof curled, and moss spilled across the surface.

The structure was about the size of a two-car garage and sat under the shade of a giant oak. What was the building used for? Storage, most likely. Currently, it was an eyesore, but the contractor in him envisioned a renovation that restored the building to its former beauty.

Avery returned, taking the deck stairs with a light step and settling into the chair she'd vacated.

"Everything okay? Not another emergency on your day off?"

"No, it was my friend Katie. She's also my nurse, so you might meet her in the morning. Enjoying the peace and quiet? Wait, you've had plenty of that on the trail. You're probably bored silly."

"I'm too tired to be bored. I'm not used to feeling so weak."

"Listen to your body. It needs time to recover."

That was an understatement. He felt tired just sitting here. But the thought that had been forming before she returned was beginning to solidify into an idea.

He gestured toward the carriage house. "What do you use that for?"

"Well, nothing much at the moment. A previous owner turned it into . . . I guess you'd call it a mother-in-law suite. I did give it a thorough cleaning—I was hoping to offer it up as partial salary for the doctor I need to hire. I thought a good cleaning would bring it up to acceptable standards, but no."

"Seems like it needs some TLC."

"I'm afraid it's stuck in the eighties, inside and out."

Wes sat on that information a long minute. She needed a restored carriage house, and he needed to settle a debt. The trade would set him back a couple of weeks, a real drawback. But it would also allow him to approach Lillian and his life in Albany almost debt-free.

He was also eager to settle up with Avery, who seemed to work hard and have financial struggles of her own.

His gaze sharpened on the young doctor.

Seeming to feel his appraisal, she met his gaze. Their eyes locked for a long beat, a question shifting the expression on her face.

"I have an idea," he said.

Six

Avery leaned forward, curiosity getting the better of her. "Okay, let's hear your idea."

"You asked me before what I do for a living. I was a residential contractor before I went overseas. I worked for a builder in Indianapolis. I've spent the past several years in Colombia building shelters for refugees who flood in from Venezuela. Converting hotels, that kind of thing. So . . . I noticed your carriage house there and remembered what you'd said about wanting to renovate it."

"Ah . . . You're interested in a trade of some kind."

"Maybe. I'd have to take a closer look, make sure the building's structurally sound."

"Well, trust me the renovations will far exceed your medical bill."

"I can see right off you need new windows and a new roof, some fresh paint. And I'm sure the interior could use some help, depending on how much updating you want done. But maybe I could get it going at least. Labor in exchange for what I owe you."

It would be ten times easier to find a doctor if she could offer attractive housing. Of course, there was still the cost of materials, but she had a little money set back. "I have to say I like the sound of this. But what about your hike? And don't you have something you have to get back to?"

"I want to finish the trail, of course, but I can delay it awhile. And there's nothing too pressing in Albany. It's more important that I pay what I owe you."

She tilted her head and stared at him. He was a curious man. Paying your own way was a noble trait, but Wes seemed to take the discipline to a new level. "You really don't like debt, do you?"

"Does anyone?"

"Touché." But was Wes really qualified for the work? She had no idea what his skills were or even how to rate them as she was mechanically challenged herself and knew nothing about construction.

As if reading her mind, he said, "You're welcome to call my previous employer, Dave at Carter Construction. I worked for him for several years before I went to South America. You could also check with ESI. I can get you the numbers."

That was encouraging. "Okay, thanks. Do you feel up to having a look-see?"

"Sure."

Wes pointed to a ceiling tile over the living room. "You've had a leak there sometime in the past. Couldn't say if it's been repaired.

But I could check the wood when I replace the roof. Hopefully it's not rotted through."

Avery had opened a window to air out the hot, stuffy room. The space consisted of a living room and a closed-in kitchen. A bed and bathroom took up the back part of the building.

"What about the plumbing?" Wes asked.

"It still functions, believe it or not. But I have the water turned off. The baseboard heating works too, but the only means of cooling is that one window air conditioner."

"If you added one in that bedroom window, that would probably be adequate. You might think about walling off the bedroom for privacy. Depends on what your vision is for the space though."

"I like that idea."

Once back in the living room, Wes peered behind a piece of paneling that had been peeled back from the framing at some point. "It's well insulated. This two-by-six framing was meant to last, and there's no beating native timber for strength and durability. All that's to say, the construction is solid, which is no surprise, given the era it was built in."

She was starting to get excited about this project. He seemed to know his stuff. Maybe he could get it far enough along that Cooper and Gavin could help her complete the project. And by help she meant she'd provide pizza and drinks in exchange for their labor.

He seemed to be finished with his assessment so she closed the window, led him back outside, and locked up behind them. "You've got me very intrigued, Wes. What's your usual hourly rate?"

He named a figure that seemed reasonable. Some quick

math told her it would take about two weeks to work off his debt. "How far do you think you could get on this?"

He examined the exterior of the building. "If the windows are standard size, and I think they are, I could get the exterior done. Probably more if there's no rot under those shingles. Obviously, I don't have my tools with me though."

"You could borrow my brother's. But where would you stay while you completed the work?"

"Thought I'd grab one of those campsites you mentioned."

She frowned, still not liking the thought of him sleeping on the ground as he recovered. He obviously didn't have the money for a hotel room. But even the campsite fee would add up over two weeks, and he was obviously concerned about his finances.

She had an idea about that. Starting tomorrow he'd no longer be her patient, and that cleared the lines of professionalism she'd blurred a little. He'd just be her contractor.

"What if you stayed in the carriage house? I know it's not much at the moment, but it's clean, furnished, and it beats a tent."

"Well . . ." He rubbed the whiskers over his chin. "I have to admit a bed and shower hold plenty of appeal. But I couldn't take you up on that without compensating you for it."

Avery chewed on the corner of her lip. He wasn't one to take charity, never mind that the structure had just been sitting empty for years. She named a cheap nightly rate and awaited his response.

Breathe. Why was she so invested in having him here? Was she really that lonely?

Wes finally gave a nod. "All right. If you're sure. I'll add that to the bill I'm working off, if that suits you," he said this through teeth that were almost chattering.

Now that they were back in broad daylight, she could see his flushed cheeks and the way his body sagged a bit.

"Suits me fine." She took his elbow and steered him toward the house. "But let's get you back to bed. I think your fever's returned."

"You call my references tomorrow, and if you're satisfied, I'll move my things back here in the morning and get started on your project."

She speared him with a glare. "No working until you're over this virus—and as doctor in residence, I get to be the judge of that."

"Deal."

A smile bloomed on her face. "See? Told you we'd work something out."

Seven

It was amazing how much could change over a weekend. Avery glanced at the closed exam room door as she continued down the hallway toward her office. She'd checked on Wes at dawn, and his fever was breaking again. But all had been quiet in there ever since. She hadn't had the heart to wake him after his restless night's sleep. With any luck he'd slip out to the carriage house during her staff meeting—she'd left the key on his side table.

She was setting up the chairs when she heard the chime, indicating an arrival. A moment later Katie appeared with a box of donuts. She wore fuchsia scrubs and her long blonde hair was up in a messy bun. "The bakery was packed this morning. I thought I'd be late."

Another chime sounded in the distance.

"Good morning to you too," Avery said.

"Good morning. Where's the coffee? I woke up late and I'm uncaffeinated."

"Brewing now."

"What's wrong? You look tired."

Sharise entered, her floral tunic fluttering behind her like a flag. The middle-aged nurse practitioner was forever cold. She wore her black curls cropped close to her head and had a wide smile that brightened the room and put patients at ease. That smile was a little dim this morning.

They exchanged greetings, then Sharise hit the donuts. "If y'all ever decide to have a teenage girl, don't. Just don't. She's crazy about this boy, and he can't decide what he wants, and my girl just won't have it any other way no matter how much I tell her to drop him like a hot potato. Who took the twisted glaze?"

The coffee finished brewing and Katie helped herself to a cup. "They were out. Isn't Charlotte just thirteen?"

"That's another thing, the girl is just thirteen! Too young for all this romance drama. Girl's gonna to be the death of me."

The chime sounded again and a moment later their office clerk, Patti, walked in. Greetings were exchanged and small talk commenced as they collected their donuts and coffee and settled into the chairs.

Avery loved the relaxed camaraderie between the women. Having experienced a cold work environment during her residency, she'd intentionally fostered an easy companionship in the office. As a result she'd grown close to the women, and they seemed comfortable coming to her with problems. They even went out together on occasion. Mixing business with pleasure didn't work for everyone, but the staff of Riverbend Medical Clinic thrived under these conditions.

"All right," Avery said. "Happy Monday, everyone. I hope you all had a good weekend. Who'd like to start?"

"Any promising applicants for the doctor position?" Sharise asked.

"Sadly, no. But eventually somebody will respond. "

"On another note," Katie said, "we're almost out of the tetanus vaccine. I gave the second-to-last dose to a guy who stepped on a nail Friday. It must've been four inches long. Went all the way through and came out the top of his shoe."

Patti, who was really too squeamish to work in a clinic, winced.

Katie grimaced. "Sorry, Patti."

"Thanks, Katie." Avery listed a couple more things that needed restocking while Patti, who stocked the medical supplies, noted them on her clipboard. They moved on to the schedule and talked a bit about athletic physicals, which were starting to come in now that summer was in full swing.

They were twenty some minutes into the meeting by the time they'd covered all the pertinent details. Avery just needed to let them know about the construction that would soon be starting out back. "Thanks, ladies. There's one other thing I wanted to make you all aware of."

A quiet knock sounded at the door, making Avery's shoulders tense.

A *Who's that?* question appeared in each pair of eyes.

Avery cursed her luck—she'd been just about to explain. "Come in," she called.

The door opened and Wes appeared, filling the space. His backpack hung from one shoulder. He didn't look one bit ill this morning in his snug black tee and well-fitting jeans. In fact, he looked very . . . healthy.

She could practically hear three feminine sighs as Wes's

gaze slid around the occupants in the room, then settled on Avery.

He gave her an apologetic grin. "Sorry. Didn't realize you were having a meeting."

Was it just her or did his voice seem deeper this morning? Avery arranged her features in a professional expression. "That's quite all right. What can I help you with?"

"I'm heading out to the carriage house now."

"All right. Thank you."

He nodded. "Ladies."

The door closed behind him and dead silence expanded around them. The room seemed to hold its breath for a solid ten seconds before three pairs of eyes swung back to Avery and everyone seemed to speak at once.

"Shoo—ee, girl," Sharise said. "I think you left something out of your update."

"I was just about to—"

"Like she has a gentleman friend she didn't even tell her best friend about?"

Patti nudged Katie. "Or the fact that his muscles have muscles?"

"Or that you can see clear to heaven in those blue eyes?"

"No wonder she's hiding him out back."

"All right, all right." Heat flooded Avery's cheeks, and she cursed her fair skin. "He was a patient over the weekend, that's all. He came in Saturday night, burning up with fever and—"

"Are you sure he was the one who was feverish?" Katie said. "Sometimes it can be confusing."

Laughter rolled through the room. Avery forced herself to roll with it. "Haha. Hot male patient, single female doctor.

Very funny. I get it. But he had—has—a URI and was severely dehydrated so I kept him overnight. Long story short, he's a contractor and he'll be starting the carriage house renovation, so he'll be hanging around a couple weeks."

"Is he single?" Sharise asked.

"I have no idea. He was my patient—and now he's here to work and I'm not interested."

"I wasn't asking for you." Sharise fluttered her lashes.

"All right, you've had your fun." Avery checked the time and stood as the phone rang. "It's that time. Let's have a great day, everyone."

Patti and Sharise filed out, still laughing over the hottie in their backyard as Avery slid behind her desk.

Katie approached, head tilted, coy smile curving her lips. "So, what was all that about?"

"All what?"

"Attractive mountain man, hiding away in the clinic with you all weekend . . . Ringing a bell?"

"I told you, he was severely dehydrated. And he didn't have insurance so he wouldn't go to the hospital." She opened her mouth to say more but decided to stop before she overexplained.

"You don't normally keep patients overnight."

Avery crossed her arms. "I've done it before."

"You said he came in on Saturday night, so you kept him two nights, and we both know it doesn't take that long to rehydrate."

"He was ill and he didn't have anywhere to go, being Fourth of July weekend, and you know what? Sometimes having a best friend working for you is a pain in the butt."

Katie chuckled, then her gaze homed in on Avery's face,

which was probably an unflattering shade of pink. "It's nice to see you interested in someone, that's all."

"I am not interested in him." She wasn't. He'd just been pleasant company this weekend. It had been a minute since she'd enjoyed the company of a male who wasn't related to her.

Katie stared at her for a long moment. "Okay. Good. Then I hope you'll give Rick Rodriguez a real chance. Keep Friday night free. It's going to be so fun, double dating. Just like when we were in college." And with one last smile Katie exited her office.

Eight

It was almost 6:00 p.m. when Wes awakened from a nap he'd never intended to take. His fever had returned in the afternoon, and his plans to measure the windows went right out the, well, window.

He sat up and ran a hand over his face. The beige sofa wasn't much to look at, but it had embraced him like a warm, soft woman. He felt much better now. Definitely well enough to start on the windows.

Avery wouldn't approve, but she didn't have to know. If the openings weren't standard size, he'd have to order the windows, and he wanted to make sure he got them installed for her. Besides, he'd been bored silly today. He wasn't used to sitting around. Sick or not, he needed something to fill the hours. He still had a long evening ahead.

A knock sounded on the front door. He ran a hand through

his snarled hair as he made his way to the door. Avery stood on the stoop. He hadn't seen her since he barged in on her meeting, though she'd checked up on him via text.

She'd exchanged her lab coat for a long tee and yoga pants, and her hair gleamed red in the afternoon sunlight. A black cat with white paws snuggled in her arms.

"How are you feeling? Looks like you just woke up."

"I'm feeling well. Best I've felt yet."

"Good. I took the liberty of ordering pizza, and it'll be here in ten if you want to join me on the deck."

"You don't have to feed me, Doc. The food you left in the fridge will tide me over till I can get to the store. Thank you for that, by the way."

"You can't subsist on lunch meat and canned soup for days on end. Come on, I ordered plenty. You do like pizza, don't you? Poppy's Pizza is legendary around here, and I ordered deluxe—their biggest seller."

"All right, thank you." His eyes dropped to the feline. "This must be the kitty you got in a bargain."

"Wes, meet Boots. Say hi, Bootsie." Her voice had gone up an octave, and she waved the cat's paw in greeting.

"Boy or girl?"

"Girl."

Wes let the cat sniff his hand, smiling at the woman's obvious affection for the animal. Boots received his attention with a steady purr and half-lidded appreciation. "I didn't think cats were affectionate."

"This one is. I can't sit down without her curling up on my lap—or my laptop."

Avery checked her watch, then excused herself to intercept

the pizza at the front door. He agreed to meet her on the back porch in a couple of minutes.

After freshening up, he joined her. His stomach gave a hard growl at the smell of pizza. "Man, that smells good."

"I would guess so. You've been on a steady diet of trail food for weeks. Restaurant food is the best part of finally reaching a town."

He placed a slice on the paper plate she'd brought out. "The mattress and shower run a close second and third."

"There's a lot to appreciate about civilization. So, hiking the AT . . . It's a huge commitment. Is it just something you've always wanted to do?"

He finished chewing a bit, thinking through his answer. He'd been asked this a lot along the trail, and he gave a generic answer that kept him from having to open up about his friend. But he was going to be here at least a couple of weeks—and she had practically saved his life.

"I had a friend in Colombia named Landon. He worked for Emergency Shelter International too, and over the years we got pretty close. Hiking the AT was a bucket list thing for him. He'd already hiked from Maine to Harrisburg and planned to finish it after our contract was up. I committed to doing it with him. Figured, why not? Sounded like fun, and I didn't have anything urgent to get back to."

Avery had stopped eating and was regarding him intently.

"One day there was a terrorist attack where we were working—suicide bomber. I was tuned in to my work on the hotel's exterior and didn't see the car's approach. Next thing I knew I was facedown in the dirt." The moment's confusion and panic returned just like that, making his heart jolt in his chest.

"Landon had thrown himself on top of me. I came out of it unscathed—but he didn't make it."

Avery's lips parted. Her eyes swam with tears. "What a friend."

Wes swallowed hard. Sometimes it still rendered him speechless that Landon had sacrificed himself for Wes. He'd like to think he would've done the same for his friend. "He really was. That split-second decision changed everything."

Avery regarded him silently for a moment. "I'm sorry for your loss, Wes. I can't imagine being on the receiving end of a gift like that. How it must make you feel."

"It's very humbling." That didn't begin to cover it. It was a debt he'd never be able to fully repay.

"And you're finishing the AT in his honor. That's a wonderful gesture."

"Not an hour goes by that I don't think of him. All these weeks of hiking has given me a lot of time to process everything. Do a little healing." He gave her a little smile. "Sorry. Didn't mean to get so heavy."

"Well, I did ask. And sometimes life is pretty heavy." One glance in her eyes told him she knew that better than most. What secrets did those green depths hold? He regretted he wouldn't be here long enough to unearth them.

———

Though Wes had lightened the moment with that easy grin of his, a heaviness still hung in the evening air. His revelation about his friend had moved her. She always enjoyed hearing what prompted people to hike the AT—it was such a rigorous and time-consuming undertaking. But his answer had struck something deep in her core. Maybe it was the guilt she sensed he carried.

She knew about guilt.

They ate the pizza mostly in comfortable silence, just interjecting a comment here and there. Avery was full after two slices, but Wes only wound down after finishing five.

Finally, he set his plate on the table between them and settled back in the chair. "That was amazing. I'm stuffed."

"You needed a good meal. Are you drinking plenty of fluids?"

"Yes, Doctor," he teased. "The eight-pack of Gatorade and case of bottled water you put in the fridge clued me in."

"We can't have you getting dehydrated again. Did you run a fever again today?"

"For a while. I slept it off though. I think I'll be back to normal tomorrow."

Avery's lips twitched. Sounded just like her brothers when they were sick, as if they could just wish the virus away. "I'll be the judge of that."

"I haven't forgotten our deal."

"A couple years ago my brother Cooper felt a virus coming on and decided to go for a jog to 'sweat it out.'"

"How'd that work out for him?"

She snorted. "Oh, he ended up in bed for a week. God forbid he should ask his sister—a doctor, for crying out loud—for medical advice."

Wes grinned. "Generally speaking, we men don't like to ask advice."

"And see what happens?"

"You're not wrong." He took a long swig of water. "Is that what made you decide to be a doctor? The stubborn men in your family who clearly need medical direction?"

Avery's smile slipped a little before she bolstered it back into place. "I can't blame it on them. I decided to be a doctor before my stepbrothers ever entered my life."

Should she tell him where it all started? This drive to protect those she loved? Her gaze locked on his face. He waited patiently for her to continue. Something trustworthy and patient infused those blue eyes. And his own vulnerability gave her the courage to open up.

"I told you my mom passed away, but I didn't tell you I was the only one with her at the time. She had a—a progressive disease." She intentionally omitted the name of it—and the fact that she had a 50 percent chance of developing Huntington's herself. It had weighed heavily on her recently since symptoms could appear as early as thirty (and had for her mom).

"I was alone with her, and she was choking, and I didn't know what to do. I called for help but the hospital was forty-five minutes away. She didn't make it."

"That's awful. You must've been so scared."

She'd never forget the terrible gurgling sound. Or the way her mother's eyes filled with panic and pleas. As Avery made the call, a rosy blush bloomed on her mom's face, but by the time help arrived, her lips were a ghostly shade of blue and she'd passed out.

Her mom died on the way to the hospital.

In the days after her passing, grief had swallowed her dad. It took him a while to realize the depth of Avery's suffering. The weight of her guilt.

"The whole thing paralyzed me. Eventually my dad got me some counseling, which I'm sure I needed. That helped, but I never wanted to feel that kind of helplessness again."

"So you became a doctor. And you opened a clinic so your community would have the help they needed."

"In a word, yes."

He observed her for a long moment.

She resisted the urge to squirm in her chair.

"You took something terrible and made something good out of it. I admire that. I'm sure med school was rigorous, and everyone knows residency is no cakewalk. You're awfully young to have opened your own clinic."

"I'm over the hill, remember?"

"A matter of perspective, I guess." They shared a smile.

A person tended to move quickly when she didn't know how many good years she had left. Yet another reason she needed to find that doctor. She needed this clinic to survive—even if her health eventually failed her.

Genetic testing could answer the question once and for all. She had a 50 percent chance of *not* having the gene. But the decision whether or not to get tested was difficult and complicated, and the results of testing had the potential to be traumatic. Genetic counseling was highly recommended prior to testing to help a person determine if she even wanted to know what miseries the future might hold.

It had not been an easy decision, but last year Avery made it: She didn't want to know if she carried the Huntington's gene. Instead of potentially living in dread and imagining every memory lapse was the beginning of the end, she was going to live her life to the fullest.

It was better not to know.

She'd informed Katie of her decision and, bolstered by her friend's support, had told her family over the winter. She hadn't yet disclosed the rest of her decision to anyone though—that she wouldn't drag a husband and children into this cycle of uncertainty.

Her new motto was, "plan for the worst, hope for the best." So, yeah. No adoring husband, recalcitrant toddler, or angsty teenage daughter in her future. Just a cat with terrible taste in food and a penchant for gnawing on her favorite running shoes.

Speaking of the cat, Boots wound between her legs, rubbing against her calves, back arching high. Avery picked her up and the feline curled into her stomach like a lapdog.

A squirrel hopped across the yard and scuttled up a tree, nattering, and farther back, the river rippled by, constant and comforting.

Wes finished off his water, the bottle crackling. "What do you usually do in the evenings after work?"

"Well, if there are no emergencies, I catch up on paperwork." Then because she realized how lame her life sounded, she added, "And sometimes my best friend Katie comes over for supper or we go out. Occasionally Gavin stops by to mooch a meal. What do you like to do in your spare time?"

His deep chuckle strummed her heartstrings. "I can hardly even remember. We worked long hours in Colombia, and I've been hiking virtually every hour of daylight since May. But I have a vague recollection of enjoying a game of pickup basketball now and then or shooting pool at a local hangout."

"There's a poolroom at the Trailhead downtown. When

you're feeling better, you'll have to check it out. Watch out for a guy named Stewie though. He's a shark who takes great delight in suckering the tourists out of their pocket change."

"Thanks for the tip." He gave her a sidelong look. "I hope you don't get this virus. Sounds like you've got your hands full around here."

"Don't worry about it. My dad says I have the immune system of an ostrich."

"Is that a good thing?"

"Apparently. But yes, the town's medical needs certainly exceed the hours of this clinic. My goal is to eventually keep it open twenty-four hours. It seems as if a disproportionate number of emergencies occur in the middle of the night."

"Hopefully once we get the carriage house renovated, you can find that doctor you need."

"That's the hope. It'll be a tall enough order, finding a good doctor who wants to practice in such a small town."

He glanced at the mountains in the distance, then returned his attention to her, lingering on her face for a beat. "I don't know, from what I can see this place has plenty to offer."

Was he flirting with her? The corner of his lip curled up, and his eyes softened in the evening light. It had been a while, but yes, he was definitely flirting.

A bubble of pleasure swelled inside. "You *are* talking about the landscape . . ."

"Of course." His eyes sparkled. "What else would I be referring to?"

"I think your fever's back. You seem a little delusional."

"Never felt better. In fact, I should be ready to start work in the morning."

"You're definitely delusional. I'm not releasing you to work until your fever's been gone twenty-four hours."

He let out a deep sigh. "You're going to be a stickler about this, aren't you?"

"I'm going to be a doctor about this."

She'd missed this—the easy banter with a man. She hadn't dated seriously since undergrad. In med school she'd been busy keeping up her GPA and working as a teacher's assistant for one of her professors. According to two men she'd gone out with, she could be a bit intimidating. That assessment had shocked her as she didn't see herself that way at all. Her girlfriends suggested it was her grades and her single-minded ambition that scared men away. Whatever.

Avery recalled the ruckus her staff raised when they'd caught sight of Wes this morning. No doubt the man had stunning blue eyes and a nice physique—broad shoulders, flat stomach, and long, muscle-thick legs. But she'd never been into the mountain-man type. She'd always preferred her men clean shaven. Well, a little scruff never hurt. But big, bushy beards and overgrown hair? Not so much. Not that she was in the market for a man.

"What?"

The word startled her from her thoughts. She'd been caught ogling. "What?"

"You were staring."

"Just wondering what you look like under all that scruff." Her tone and the accompanying smile were flirtatious. But what was the harm? He wouldn't be here long anyway.

He rubbed his beard. "Underneath all this, I'm hideous. All scarred and grotesque. I'm like the phantom, and this is my mask."

She chuckled. "I highly doubt that. Do you normally wear a beard?"

"Nah. Just too much bother to shave on the trail."

A text came in and she checked her phone. It was Rick, confirming the time for their double date Friday. He'd called last night to make the invitation official—and to flirt for a few minutes. Why didn't she enjoy flirting with Rick as much as she enjoyed flirting with Wes? Probably because Rick flirted with every human being with double X chromosomes, whereas Wes . . . well, she didn't really know who he was, did she?

But for some reason she wanted to find out.

Nine

"You're letting some vagrant stay in your backyard?" Gavin stood on her doorstep the next morning before the clinic opened, hands perched on his narrow hips, wearing a dark scowl.

"Good morning, Brother. Come inside. Would you like a cup of coffee?"

He entered her apartment and frowned at her innocent Keurig. "That's not coffee. Who is this guy, and why's he staying in your shed?"

Here we go again. Her family was overprotective of her. She was the baby of the family—and the potential disease didn't help matters either, especially as she'd approached thirty. They were always after her for working too much, and they went on high alert if she had a memory lapse, stumbled over her own feet, or was simply in a bad mood.

Avery scooped Boots's generic kibble into her dish, and the

cat pranced forward. Katie must've told Cooper about Wes and Cooper had told Gavin. She was surprised Cooper wasn't on her doorstep too.

"Not that I owe you an explanation, but he's not a vagrant, and he's down with a bug at the moment. He needed a place to crash, what with it being a holiday weekend."

"And then you invited him to stay and renovate your shed? I can make room for him at the campground if that'll help."

"He's fine where he is, thank you. And it's a carriage house."

"What do you even know about this guy?"

Avery crossed her arms over her chest. "I'm perfectly capable of screening people, you know. I run a business, remember? I made the necessary phone calls to insure he was a capable contractor and decent human being, and I really don't appreciate being underestimated."

His shoulders lost some starch. "I was just worried about you having a stranger on your property. This neighborhood is all but deserted after business hours, and you're here all alone."

"That's what locks are for."

"And why didn't you ask me to handle the renovation? I was a highly sought-after contractor in my former life, you know."

She narrowed her eyes. "I did ask you. Twice. You put me off."

"I'm building that big cabin at the campground. But maybe I can squeeze your shed in on my day off."

"Not necessary. But I need another doctor at this clinic ASAP." According to her Fitbit she was averaging five and half hours of sleep per night. Better than during residency, but still. She was too old for this.

"I didn't think you were in that big a hurry. Or that you were serious about using that shed"—when she gave him the evil eye, he said—"*carriage house* for a living space."

"Well, I was serious, and now the job's getting done—or at least started. Keep feeling guilty though, since I'll need your help once Wes leaves. And he'll need to borrow your tools too. Whatever he'll need to install windows and a new roof."

"He'll need to pull a permit."

"He's well aware."

Gavin glanced out the kitchen window toward the backyard. "I'd like to meet him."

"It's seven forty-five in the morning and he's sick." She held his gaze, not backing down.

"Later then."

"Whatever. It's not changing anything. Now, are you finished interrogating me or can we move on to more pleasant subjects?"

He leaned back against the island. "Sorry. Sometimes I forget you're all grown up."

She almost mentioned she'd just had her thirtieth birthday, but that would be counterproductive. She placed the French vanilla pod in the machine and pushed the Brew button.

"Cooper said you're going out with Rick this weekend."

"The family grapevine is definitely alive and well." She wished she'd just held firm with Cooper, but she hadn't, and now, short of coming down with a virus, she would have to suffer through. At least Katie and Cooper would be along. They were fun and their presence would keep things casual.

"Watch out for Rick. I know Cooper thinks a lot of him, but he seems like a player to me."

Avery raised an eyebrow. "Again, give me some credit."

"Can't seem to help myself. Over the hill or not, you'll always be my baby sister."

She cut him some slack, an old habit. Gavin was only trying to spare her the heartache he'd suffered. It couldn't be easy being thirty-three with a failed marriage in your rearview mirror. Especially when his brother was currently engaged to the woman he'd wanted for himself.

"Well, try. I can handle my own life."

A few minutes later Gavin gave her a quick hug and left. Avery took a few minutes to enjoy her second cup of coffee as she read her daily devotion at the island while Boots nipped at her kibble.

When Avery was finished reading, she glanced out the kitchen window. Was Wes up yet? How was he feeling this morning?

That she'd opened up to a stranger the previous night surprised her. It was probably only because he wouldn't be here long. He was practically a vapor, here for a moment, then gone. If befriending him (and flirting a little) eased the ache of loneliness and tediousness of her workaday life for a couple of weeks, why shouldn't she indulge?

Ten

Wes was dying—not of a virus but of sheer boredom. At four o'clock he shot Avery a text. It's been 24 hours. He didn't expect to hear from her until the clinic closed at five, but he was raring to go. He'd already measured the windows and made a list of the supplies he'd need.

He went to the sink to wash his lunch dishes. He should've asked Avery last night if she'd be free to run to town tonight. Surely she'd want to pick out the windows and roof shingles.

His thoughts went back to the pleasant evening they'd spent on the back deck last night. Avery had loosened up and he found himself enjoying her company. Enjoying the southern cadence of her voice.

Okay, so he was attracted to her. Big deal. She was an intelligent, warm, beautiful woman. Maybe he should've mentioned Lillian. But why would he do that? He was out of here in a couple of weeks. He'd get on with his life, and the doctor would get on with hers.

The story of her mother's sudden passing made him ache for her. In many ways the traumatic event had determined who she'd become. He wasn't so different. He didn't even remember his mother, but the nomadic lifestyle his dad had inflicted upon him certainly affected him.

As he turned off the tap, a knock sounded at the door.

Avery stood on the stoop, wearing a lab coat over peach scrubs. A stethoscope snaked around her neck. Silky strands of hair had escaped her ponytail, and pale freckles peeked through any makeup she might be wearing.

"No ibuprofen in the past six hours?" she asked by way of greeting.

"Nope."

"All right, let's have a look at you."

He sank onto a kitchen chair that seemed old enough to make him question its sturdiness. It only gave a minor complaint as he eased his weight onto it.

Avery whipped a thermometer from her pocket and stuck it into his mouth, then proceeded to listen to his heart and lungs. She set a hand on his shoulder as she moved the stethoscope to his back. She had steady hands and a gentle touch. A good bedside manner. She cared about people—even a smelly, hairy stranger who showed up unexpectedly on her porch. On her birthday.

From beneath his lashes he watched as she listened through the earpieces. Sunlight flooded through the kitchen window, making her green eyes appear as deep and mysterious as a secret swimming hole. A closer study revealed spokes of amber and a dark limbic ring encircling her iris. The pink tones of her high cheekbones appeared natural, and her cute nose seemed to have been custom sculpted for her delicate face. Her lips appeared soft and lush in their relaxed state. If he hadn't already committed himself to Lillian—

The thermometer beeped.

Avery curled the rubbery stethoscope around her neck and slid the thermometer from his mouth. "Ninety-eight point eight. Looks like you're officially well, Mr. Garrett."

"I was hoping we could head to Asheville tonight and get the windows and roofing supplies. The windows are standard size so that's good news. You mentioned borrowing your brother's truck?"

"Right. Yes, Cooper said we could use his truck but . . ." Something flickered in her eyes. "I can't go with you to Asheville. I'm on call."

"I was hoping to start installing the windows in the morning."

"You may as well go by yourself; I'm always on call."

A forty-five-minute drive didn't seem very far, but maybe something else was behind her refusal. Maybe she didn't feel comfortable being alone with him. He was a virtual stranger after all. "Don't you want to pick out the window and shingles? Asheville seems to be the closest town that carries what we'll need."

"No, you're right, it is. But you can pick out everything."

"Is your brother okay with me driving his truck? I can charge the supplies to my credit card and give you the receipt."

"Cooper's fine with that. And yes, I'll reimburse you as we go. And as far as the product, just try and match it to the house as much as possible."

"White double-hung windows and a three-dimensional roof shingle. What about quality?"

"I'll trust that to your expertise. I don't want cheap but I don't need extravagant either."

"Got it. I can text you pictures if I'm unsure."

"Sounds good." She shifted on her feet and her gaze dipped to the floor before returning to his face. "I should get back to the clinic. I'll take you over to get Cooper's truck." She checked her watch. "Say, five thirty?"

"All right."

With one last smile Avery exited the apartment and Wes jotted a couple more notes on his phone. He pushed aside the disappointment that she wouldn't be joining him tonight. He was only lonely from the solitude of the trail. He'd call Lillian on his way to Asheville and check in.

───────────

The baby's wails filled the exam room as Avery exited. Katie had just given the sweet infant her first vaccination, and the poor thing was furious.

It was barely ten in the morning, but the waiting room was half filled with patients. However, the other exam rooms were empty. She went to the front desk, but Patti was nowhere to be found—and neither, come to think of it, was Sharise. Avery headed down the hall and found the two women in the office, peeking through the French doors into the backyard.

Avery cleared her throat and the women whipped around, the remnants of their laughter hanging in the air and lingering on their flushed faces.

Now that they'd shifted, Avery had a clear view of Wes lifting a window into an opening in the carriage house. His white T-shirt clung to the broad expanse of his shoulders, and his sun-bronzed skin stretched taut over the rippling muscles of his arms as they shifted under the weight of the window.

Avery regarded the women. "This isn't a peep show, ladies."

Patti glanced longingly out the window. "But did you see—?"

"That there are five patients in the lobby and none in the exam rooms?"

"Right, Boss." Sharise headed toward the door. "On it."

Patti followed in her wake. "But did you see—?"

"Back to work, Patti." Avery's lips twitched as she watched the women leave.

Avery took a water bottle from the mini fridge and chugged it down, making a point of not peering out the window. *Not* seeing what had captured the women's attention. But the mental picture was already stuck in her brain, and she couldn't seem to eradicate it.

———

Wes dashed through the pummeling rain and headed up the outdoor staircase to Avery's apartment. Daylight had faded but the weather had sidelined him hours ago. Even though the fatigue made him feel as if he were moving through molasses, he busted his butt to get the windows in before the rainstorm arrived.

When he reached the top of the stairs, he ran a hand through his damp hair and knocked.

A moment later Avery appeared in the doorway, wearing a loose, pale-green T-shirt that draped on one side, revealing an ivory shoulder. As usual her hair was swept back into a ponytail. "You got rained out today, huh?"

"I got all the windows in before it started. But yeah, the roof'll have to wait till tomorrow."

"I hate to tell you, but they're calling for rain tomorrow too."

"All the more reason to talk about the interior. You got a minute? I'll need to order the flooring if it's to arrive before I finish the roof."

"Sure, come in out of the rain. Have you had supper?"

"I did. Is that coffee I smell?"

She opened the door wider and winced. "I forgot there was no coffee maker out there. I'm so sorry."

"The gas station down the road sells it."

"Even I have my standards."

"Yeah, it wasn't great." But it had given him the fuel to make it through today. He took in the open apartment. A gray leather sectional took up a large chunk of the living area. The original wood floors had been restored to a sheen, but the wide base-board was sporting several coats of paint—currently white. The kitchen lay just beyond and a short hallway ran alongside it. The walls sported a neutral shade of gray, but pops of color appeared here and there: pillows, wall hangings, and throws. An eclectic collection of picture frames propped up photos on the end tables and bookshelves.

"Make yourself at home. I have a Keurig and pretty much any kind of coffee you could want."

"A dark roast if you have it. Any chance you have real cream? I've missed it."

"Half and half?"

"Perfect." Curious, he wandered over to the bookshelves.

You could tell a lot about a person by the books she read. Unsurprisingly, Avery had two shelves full of medical textbooks. Below that, in alphabetical order by author name, were four rows of fiction. The genres were varied, everything from thriller to historical to romance. Classics like Austen and Brontë stood alongside the latest best sellers. He'd read four or five of the novels himself. Biographies and memoirs took up the bottom shelf.

A few minutes later Avery returned, coffee in hand.

"Thank you." He took a sip, savoring the best coffee he'd had since his stop in Erwin.

"Do you like to read?" she asked.

"Very much. I brought a paperback on the trail, hoping it would keep me company at night. But it was too good—I finished it inside of a week."

"You're welcome to borrow any of these."

"I'll take you up on that. The nights can get boring. I've been playing solitaire to keep my brain busy."

He followed her to the sectional, and his body ached as he lowered himself at one end of the beast. "This must've been a bear to get up that staircase."

She chuckled. "It took both my brothers and me to make it happen. There were some unfortunate verbal exchanges involved, but in the end, I saved the relationship with a large deluxe pizza from Poppy's."

"Smart woman."

Avery settled in the corner, pulling her legs underneath her. She cupped a pink insulated mug between her hands. "How are you feeling? I hope you didn't overdo it today."

"The rain saved me from working too long. I got a peek at the roof, and I'm pretty sure it has three layers."

"Is that bad?"

"You really shouldn't go beyond two. They'll have to be torn off, and for that I'll need a dumpster. I took the liberty of ordering one. I'll reschedule if it looks like rain tomorrow. No sense paying for days we won't be using it."

"I didn't even know you could order a dumpster."

He grinned. "Well, I didn't know URIs could be viral or bacterial."

"I thought everyone learned that in school."

The thought of his upbringing dimmed his smile. "I'm afraid I didn't do very well in school."

"You're a self-professed avid reader, and you have an excellent vocabulary. Were you an underachiever, Wes?" Her voice was slightly flirtatious.

"Something like that. I should add that by high school, my motivation did pick up. I actually became fairly studious." He took a sip of his coffee, waiting for her to fill the silence. When she didn't, he filled it himself. Why not? "I moved around a lot, growing up. Attended four different elementary schools and three different middle schools. Seemed like by the time I got things figured out at one place, it was time to move on again."

"Seven different schools? Was your dad in the military?"

He chuckled. The idea of his dad being anything that noble was literally a laughing matter. "Definitely not. Holding down a job of any kind wasn't high on his list of objectives. He wasn't a very honorable person."

"I'm sorry. That sounds like a difficult way to grow up." She tilted her head as she studied him. "I wonder . . . how did the apple fall so far from the tree?"

"The apple rolled as far from that tree as it could get."

"You spoke of him in past tense . . ."

"Shortly after I graduated high school, his lifestyle finally caught up to him and he was sent to prison. He died there five years ago." Wes had visited him monthly. He hadn't been much of a man or a father, but he'd never left Wes. That counted for something, he supposed.

"I'm sorry. Do you have any other family?"

"I had a great-aunt—Cordelia—my dad's aunt. She was like a mom to me. We ended up crashing with her when we were between places, which was often. She used to beg Dad to let me stay with her. I would've loved that." He'd always planned to move in with her when he turned eighteen, but she'd passed away before that. Until Landon's death, that had been his greatest loss. He'd cried until his dad grew frustrated and gave him chores to keep him busy.

"That's good you had someone like her in your life. I'm thankful for my stepmom, Lisa. She really filled the gap in my life."

"You're lucky to have family close by." He regarded her as he took a sip of coffee. She looked adorable, sitting pretzel-style in the corner of the overstuffed sofa.

"And most of the time I appreciated it." She pursed her lips. "So you wanted to talk flooring? I've been doing some research online."

"Show me."

She retrieved her laptop and settled beside him, then pulled up a website and showed him some of the flooring she liked. She wanted a wood-plank design, and he advised her on the pros and cons of different material types. She settled on planks of laminate flooring in gray tones.

Wes leaned back against the sofa. "If it's raining tomorrow, I'll head back to Asheville and pick up some flooring samples. What color paint were you thinking of for the walls? I'll bring back some color swatches too."

"I was thinking of using the same color I used in here—Agreeable Gray by Sherwin Williams."

"I'll pick up what we need."

His gaze connected with hers, and he felt that pull tightening between them. It had been there from the start. But now that he was well and thinking clearly, he couldn't deny the magnitude of his attraction. She was a beautiful woman, with her arresting green eyes and soft features. But it was more than that. For all her intelligence and independence, there was something inherently vulnerable about her. And it drew him like a magnet.

Why was that? She didn't need someone to solve her problems or take care of her—she was perfectly capable. He just desired to know her in a deeper way. He was suddenly aware of her knee, pressed against his thigh. Her elbow, touching his arm.

"So . . . ," she said softly, breaking the silence but not the eye contact. "After all that moving around you must have a strong urge to settle down. Why Albany?"

He blinked at the topic that had been far—too far—from his thoughts. He cleared his throat, a prick of guilt poking his insides. "I have a friend there. And yes, I'm definitely longing to get a steady job and put down some roots."

"Albany's a nice-size city. You should have decent job opportunities there."

"That's the hope." He needed to get out of here—but he wanted to stay. The contradictory options played tug-of-war in his head.

Avery snapped her laptop closed and bounced to her feet. "You want to play cards? I'm a master of rummy, but I'm also passable at poker, euchre, and hearts."

He couldn't resist her hopeful expression. And let's face it, he didn't even want to. "Poker, huh? What are the stakes?"

She cocked an eyebrow. "Something cheap."

"Dinner? Loser cooks."

"Are you any good?"

He followed her to the dining room. "At cooking or poker?"

"Both."

"I'm proficient enough at both."

"All right then." She pulled a deck of cards from a drawer and slapped them down. "Your deal."

Eleven

"No." Katie shook her head. In the floor-length mirror, her gaze traveled the length of Avery's body. "No, no, no."

Avery took in her outfit: stretchy jeans, a nice black top, and flip-flops. Okay, maybe the sandals had seen better days. "It's just a casual dinner, and I'm really not looking to impress Rick."

But Katie was already at the closet door, still in her scrubs, riffling through Avery's clothes. "It's your first date in ages. Do it for yourself. You used to enjoy getting dressed up. You've just grown accustomed to the scrub life and forgotten what it feels like get all dolled up."

Avery studied her appearance. "It's not that bad."

"You're a beautiful woman with a great body." Katie's voice echoed from the depths of Avery's closet. "You shouldn't hide it with baggy shirts and unflattering jeans. If I had long legs like yours, I'd wear dresses twenty-four seven."

Katie might not be tall, but she was adorably petite. Add in her almond-shaped blue eyes and gorgeous blonde waves and Avery could see why both her brothers fell for her.

"Good grief, have you bought anything new since college?"

"I've been a little busy with the clinic."

"Do you even have any dresses in here? I had no idea scrubs came in so many colors—or that people actually hung them up."

"That's why they're never wrinkled."

"Aha! Ugh, never mind. Positively shapeless. Just for tonight you need a new look."

"There's nothing wrong with my look. It says . . ." Avery met her own gaze in the mirror and lifted her chin. "It says I'm confident. I'm comfortable with myself."

Katie tossed a glance over her shoulder. "It just says you're comfortable. Oh! Here we are. How about this one?" She held out a hanger, holding a short black dress.

"I bought that for med school graduation."

"Well, it's perfect for tonight. Put it on. Where are your shoes?"

Avery took the dress. "Right there on the floor."

"This is it? You have four pairs of shoes?"

"Five, if you count the ones I'm wearing."

"I don't," Katie muttered. She heaved a sigh and grabbed the black flats. "Luckily with your height, you can pull these off."

Avery went into the bathroom to change into the dress. It slipped up her body and she managed to get the zipper all the way up.

"This is just like college!" Katie called through the door. "Except back then I didn't have to beg you to dress up. How's it look?"

"Okay, I guess." Avery pulled at the hem. She didn't remember it fitting so snugly. It was modest for a little black dress: a sleeveless, fitted number with a gently scooped neckline and a hemline that showed off her long legs. Katie was right. Avery didn't know why she'd left it hanging in the back of her closet so long. Maybe she didn't have anyone to impress, but she did like dressing up on occasion. She just didn't want to send Rick the wrong message.

"Let's just keep things fun tonight, okay?" Avery said. "I'm not interested in anything serious." Or anything at all.

"Of course it'll be fun. Cooper and I are fun, aren't we? And Rick seems like a good time too. Just relax. It'll be a blast."

Avery found herself thinking of Wes. Of the low scrape of his voice. Of his deep chuckle as they'd played poker the past two nights. He was an easygoing kind of guy. Their conversation flowed effortlessly, and the low-key flirting was fun and stimulating. His love of reading made him knowledgeable in a lot of areas, from politics to astronomy to world history.

She stared at her reflection. What would Wes think of this dress? He'd only seen her in scrubs and jeans.

"Let me see," Katie called.

Avery gave her reflection one last glance before she opened the door.

Katie's smile bloomed. "There are those curves. And I'd forgotten what great collarbones you have. Skip the necklace. Let's find some dangly earrings." She glanced at Avery's ponytail. "And we need to do something else with your hair."

"It's a chic ponytail. I even wrapped a strand around the elastic."

"I can hardly even remember what your hair looks like down. Pleeaase?"

"Fine, but I'll curl it myself. You still have to run home and get ready."

Katie checked her watch. "Ooh, you're right." She snatched her purse off the sofa and turned at the door, a twinkle in her eyes. "And don't forget, a little mascara and lipstick never hurt anyone."

Avery grabbed a throw pillow and tossed it at her friend. It hit the back of the door and fell to the floor as Katie's laughter carried through the walls.

Avery should've just agreed to meet Rick at the restaurant. But it was too late now. As she secured her earring, the second knock sounded on her door. She grabbed her purse, slipped into the flats, and opened the door.

Rick's eyes made a quick sweep of her figure and his dark eyes lit. "Wow, I am one lucky man."

"Good to see you, Rick. You look nice too." His thick jet-black hair, rich bronzed skin, and athletic build attracted plenty of female attention. His Spanish accent and flirtatious ways didn't hurt matters either.

They made small talk as he escorted her to his Chevy truck. Even in jeans and a button-down, Rick walked with a confident swagger that screamed law enforcement.

Avery made an effort to keep the conversation flowing on the short ride to the Trailhead, and soon they were pulling in to the parking lot. Cars packed the lot tonight since a band was playing, but Cooper had managed to reserve a table—a perk of holding a county office.

Ever the gentleman, Rick helped her from the truck and led

her inside. The welcome coolness of air-conditioning swept over Avery's skin as she entered, and the delicious aroma of smoked brisket beckoned her. The lobby was elbow to elbow with people, but Rick took her hand and led her through the throng and toward a booth along the wall. They exchanged greetings with Cooper and Katie.

"You look great," Katie said over the streamed-in music.

"Me? Look at you." Katie wore her long blonde locks in beach waves, and her makeup was spot on. "How do you go from nurse to knockout in fifteen minutes flat?"

Katie waved off the compliment as they picked up the menus and debated the specials. When they'd decided, they put in their order with the busy server.

After she left, Avery directed the conversation toward Cooper and Katie. "How goes the wedding planning? Did you make any progress this week?"

"The invitations came in yesterday," Katie said. "I forgot to tell you. They're beautiful."

"Lucky for you," Avery said, "Cooper has good handwriting."

"Hey, I'm doing my part."

Katie wrapped her arm around his. "You are, sweetheart. You've been a great help."

"When's the big date?" Rick asked.

Katie frowned. "Didn't you get your save-the-date card?"

"I did but"—Rick shrugged—"I'm not sure where it went."

"Typical bachelor," Avery teased.

Rick gave her a saucy smile. "If only you'd put me out of my misery and marry me."

"I think that's your third proposal."

Rick pouted. "And still it's a no."

"The wedding's September third," Cooper said.

"It's really coming up fast," Avery said. "Then again, what do you expect when you have a six-month engagement?"

Cooper had proposed on Katie's birthday in March. Avery loved that he'd talked it over with Gavin first. It had been clear to all of them where Cooper and Katie's relationship was headed, and Gavin, who'd dated Katie first, had graciously given his blessing.

Cooper gave Katie's hand a squeeze. "When you know, you know."

"That's right. I can't wait." Katie leaned into Cooper.

The couple gazed into each other's eyes as if they were the only ones in the room. Big changes awaited these two. Since Katie owned her home, Cooper was moving in with her. The thought of her brother living in that feminine yellow house made Avery's lips twitch. Her brother was totally smitten.

"So . . . ," Rick said to Avery after a long moment. "How 'bout them Braves?"

"You know, I don't really follow the MLB, but I admire your attempt to fill the awkward silence."

Katie chuckled. "Sorry, you two. We'll behave."

"Speak for yourself."

Katie gave Cooper a nudge. "Avery's my maid of honor, Rick. Wait'll you see her in that dress. The sage green looks fabulous on her."

"Does it match her amazing eyes?"

"To a tee." Katie grinned.

Avery gave her friend a pointed look. "No one will even notice me when you enter the room. That gown is stunning on you."

Katie covered her fiancé's ears. "Shush. Cooper knows nothing."

"I know nothing."

The microphone gave a loud squeal as Lonnie Purdy, the restaurant's owner, gave the band an introduction. After enthusiastic applause, the Silver Spurs kicked into their first song, making conversation almost impossible.

They listened to several songs before the server delivered their food. The brisket was divine but there was so much of it, she passed her leftovers to Rick, who was on his way to consuming his weight in beef. Soon after they finished their meal, the band segued to a slow song, and Cooper led Katie to the dance floor.

"Would you like to dance?" Rick asked.

She loved dancing but didn't necessarily want to encourage him.

"Come on. Just one dance. You have to give me a chance to show off my moves."

She had no doubt he had them. Avery dropped her napkin on the table. "All right. You talked me into it."

Twelve

Wes could hear the loud bass thumping a block away from the Trailhead Bar and Grill. He'd nearly ordered pizza and stayed in, but a long evening alone held no appeal. Even though he knew virtually no one in town, he'd rather be surrounded by people tonight. And he remembered Avery mentioning a local pool hall.

Apparently there was a popular band on tap tonight. When he reached the entry, he opened the door to a sea of people. The bar was also packed with diners, sitting shoulder to shoulder. He should just run across the street and order a pizza. But the savory smells emanating from the kitchen convinced him the wait would be worth it.

He would order a drink and head for the poolroom, which was just off the main dining area, next to the restrooms. After he played a game or two, he'd check for space at the bar. If that didn't work out, he'd order carryout. He made his way toward the bar and waited for service.

Ten minutes later, drink in hand, he made his way through the restaurant toward the poolroom. The band was playing a slow country song, and the dance floor was packed with couples, swaying to the—

His gaze stopped on a familiar face. His footsteps slowed. He almost hadn't recognized Avery in the dim lighting. Her brown hair tumbled over her shoulders, and the form-fitting dress did something for her figure that no lab coat could ever do.

As he progressed toward the poolroom, he glanced back at the couple. The man held Avery close, his hand at the small of her back. His smile seemed a little slick for Wes's liking.

Of course men were interested in her. She was an intelligent, successful, and beautiful woman. For all Wes knew, that man could be her boyfriend. He'd never even asked if she was in a relationship.

The heavy weight in his gut unsettled him. He had no claims on Avery and certainly no future with her. It was just a harmless flirtation. A way of passing time while he was in Riverbend Gap. Then why the disturbing feeling?

The poolroom walls bore all the token decorations you'd expect: old license plates and neon signs. A handful of spectators gathered around two tables, both in use. He leaned against the doorjamb and watched the action at the first table, where a twentysomething man played an older guy. Wes's ears perked up when the younger man called his opponent Stewie. Wes's attention sharpened on the pool shark Avery had warned him about.

The young guy came up empty on the break, so Stewie took his turn, easily sinking a ball. He missed his second shot.

Wes fished a quarter from his pocket and set it on one of the rail cushions, then returned to the doorjamb, forcing his attention on the game. It would do no good to torture himself with the sight of Avery and her date. The image of her in the man's arms was already set in concrete. He was glad when, a couple of minutes later, the slow song ended and the band kicked up a rousing country tune. But he didn't let himself check to see if the couple remained on the dance floor.

Stewie was up again and sank two shots—one of them difficult. The younger man must've had money on the game—he seemed more depressed by the minute.

Wes wasn't sure what made him turn, but the moment he did, Avery was there, making her way toward the short hall.

At the sight of him she stopped in her tracks and her eyes widened. "Wes. Hi. I didn't expect to see you here."

"Decided to check out that poolroom you told me about." He took in her dress, those legs, in one fell swoop. "Wow. You look amazing."

She released a nervous chuckle. "A step up from scrubs, I guess."

"See?" Katie had come up behind Avery. "You should dress up more often."

"Hi, Katie." Wes had run into her a few times this week. "You look nice too."

"Thanks. How are you, Wes? You wanna join our table? We could pull up another chair."

Sit and watch Avery canoodling with her date? Pass. "Ah, no

thanks. I'm just here for a game or two, then I'll probably grab some takeout and head back to the house."

"Go for the brisket special," Avery said. "It's delicious."

Katie excused herself and headed for the restroom, and Avery's gaze returned to Wes. Her lashes seemed impossibly long tonight, framing those beautiful eyes. But it was her full red lips that commanded his attention.

Avery shifted. "Um . . . you should come over to the table and meet my brother Cooper."

"I've already met him, actually—and your other brother too."

She blinked. "What? When?"

"They came over this week—separately—while I was working on the carriage house."

"Oh, jeez. I hope they were nice."

"They were . . . fine."

"Oh no."

He didn't mention that Cooper had showed up in uniform. "They just wanted to make sure I knew they were keeping an eye on their baby sister."

She closed her eyes. "For crying out loud."

He chuckled. "No worries. I'd probably do the same if I had a little sister."

"Their little sister is a thirty-year-old doctor who owns her own business."

"All the same . . . You're blessed to have people who care about you so much."

"When you put it that way . . ."

Wes glanced over her shoulder where her date waited at the table. He was watching the band, seemingly unaware Avery had been sidetracked. "I should probably let you get back to your boyfriend."

"Oh, he's not . . . it's just a date. We're not . . ."

"Hey, buddy," someone behind him called. It was the young guy who'd just played. "You're up."

Avery backed away. "I should let you get on with your game. I guess I'll see you tomorrow."

"See you." He watched her retreat down the short hall and into the restroom. Only when the door closed did he return his attention to the table.

"What was that?" Katie asked the moment the bathroom door closed behind Avery. Her friend straightened from the mirror, holding an open tube of lip gloss.

"What was what?"

"You like him."

"Who?"

"Who," Katie scoffed. "Your backyard buddy, that's who. That's why you're not interested in Deputy McDreamy."

"No, that's not at all—"

"Did you see the way he gawked at you?"

"Not really." Actually, the way his gaze raked over her had given her chills. Just the thought of it made her arms prickle with gooseflesh all over again. Avery pulled her lip gloss from her purse and began applying it.

"Please. He was staring at you like a starving man eyes an all-you-can-eat buffet."

"Nice analogy."

"You should go out with him. I mean it's clear you're not really into Rick. You could've fit a semitruck between you when you were dancing. Why didn't you tell me something was going on between you and Wes?"

"There's nothing going on. He's just passing through. And anyway, I'm not looking for—"

"—anything serious right now." Katie rolled her eyes. "I know, I know. But, honey . . . sometimes love just comes a-knockin'. And you definitely want to answer that door."

Avery capped her lip gloss. "Spoken like the besotted woman you are. Come on, let's get on with this date."

"Spoken like a woman with a checklist. You're hopeless."

"Please keep that in mind next time you're tempted to set me up."

Katie huffed as they exited the restroom. Avery didn't even glance in the poolroom as they passed.

But ten minutes later she couldn't resist sneaking a peek. Wes bent over the table lining up a shot. His opponent stood nearby. Stewie Mason—the man she'd warned him away from.

Before she could look away, Wes straightened from his shot, and his gaze locked on her.

Trying to telegraph a warning, she cut her eyes to Stewie, then back to Wes and gave her head a sharp shake.

The corner of Wes's lip lifted and he winked at her.

Avery took the steps to her apartment, Rick on her heels. Night sounds carried on around them: the warbling drone of cicadas, the chirp of a nearby cricket, and the deep croak of a bullfrog down by the river. But the cacophony was simply background noise for her internal thoughts.

No doubt Rick was used to getting what he wanted where women were concerned. But Avery was certain his healthy ego would easily sustain the blow of rejection. Once she reached the top of the stairs, she unlocked her door and turned to face him. The interior light she'd left on cast a dim glow over his attractive features.

"I had a great time tonight," he said. "I'd like to go out with you again."

She gave him her best *bad news* smile. "Listen, Rick . . ."

"Oh no. You had a terrible time. You never want to see my ugly mug again." A shadow pooled in his dimple.

"No, no, not at all. It was fun. You know how to show a woman a good time."

"I hear a big *but* at the end of that sentence."

"It's nothing personal, I promise. I'm just not looking for anything serious right now."

"Let's just go out and have a good time then. I won't rush you."

She shook her head, letting the silence lengthen. Letting the action speak the words.

That charming smile never faltered. "Okay, you're focused on your career right now. I get that. I respect it, even. I can wait."

"And disappoint all the single women of Riverbend? That would just be cruel."

"Aw, Robinson." He palmed his chest theatrically. "You're breaking my heart."

"I can see that." She extended her arms. "Come here. Let's hug it out."

He stepped into her embrace. "This isn't how I saw our good night going."

"No doubt." She chuckled as she wrapped her arms around him. "You're a swell guy, Rodriguez."

"Ouch."

"I really do want to be friends. I'm not just saying that, you know."

"You're killing me here."

She stepped away, stretching her lips in a wide smile.

His eyes twinkled in the shadows. "All right, all right, I can take a hint."

"Did you miss that whole part about friendship?"

"Okay, *friend.* I'm sure we'll see each other around—this town being the size of a Monopoly board and all."

She tilted a wary look at him. "You're going to pull me over and give me a speeding ticket, aren't you?"

"Not if you don't speed."

Avery laughed. "Thank you for a very nice evening."

He flashed a smile as he turned to go. "You change your mind, you know where to find me."

The guy was persistent, she'd give him that. She slowly shook her head. "Good night, Rodriguez."

"Good night, Robinson."

She remained in the shadows as he descended the stairs. At the bottom, as he made a U-turn for the parking lot, the streetlight pushed back the shadows on his face. His guard had dropped, and his dimple was gone. His eyes turned down at the corners, his face crestfallen.

She blinked. Beneath that cavalier exterior was a man who actually cared for her. The revelation stole her breath. Avery stepped quietly inside, closed the door, and leaned against it. The attraction had never been there for her, and still she'd agreed to the date, given him false hope.

Guilt tightened her chest as she closed her eyes and exhaled a long breath. "Well, crap."

Thirteen

"How'd your date with Ricky Rodriguez go, honey?" Lisa heaped a serving of broccoli salad onto her plate and passed the bowl to her husband.

Avery had been wondering when that would come up. The Robinsons had been gathered around the table for a whole two minutes. "It was fine. Rick was a perfect gentleman. We had fun."

"She shut him down," Cooper said with a full mouth.

"I told him I'd like to be friends."

"Ouch," Gavin said.

All the men around the table displayed some form of a wince, even her dad. "What is so wrong with being friends? Everybody needs them and you really can't have too many."

"No man wants to be friend-zoned by the woman he has the hots for," Gavin said.

Avery opened her mouth to refute the statement, then

remembered Rick's crestfallen expression last night. "It's nothing personal. I'm just not interested in a relationship right now."

From across the table Lisa touched Avery's hand. "I've been wanting to introduce you to a man I met this week, but I thought I'd wait and see how things panned out with Ricky. His name's Jeremy and he's new to town—he works over at the radio station with Katie's mom."

"Oh!" Katie said. "Jeremy. Why didn't I think of that? He's really cute, Ave, and he's super smart. Mom said he attended Cornell, and he moved here to look after his mother who's not faring well—very sweet."

Katie continued extolling the man's virtues while Avery gave her friend a pointed stare. Seriously, what part of "not interested in a relationship" did people not understand? She supposed she should just be glad Katie hadn't mentioned her supposed crush on Wes.

"I have to run over to the station this week," Lisa said. "I could feel him out, see if he's interested."

"Thank you, but no. I'm fine on my own." Though Avery managed a temperate tone, she could feel her blood pressure increasing. Why did everyone feel the need to set her up?

"Have you tried a dating app yet? Flutter's the best, in my opinion." Gavin knew his way around the apps. But since losing Katie to his brother last fall, nothing solid had materialized.

"I've heard EHeart is pretty good too," Cooper said.

Avery's dad gave her a knowing smile. "Or she could just focus on her career for now."

"Thank you, Dad."

"Well, of course, it's up to you," Lisa said. "But I think you'd really like Jeremy, if you just gave him a chance. It's great that you're not actively looking—that's when the best opportunities come along."

Her stepmom meant well, she really did. But Avery only had to remember the deflating end to last night's date to steel herself against Lisa's persuasion. Avery would not be pressured into this.

"Let me just find out if he's single. I can ask Beth to do a little digging—subtly, of course."

"That's all right. Let's just leave it alone for now." Avery balled the napkin in her fist and forced slow, even breaths. Even though her appetite was long gone, she forked a couple of green beans and slid them into her mouth. "How are those wedding plans coming along, Cooper?"

"We just talked about that last night."

"I brought the invitations," Katie said. "I'll show you after lunch."

"Oh, I know." Lisa sat up straighter. "We can organize a spontaneous meetup. Jeremy grabs coffee every morning at Millie's. You could show up at the same time and see if there are any sparks."

"Good idea," Cooper said. "More natural that way."

"Right?" Lisa said. "That way no one's put on the spot, and you'd get to see him before—"

Avery's thumped her fist on the table, making the silverware jump. "I'm not getting married!"

Five pairs of eyes darted her way as everyone froze in place. Their expressions would've been comical if not for the fact that her outburst had come from a place of deep hurt and grief. Her face heated under their scrutiny.

"Well . . . ," Lisa said. "Of course not, honey. I was only talking about a little ol' date."

Avery scanned the concerned expressions around the table. No doubt they were wondering if her sudden outburst could be considered a mood change—a symptom of Huntington's disease.

But she didn't want to deal with that right now. However, it was definitely time to put an end to all the setups. All the false expectations. She'd made her decision and now she needed to include her family. She shouldn't have put it off this long.

"What I mean is . . . I've decided that I'm going to remain single." Avery loosened her grip on the napkin and calmly set it on the table. "For life."

Silence swelled at the table until the air fairly vibrated with tension. Her dad's brows drew tight over his blue eyes. Lisa's mouth gaped. Her brothers stared at their plates. Katie touched the base of her neck, peering at Avery with a heart-wrenching expression.

Avery took a deep breath. "A few months ago, I told you all that I'd decided not to get tested for Huntington's . . . Well, I've also decided that I won't put a husband and children through all the uncertainty I'm forced to contend with." There was so much more to it than that. The threat of losing her mental health, of becoming dependent on the people she loved most, the shortened lifespan.

"Oh, honey," Lisa said. "That is such a big decision."

"And one I've not come to lightly."

Lisa's eyes went glossy. "You're still so young."

Beneath the table Katie took Avery's hand.

"Have you thought about in vitro fertilization?" Lisa said. "There are lots of options these days."

Today's technology allowed the testing of harvested eggs for the Huntington's gene. They could implant only the ones devoid of the gene—without informing Avery if she was a carrier. But that only solved part of the problem.

"Even if I went to the expense of IVF, I can't guarantee I'll be around for a child. I won't risk leaving him or her parentless." She met her dad's gaze, willing him to understand. To not feel guilty.

"Oh, honey . . ." Lisa's words broke off as her face crumpled. She was, no doubt, considering all Avery would sacrifice: the love of a good man, the joy children brought into a mother's life. Avery could only know in theory what she would sacrifice; Lisa knew firsthand.

Still, Avery would have her work. She took in the somber expressions around the table. "Come on, you guys. Stop looking so morose. Many lifelong singles go on to lead very productive and meaningful lives. I don't need a man to be happy."

"Of course not," Katie blurted, then shot Cooper an apologetic glance.

"Well . . ." Dad cleared the tremor from his throat. "Look what you've already accomplished. We're very proud of you, sweetheart. You're a bright woman and obviously you've thought this through."

Lisa took Avery's hand. "Of course your dad and I will support your decision. We're here for you no matter what."

Gavin gave her a smile. "That goes for all of us. Right, Coop?"

"Of course. We're family."

"Me too." Katie gave an unabashed shrug. "Well . . . I will be soon."

Avery sank back against her chair as she blinked away tears.

"Thanks, you guys. I'm so relieved to have this out in the open, and I really appreciate your support. I'll be fine, I promise. You know how dedicated I am to the clinic. My work is important to me, and it's enough to fulfill me." The words came out with a confidence she didn't quite feel. Would her family see right through the bluster?

Fourteen

Wes hoped to high heaven this meal would be edible. He gave the boiling pasta a stir, dumped the spaghetti sauce into a pan, then buried the Prego jar in the trashcan. He was more of a frozen pizza kind of cook. But after losing the poker game to Avery, he owed her a decent supper.

He searched her kitchen for a baking sheet for the breadsticks. She'd worked till noon and had someplace to be this afternoon, so she'd told him to help himself to her apartment since his kitchen wasn't well stocked.

He'd had a busy day himself. He spent most of it ripping old shingles off the carriage house—he'd been rained out since Thursday. Some of the shingles were so old and rotten they crumbled in his hands. Cleanup would be a bear. All told, the tear-off alone would take two or three days. Which was why when he went into town for groceries, he really hadn't had time to visit the barber.

He rubbed his jaw, the feel of smooth skin both unfamiliar and welcome. He told himself the grooming had nothing to do with Avery or her date last night. His beard had been getting downright bushy, and his hair, hanging in his eyes, distracted him while he worked.

"Keep telling yourself that, Garrett." He turned the bubbling spaghetti sauce to low and added the cooked ground beef while Boots wove between his legs.

He'd walked home from the restaurant last night just in time to catch Avery and her date embracing on her stoop. He retreated into the carriage house before he could see if the man followed her inside. None of his business. But that didn't stop him from torturing himself with thoughts of the two of them alone up there.

Wes shook the image from his head and replaced it with one of Lillian. Specifically, the one in the photo she'd sent her brother months ago. She was riding a bicycle, smiling. Her filmy white shirt blew in the wind, and her curly brown hair flowed over her shoulders.

He hadn't called her since Tuesday, and with all the rain they'd had, there was no excuse. He'd call her tomorrow. The resolution alleviated the momentary prick of guilt.

The pasta sauce was bubbling again, so he gave it another stir. After putting the breadsticks on the baking sheet, he slid it into the preheated oven. The timer was already set for the pasta so he just made note of the time.

He considered the table he'd set earlier. Seemed kind of plain, but he was no good at this type of thing. Flowers would help, maybe. A plethora of wildflowers grew behind the carriage house.

But no, flowers would be too much. This wasn't a romantic occasion, just the payoff of a friendly bet.

Boots came as far as the threshold and peered up at him with wide amber eyes.

"What do you think, Boots? Does it look all right?" His gaze swung back to center of the table, where a lone salt-and-pepper set stood. "It's missing something, isn't it? Should we pick some flowers for your mom?"

Boots gave him a slow blink.

"Yeah, we definitely should. You watch the stove. I'll be right back."

Avery grabbed her library bag from the blue Jeep and headed toward her apartment. Though the lunch with her family had been heavy, she now felt extraordinarily light. Maybe she hadn't planned on doing the big reveal today, but it was over now.

Plus, she was set for two weeks with her library haul and in possession of the book she'd had on hold for more than a month. She could definitely put her Jane Austen marathon on pause for a while. Oh, and a freshly cooked supper awaited her upstairs.

All in all, not a bad day.

Avery took the steps and opened her door. The savory smells of garlic and yeast greeted her. Steam rose from a pan on the stove, but Wes was nowhere to be found. She closed the door and dropped the library bag on the couch. "I'm home!"

Boots pranced across the living room, and she swept her up in her arms.

A stranger popped up from behind her kitchen island.

Avery jumped. A scream crawled up her throat.

Then her gaze locked on familiar blue eyes. Wes. She stifled the scream and threw a palm against her thrashing heart.

He held up his hands, palms out. "Sorry. Didn't mean to scare you. I was just checking on the bread."

She made an effort to slow her breaths as she took in this barely recognizable man. His bushy beard had concealed a set of chiseled cheekbones and a very masculine jawline. His mustache had hidden a very nice upper lip.

His hair had also been cut. The faded style was very short at the nape but kept a little length on top. He looked . . . as if he belonged on the cover of *GQ*. Or perhaps—since he was currently sporting her favorite apron—*Bon Appétit*.

"You shaved." There was all that higher education at work.

He rubbed his face as if just remembering. "Stopped by the barber while I was in town. Tired of all the scruff."

Oh, and he had a cleft chin also. Good heavens. Avery blinked and set down the cat. "You look so different, I hardly recognized you." She still had a good case of tachycardia going, but it was no longer shock that had her circulatory system in overdrive.

"I was definitely starting to resemble a caveman. Too hot to have all that hair anyway."

"I imagine so." She approached the kitchen. The evening light cast a golden glow over the table setting. He'd picked flowers: red cardinals and white asters. Her everyday plates and paper-towel napkins kept it casual. "How nice. Everything looks wonderful. And smells good too."

"It's just pasta—nothing fancy. Oh, shoot. The breadsticks."

He whipped on a glove and opened the oven. "They're a little overdone."

"It's my policy to appreciate any food I don't have to cook myself."

"That's a relief. I may have overstated my cooking abilities. I'm a little out of my element here."

A few minutes later the food was on the table. Avery wound the spaghetti around her fork. She'd purposefully eaten little at lunch to save her appetite, and she was ravenous now.

"It's delicious," she said a moment later. The garlic and oregano balanced the tang of the tomato sauce.

"I should've made a salad to go with it."

"You've seen my typical supper—I'm lucky to fire up the stove once a week. This is a treat." She grabbed a breadstick, took a bite, and closed her eyes. "Bread is my weakness. Well, that and brownies."

"Not that I snooped or anything, but I did notice four boxes of brownie mix in your pantry."

She jutted out her chin. "They were on sale."

"No judgment here. I've been around enough to know sometimes a girl needs her chocolate."

She tried to find offense, but well, it was true. "Fair enough."

They ate in silence for a few beats as Avery thought back to the night before, to bumping into Wes at the Trailhead. To the rest of the evening when she'd been hyperaware of his location. She thought of her parting with Rick at the end of the evening and the guilt that consumed her. Then she thought of Wes and the time they were spending together. She didn't want to lead him on.

But this wasn't the same thing at all. They both knew he was leaving soon.

She shook away the thoughts. "So, how'd that pool game go last night? I was concerned when I saw you neck-deep in a game with Stewie."

"He's not as good as he thinks he is. I won the games, at any rate."

"Good for you. Did you wager anything fun? Supper? Money? Your firstborn?"

"Nothing as serious as that. But we did get to talking while we played. Did you know he's a certified plumber?"

Avery frowned, chewing. "Doesn't he manage the Shady Pine Motel?"

"Yep. But back in his twenties he worked for Bleeker Plumbing—I confirmed that information this morning as he'll be installing that new tub and sink of yours for free."

"What? You're kidding."

"Nope."

"That is great. Plumbers charge a fortune. We'll definitely deduct that from your tab."

"Not necessary. It only cost me a few games of pool."

But he could've won something for himself—he obviously wasn't swimming in cash. Her heart squeezed tight at the gesture. "That was very kind of you."

"Well"—his lips tilted in a sideways grin—"you've been very kind to me as well."

She shrugged. She'd only been neighborly, offered him a meal here and there. He'd saved her a heap of money with that bet.

"So help me understand," he said. "How does a woman your age own a medical clinic? It takes so many years to get an MD. Shouldn't you still be in residency or something?"

"I got an early start on college—skipped fourth grade—so I graduated high school at seventeen. And I had life insurance money to fund my higher education, so I didn't have to work much in college. Four years of undergrad, four years of med school, and three years' residency in Pennsylvania. Came back home, opened the clinic, and here we are."

"You make that sound pretty simple, but you're not fooling me. You've been on quite the career track, Doc."

She smiled wide. "I'm a very determined woman."

"I can see that." He held up his glass, his eyes smiling. "To strong women who know what they want and how to get it."

She clinked his glass. "Hear, hear." His words warmed her. After having been treated like a delicate flower by her family and written off as intimidating in college, she appreciated his perspective.

Why *had* those college boys found her intimidating? Because she was strong? Because she knew what she wanted? She loved that Wes didn't seem put off by those qualities; instead, he seemed to admire them.

"So, the next phase in your plan includes a second doctor?"

"Among other things. Eventually I'd like to become a full-service clinic."

"What would that entail?"

"Longer hours. More equipment, such as an X-ray machine, a small lab machine, and an ultrasound machine. I've been trying to get funding through grants, but there's a lot of competition for those dollars."

"I have no doubt you'll keep at it until you've succeeded."

"Thanks." They'd only known each other for days, but he had such a high opinion of her, and she didn't want to do anything to alter that. His words gave her a much-needed shot of energy. And after being weighed down by the responsibility of the clinic for months, his optimism was an adrenaline rush.

Avery set her fork down. "Getting that carriage house remodeled is crucial to finding a doctor, so I can't tell you how much I appreciate your help."

"Trust me, it's a win-win."

"I'm just sorry your hike got delayed. And the rain this week certainly didn't help matters."

"First of all, have you hiked in the rain? By Friday I was glad just to be dry. And it wasn't a complete loss. I was able to get started on the interior painting."

"And now you have to endure paint fumes all night long."

"It isn't so bad with the windows open. I was glad to tear into the roof today though. So far I haven't found any rotted sheeting."

"That's good news. How long will the roof take?"

"If all goes well, another day or two. The cleanup is time consuming."

Avery considered a second breadstick, then remembered the snug dress she'd worn the night before and decided against it. She'd filled out a little in past year or so and hadn't realized it—the perils of scrub life.

Then she remembered the way Wes stared at her figure—he sure hadn't seemed to mind the extra pound or two. Her face heated as her eyes flashed up to his.

He was watching her. He'd finished his food and propped his elbows on the table, leaning forward. "Sounds like you were pretty busy in college. Did you make any time for dating?"

Her antennae went up at the personal question. But what

was the harm? "Not much. I dated casually and had one serious relationship in undergrad—Sam."

"How long were you together?"

"A little over a year. He was already in med school and serious about his grades too, so it worked out." She gave him a wry look. "There were a lot of study dates."

"Sounds romantic."

"Oh, he had his moments. I really couldn't have dated anyone who demanded too much of my time."

His blue eyes drifted over her features, seeming to take her in. "Were you in love with him?"

Avery considered that, not for the first time. "I think I was. And he seemed to return the feelings. He could be fun, and I probably needed someone to remind me life existed outside the classroom. He made me smile." She'd been seriously considering a future with him until—

"That's a great quality. What happened between you?"

She let out a grim laugh. She had revealed she was a potential Huntington's carrier, that's what. But she wasn't about to disclose that information. Except for Katie, she no longer told people about her potential diagnosis. Once they knew they treated her differently. They stared at her with pity or—as Sam had done—made a quick exit from her life.

After she'd broken the news to him, he tried to convince her to have the test. Made it sound as if taking it was obviously the right thing to do. But he wasn't the one whose future could be doomed with the results. Wasn't the one who'd had to watch her good-natured mother evolve into a stranger who screamed and pounded the walls in anger, her speech so garbled she was, at times, incoherent.

When Avery had refused to be pushed into taking the test, Sam got angry. *Why didn't you tell me sooner? You hid this from me. This is a big deal, Avery.* As if she hadn't known that. In the end he blamed her for the demise of their relationship.

She'd had plenty of time to reflect during her remaining years of school. Maybe she should've told Sam sooner. But when exactly was the right time? Before they'd become exclusive? Before they fell in love? Scare him away before they'd even had a chance?

That line of thinking only reinforced her decision to remain single for life. That was the only way to keep anyone from getting hurt.

"Sorry," Wes said. "Didn't mean to pry."

Avery blinked away the memories. She hadn't meant to get stuck in the past. "Not at all. I just—I guess you could say we had irreconcilable differences. That sounds lame, but it's true nonetheless. Anyway, I don't think he could've settled here in Riverbend. He was more of a city guy. He ended up taking a residency in Chicago."

"Where is he now?"

"I have no idea. We're not Facebook friends anymore."

He tweaked a brow. "You've never stalked him a little just to find out? I thought everyone did that."

She grinned. "I don't spend much time on social media. But that raises the question: Do you have a former girlfriend you're prone to stalking online? Inquiring minds want to know."

He chuckled. "I guess I asked for that. But no, I'm not a stalker—online or in person. I do have a couple ex-girlfriends though."

She grabbed her drink and settled back in her chair. "Do tell."

"Okay, well, my first real relationship was shortly after high school. Allison and I were together for a tumultuous year and a half. It was a real roller coaster."

"What made it tumultuous?"

He shook his head. "I still couldn't tell you. But the ups were way up, and the downs were way down. What I did learn from that relationship was that I still had a lot to learn about relationships."

"A valuable takeaway."

"I don't know. I guess, having no mother or sisters in my life, I was probably at a disadvantage from the get-go."

"What about your great-aunt? Wasn't she a good role model?"

"She was. She was nurturing and intelligent—she's the one who got me hooked on books. She was a self-made woman, worked her way up at the newspaper and was managing editor when she retired. Never married. A very stable woman—and I needed all the stability I could get."

"She sounds amazing." No wonder this man appreciated a strong woman. Avery filed that information away, then gave him a slow smile. "Okay, back to your ex. It was just getting good."

His lips twitched. "You're really enjoying the misery of my youth."

"Relationships are fascinating, don't you think?"

He let out a dry laugh. "Mainly I've found them confusing. But looking back, I think Allison and I were just too different."

"Opposites do attract."

"That's true—and she was definitely my polar opposite. Outgoing, excitable, a little flighty. During the time we were together, she was, at turns, a barista, a flower-delivery person, and a server at a local café. But nothing I did seemed to make her happy. I always bought the wrong gift, took her to the wrong restaurant, said the wrong thing. I was forever disappointing her."

"Sounds as if she was hard to please."

"She was young—we both were. I'm sure by now she's probably found some guy who knows, better than I ever did, how to make her happy."

Avery sipped from her glass, thinking his assessment of Allison was very generous. "Tell me about the other one. What was her name?"

He stared down at his empty plate, his brow furrowing. "Kendra came along after I moved to Indianapolis, so I was older—and presumably wiser. I met her through a mutual friend, and we clicked right away."

"What was she like?"

"Steady and driven and hardworking. She was a paralegal for a big firm downtown, but she had aspirations of becoming an attorney. She'd already passed the LSAT and was applying to law schools."

"Sounds as if she was Allison's opposite."

He smirked. "Never let it be said I'm a slow learner."

"How long were you together?"

"Two and a half years." He took a drink and his eyes glazed over, indicating he was somewhere in the past.

He seemed to think he didn't know much about women, but from her perspective, he knew plenty. He treated Avery with respect, and it didn't escape her that in telling her his dating history, he hadn't once mentioned his exes' physical appearance. It revealed what he valued most.

"Were you in love with Kendra?"

"Oh, I definitely was. After Allison I was afraid I was destined to drive women over the edge, so I avoided anything serious for years. But when I started going out with Kendra, I was relieved to discover I could maintain an even-keeled relationship."

Allison sounded like a piece of work, but it was nice that he didn't fault her for the demise of their relationship. "What went wrong with Kendra?"

"What went wrong . . . ," he mused aloud. "Well, one day she had to work late, which was pretty typical. I decided to stop by with her favorite takeout—and found her engaged in the lip-lock of the century with one of the firm's lawyers."

Avery winced. "Oh no. That's terrible."

"There may have been a few undone buttons as well. I honestly had no clue. Her expression when she saw me would've been comical if I hadn't been so devastated."

"Oh, you poor thing. What did you do?"

He lifted his shoulders. "Dropped the takeout on her desk and walked out."

"You left the food? I would've . . . I don't know what I would've done, but I wouldn't have left the food!"

"I guess I was in shock. The real anger didn't hit till later—all those 'late nights' at work—and then I wished I'd slugged the guy. But really . . . she was the one in the relationship. She was the one who'd cheated on me."

"What did she have to say for herself? Not that there was any excuse."

"She showed up at my door that night—swore it would never happen again. That she'd been attracted to the guy, but it hadn't meant anything. She didn't want to end things between us. But how could I trust her after that? I basically told her to have a nice life and closed the door. In the coming days she tried to get me to meet with her but . . . I didn't see the point. There was no future for us."

"I've never had anyone cheat on me. It must be hard to move on after a betrayal like that. How do you trust someone again? How do you let down your guard long enough to fall in love?"

"I was definitely jaded for a while. And yes, afraid to trust anyone else, or even myself—I really had been clueless. I just wanted to get away. My dad had died recently, so I started searching for a job outside of Indy. A few weeks later I came across information about ESI and their humanitarian work in Colombia. I'd always wanted to travel abroad, so I decided to go for it. I don't regret it. Building homes for refugees was rewarding work."

"I guess you'd know all about how it feels to want a home."

He smiled. "You're very perceptive, Avery. Someday I'd like to do some volunteer work with them. Take a week or two from my life and just go build a home for someone. Unfortunately, I'm not at a place where I can work for free. I had some debt to pay off, but I'm almost done with that. I'm glad I went to Colombia. I learned a lot about myself. I made some really good friends, especially Landon."

His face softened at the mention of his friend, and Avery's heart broke for him. "What was he like? What was it that connected the two of you?"

"Good question." His brows puckered in thought. "He had a rough upbringing like I did, so I think that was a point of connection. He had a sister though, and they were close. Landon had a strong sense of duty, was loyal to a fault. I'm making him sound like a bore but he wasn't. He knew how to have a good time."

Wes glanced out the window, then checked the time. "I didn't realize how long we've been sitting here. I didn't mean to take up your whole evening."

"Not at all. Supper was delicious and it's nice having someone to talk to."

He stood, gathered his dinnerware, and headed to the kitchen.

She followed him with her own dishes and stopped a foot shy of him. "Just leave them in the sink. I'll load them later."

He started to argue.

"I insist."

His features relaxed as he set his dishes in the sink. "All right, then."

The time had flown, and she felt as if she knew Wes much better after their conversation. He was good company—and suddenly she didn't want to see him go.

"Know what sounds good right now?" she blurted.

He'd turned midway between the kitchen and front door.

Avery paused. He'd only come to pay off a silly debt, and he'd been working hard all day. He was probably anticipating a nice, quiet evening alone. The risk of rejection made her heart thud heavily.

"Let me guess." He gave a wry smile, his blue eyes twinkling. "Brownies."

Her pulse settled into a normal rhythm at his positive response. Maybe he wasn't eager to be rid of her after all. Maybe he enjoyed her company too.

She gave him a playful look. "And here you claimed not to know a thing about women."

Fifteen

Wes couldn't believe his luck. He'd been having such a good time with Avery that he'd been dreading his return to the quiet little cottage. Oh, it was comfortable enough, but after months on the trail, he was lonely for company.

That's what he told himself anyway. That the conversation between Avery and him flowed so naturally didn't factor in. Nor did the fact that she was so beautiful under the golden glow of the chandelier. Stimulating conversation aside, it was a treat just to look at her.

"Can you grab two eggs from the fridge?" Avery asked.

Wes did so and returned to the island, where they'd already dumped the mix plus the oil and water into a clear glass mixing bowl.

"Go ahead and add the eggs. I'll get the pan."

As Avery grabbed a baking pan from the drawer beneath the stove, Wes cracked open the first egg, then the second.

Avery returned in time to catch his technique. "Wow, one handed. I'm impressed."

"Don't let that fool you. I subsisted on scrambled eggs for many years."

"Hmmm, you pulled off that nice Italian supper, and now I catch you cracking eggs like a celebrity chef. I'm starting to think you're a hustler."

He gave a droll laugh. "Must've picked that vibe up from my dad."

Avery raised an eyebrow as she handed him a large spoon. "He was a hustler?"

"He could've sold mosquitos to a backpacker—and he would've if he hadn't been so lazy. Such as it was, he made do with home-improvement scams."

"Oh no."

"Sad thing was, he could've actually done the work if he'd wanted to. It was just easier to rip off people."

"How'd he manage that?"

"Oh, he'd go door to door and give people bids on whatever they needed done. He'd take a deposit, then never come back." Sometimes he even brought Wes along so they felt sorry for him—single dad, trying to eke out a living.

"People just trusted him that easily?"

"He was pretty slick. And he always wore a shirt and hat with the logo of a well-known home-improvement company."

Wes wished he hadn't started this conversation. It was humiliating to admit how he'd grown up, and he and Avery were having a good time. "Mind if we change the subject? Talking about my dad's kind of a downer."

"Of course not." Avery sprayed the pan and set it out for him to pour the batter into. "I just have one more question . . . and it's a very serious one. Your response will likely determine whether or not you're invited to stay for brownies."

He lifted his gaze from his task, raising his brows. "So much on the line . . . you're making me nervous."

"I only ask that you're honest." Avery swiped the side of the bowl with her finger and stuck it in her mouth. "Do you prefer corners or inside pieces?"

A few minutes later the batter was in the oven, and Wes and Avery settled at the island with the mixing bowl between them. Boots was perched in the living room window.

Wes watched as she handed him a rubber spatula, already wielding one of her own. "What's wrong with the spoon we used to mix it with? Other than the fact you've already licked it clean."

"Amateur." Avery tilted a smile at him. "You can get every last bit of batter with one of these babies."

"You take your brownies very seriously. And don't think I didn't notice—you didn't exactly scrape all the batter into the pan."

"Well, everybody knows the batter is the best part." She scooped up a gooey blob of chocolate and sucked it off the spatula, eyes closing in apparent rapture. "Never gets old."

His lips twitched as he took a small scoop of batter. "Should I leave you two alone?"

"You were forewarned. And I'm only letting you stay because you prefer the inside pieces. That's why Katie and I work so well together."

"I see how you are." It was kind of adorable—and sexy—the

way she savored every bite. "How exactly did you and Katie meet?"

"We were in undergrad together at Duke. We bonded over our dislike for a certain English professor, and things progressed from there. Unfortunately, we lost touch after we graduated— she stayed in Asheville and I went off to med school. But when I started the clinic, I thought of her. She'd just lost her brother and liked the idea of moving to a smaller community."

"That's too bad about her brother. She's dating Cooper now?"

"Engaged." She tossed him a saucy smile. "Funny story there. Genius that I am, I'd actually set her up with Gavin. They were an item for a while."

"That must've been messy."

"You could say that. There was a love triangle, a scandal, and all the family drama you could possibly want—if you like that sort of thing, which I don't. Katie being my best friend, I was right in the middle of it all. But we eventually came through it."

"If Gavin managed to put all that behind him, he must be a decent guy." Behind all that protective bluster.

"Both my brothers are good men—love doesn't always play fairly."

He thought of Kendra. "No, it does not." Not only had she cheated on him, but looking back, she'd always seemed embarrassed by his lack of higher education. It took her many months to bring him around her colleagues at the law firm.

Wes and Avery made quick work of the batter while they talked about Avery's family and her brother's run for sheriff last fall. How had she managed to run his campaign when she was practically shackled to her clinic?

She licked the last of the batter off her spatula and set it in the bowl with his. "That really hit the spot. Something about Italian food makes me crave sweets."

A bit of chocolate smudged the corner of her lower lip. He reached out and swept it away, then licked it off his thumb.

Her eyes locked on his and darkened to moss.

The gesture had been intimate—he just felt so comfortable with her. But maybe she didn't feel the same. Should he apologize? Or act as if nothing had happened?

She wiped her mouth, emitting a husky laugh. "Is it gone? I'm so messy. Growing up, I was always the messiest. I can't wear a scarf without finding bits of food in it at the end of the day."

"You're free and clear." He was glad she'd played it off so casually. Maybe he hadn't been out of line. He would never take liberties with a woman and definitely didn't want to make Avery uncomfortable when they'd built such a good rapport.

But Avery was off and talking again, so he must not have blown it. He leaned back against the bar stool and listened, the melody of her laughter filling the space from time to time. Before he knew it, the air filled with the smell of baking brownies. The evening was almost over, and he was still loath to leave.

Sixteen

Avery settled into her favorite corner seat at the coffee shop and took a much-needed sip of her Americano. She remembered the days when she'd ordered green tea for her health. But this morning she'd had to get up early—she'd committed to watching the tots at the early service—and she'd been up in the middle of the night.

Katie entered the shop and Avery waved her over.

They exchanged greetings as Katie looped her purse over the chair. "Aw, you didn't have to get mine. Thank you though." She sank into the seat, looking like a breath of fresh air in her Kelly-green blouse and naturally made-up face. Her blonde hair was swept into a messy bun that seemed chic instead of sloppy.

"Extra sweet, just the way you like it."

"You're the best." Katie eyed her over the rim of her mug. "You look tired this morning."

"There was a call last night. I ended up sending the woman to the hospital for an X-ray. I'm pretty sure it was a fractured tibia."

"How do people get these injuries in the middle of the night, that's what I want to know."

"Apparently, she fell down the stairs."

"We have got to get an X-ray machine."

"I'm working on it. That's what I'll be doing this afternoon." She needed to spend less time fraternizing with her contractor and more time writing grant applications. But the former was so much more enjoyable.

"Let me take your hours next Saturday. If nothing else, you could sleep in for a change."

"I'm sure you have wedding stuff to do, invitations to address."

"We're doing that today. I plan to get them in the mail this week. Let me take your hours."

Avery stifled a yawn. "I'm fine, really. I had some down time last night."

"Meaning you did paperwork in your apartment?"

"No . . . I had a nice supper and finished off the night with freshly baked brownies."

"You cooked on a Saturday night? That's not like you. I mean, brownies, yes, but a meal?"

Avery took a sip of her Americano and strove for a casual tone. "Wes cooked, actually."

Katie's brows shot up. "Oh really."

"He owed me a meal, that's all."

"*Owed* you a meal?"

"We played poker this week and he lost." She was digging this hole deeper and deeper.

"You played poker this week."

"Can you stop repeating everything I say?"

"Sorry, I'm just confused."

Avery didn't particularly want Katie to expound on the thought as she was a trifle confused herself. But she enjoyed Wes's company too much to examine the situation closely. "He shaved off all his facial hair."

Katie frowned at the slight change of topic. "And this is relevant how? "

"He just looks a little different, that's all."

"A little hotter, you mean." Katie studied her with the intensity of a scientist who'd just given her lab rats an experimental medication.

Avery sighed. "All right, fine. Let's hear it."

Katie set down her mug and folded her arms on the table. "So, Friday night I could feel the sparks flying between the two of you."

Avery rolled her eyes.

"Don't deny it. And then yesterday you announced your intention to remain single the rest of your life. And then today you tell me you've been spending all this time with Hottie McHandyman . . ."

"An evening here and there."

"Anyway, you're spending time with him and seemingly enjoying his company."

"And . . ."

"And . . . I can't help but wonder to what end? He's leaving after he's paid off his bill from the clinic, right? He's finishing the trail, then he presumably has a life elsewhere?"

"Albany. And the fact that he's leaving soon is kind of the

point. I enjoy his company, and he seems to enjoy mine. There's no reason to pass up some good conversation in the meantime. There's really nothing to lose here."

"But what if you . . . ?" Katie stared off into the distance, her eyes glazing over for a moment before they swung back to Avery. Her face went soft and her voice lowered. "I'm just worried about you. I don't want you to get hurt."

Avery laughed lightly. "That's sweet but you don't need to worry about me. Wes will be here all of two weeks. Even I couldn't manage to bungle it up in that amount of time."

"Oh, I don't know, you seem to take the fast track on nearly everything you do in life."

"When I have a plan, yes, I'm full speed ahead. But falling for some guy who's just passing through? Not on my agenda."

"Love can creep up on you, you know. It can take you by surprise, change all your plans—despite your best intentions."

Katie was speaking of herself and Cooper. "I get what you're saying, but it's not like that. We're just hanging out, enjoying each other's company. And don't forget, he's helping us get one giant step closer to having another doctor around here."

"And I'm all in favor of that."

"I meant what I said Saturday: I'm dedicated to the single life. I intend to have a long, grand affair with my medical clinic."

Katie gave her a pained look.

"Stop feeling sorry for me. I'm content with my decision—no, *excited* about it. I can serve my community in a way I'd never be able to if I had to take care of a husband and children."

"The community won't warm your feet in bed."

"I have an excellent feather duvet."

But Avery reflected on the intimate way Wes had swept the

batter from her lip. The reflexive way he licked it from his finger. He didn't mean anything by it—that was obvious by his expression afterward—he simply felt close to her and reacted. She loved their warm, intimate friendship.

Avery shook the thoughts away. "Aren't we supposed to be discussing plans for a certain bachelorette party? Because I have some ideas I think you'll like."

Katie released a resigned sigh. "Fine. But I reserve the right to revisit this conversation at a later date."

"Duly noted. Now, I know we're a little limited here in Riverbend, but I made a few calls." Katie had preferred to go to Asheville for the festivities, but she couldn't drag Avery that far from the clinic. "I know you love some spa time, so what if I set that up right here in town?"

"Um . . . we don't have a spa in Riverbend—which I might add is a very unfortunate fact."

"No, but we do have estheticians and manicurists. I already called the salon about hiring them for an afternoon. The Riverview Bed-and-Breakfast has a small event room and two masseuses. I spoke to them about the possibility of renting the room for an afternoon of bliss, followed by dinner out—if that sounds like something you'd want to do." It would only be the two of them since the wedding was small, and Avery was the only bridal attendant.

Katie's face bloomed in a smile. "You are amazing. That sounds perfect."

Avery took a sip of her coffee and said smugly, "Do I know my best friend or what?"

Seventeen

A bead of sweat trickled down Wes's back. He stood up on the roof and stretched. The afternoon sun beat down, and the new dark shingles reflected the heat. But the views from up here were stunning. Toward town, the church steeple towered above the other buildings, pointing heavenward. To the back of the property, the mountains rose high, the peaks defined by the gray sky beyond it. At the base of the mountain, the river snaked past, rippling over rocks with a now-familiar *burble*.

Yesterday he'd finished tearing off the old shingles, and this morning he'd cleaned them up, tossing every last bit of the mess into the dumpster, which had been hauled away at one o'clock. He found the roof decking in good shape—no rotting—but he had to secure some loose boards. He laid the felt underlayment, nailed down the drip-edge flashing, and snapped his lines. He was currently laying shingles, but judging by the darkening sky, he wouldn't get far.

His phone buzzed in his pocket, and he checked the screen. Lillian.

He eased down to sit and answered. He could tell in only a few words that she was having a bad day.

"What happened?" he asked.

"What hasn't happened is the question. My day care is going up in smoke. I haven't been able to take on any more children, and the transmission on my car is on its last legs. And I started going though Landon's things over the weekend, thinking I was ready." She sniffled. "Obviously a mistake. I only made it through one box and I bawled all weekend. Then this morning the two kids I'm watching were little terrors, and I've been impatient with them. They're down for naps now. I'm sorry for bothering you. I feel like I only call when I'm miserable."

"Hey, now. That's what I'm here for. I have bad days too." Most of them had been on the trail when he'd had no cell reception, but he wouldn't have wanted to drag Lillian down anyway. "There's no hurry with Landon's things. Why don't you just wait until I'm there. We can go through them together."

She sighed. "I'd like that. I'm just feeling so lonely."

"Of course you are. He was your brother and you miss him."

"I hate that we were apart for the last years of his life. I feel like I—like I didn't even know him anymore, you know? Because of the distance."

"I can assure you he didn't feel that way. He talked about you all the time. He loved you so much."

"Thanks, Wes." Her voice wobbled on the words. "Can you

tell me another story? Never mind, I'm bothering you in the middle of the day—you're probably busy on that renovation."

He glanced at the threatening clouds. But what could be more important than easing Lillian's grief? She loved hearing about Landon's day-to-day life in Colombia. "I always have time for you." He launched into a story of one of Landon's pranks. It involved Wes's face Photoshopped onto the body of a bikini-clad woman and plastered all over their living quarters. An inside joke—the crew had loved it.

The story had the desired effect—Lillian laughed at her brother's antics. So he told another story and another. She was crying happy tears by the time he was finished. "Thank you so much, Wes. Talking to you always makes me feel closer to him."

"Same. And try not to worry so much. Everything will sort itself out." He wished he had the money to alleviate her financial worries. But when he reached Albany, he'd get a good job, and then he'd really be able to be there for her.

"I know they will. I just got overwhelmed, but I feel much better now."

"I should be finished here by Friday and ready to hit the trail on Saturday."

"Are you feeling good—the fatigue is all gone?"

"Yeah, I'm feeling great. Don't worry about me."

"Uh-oh, one of the munchkins is up. I should go."

"All right. Keep your chin up, hon. Everything's going to be all right." After she said good-bye, he tapped the Disconnect button and pocketed his phone.

This roof wasn't going to shingle itself. As he came carefully to his feet, a figure on the ground caught his eye. Avery's brother Gavin was inspecting the new windows.

"Hey there." Wes propped his hands on his hips. "What brings you by today?"

"Just checking in."

Checking up, more like. Gavin seemed to wear a perpetual frown—or maybe that was just Wes's effect on him.

"Home-center windows?" Gavin asked.

"Seven-eighths inch with low-E and argon. Fusion welded and Energy-Star rated. Not top of the line, but Avery didn't want to go to that expense."

The man stepped closer to inspect Wes's work. He'd meticulously wrapped the old wood trim around the window with vinyl aluminum coil and laid smooth lines of caulk to fill the seams in the window frame. His work could not be faulted, not even by a former big-city contractor.

"They'll do, I guess."

Wes gritted his teeth. "I appreciate the use of your tools."

Gavin stepped back from the house, taking in the roof's underlayment and flashing. "You took off all the shingles?"

"Every last one of the three layers."

"What are you putting the new ones on with?"

Wes held up the nail gun. As if he'd cheat with a staple gun. Some not-so-nice feelings roiled inside. Sure, Gavin was looking out for his sister—couldn't fault him for that. But surely he could see by now Wes knew what he was doing.

Funny how Wes's dad had gotten away with so many scams, yet Wes, who would never cheat Avery, was being regarded with such suspicion. It didn't set well with him. He was good at what he did. You wouldn't find a better window wrapper, and darn it, his caulk lines were smooth as silk.

"Any other questions?" Wes asked.

Gavin raised an eyebrow.

Okay, so his tone had been a little combative. But he'd spent his entire adult life trying to be an honorable person—and his work spoke for itself.

"Can't blame me for looking out for my sister."

"Has she had any complaints?"

"She wouldn't know a Phillips from a flathead. That's why *I'm* here."

Wes wanted to remind him he could've been the one doing the work since he was so qualified, but he bit back the comment. "I take pride in my work, and I'd never rip off Avery."

Gavin gave a brief nod. "I don't know squat about you other than you came off the trail and ended up in my sister's employ."

"Well, now you can see I'm capable of installing a window and know my way around a roof. But feel free to stop in any time—you won't find anything amiss."

"Fair enough."

Before Wes could respond, the sky opened up and rain pounded the roof.

"Got a tarp?" Gavin asked.

"Over there." Wes pointed to the other side of the carriage house.

Gavin grabbed a corner and handed it up to Wes who tugged and pulled until he had the roof covered. From the ladder Gavin helped adjust the tarp, then Wes climbed down, now soaked to the skin.

He ducked under the overhang by the door. "Thanks for your help."

"No problem." Gavin gave him a nod and took off toward his truck.

Wes watched the man rush off. He didn't like the way Avery's brother made him feel, but maybe that was his own problem. His own demons—God knew his father had left him with plenty.

Eighteen

Avery slipped into her raincoat and darted out her office toward the carriage house, her heart beating faster than the movements could account for. The spongy lawn gave way under her steps as she ducked her head under the rain that fell from a formless gray sky. She had thirty minutes till she was due at her folks' place for supper. Just enough time to check in with Wes, change from her scrubs, and grab the mac and cheese keeping warm in a Crockpot.

Water dripped from the blue tarp covering the carriage house and pooled on the ground below it. She hadn't really checked on Wes the past couple of nights—Katie's words at the coffee shop haunted her. It was true that Wes would be gone soon—based on their agreement he was free to leave tomorrow, debt paid.

But Avery couldn't deny the strong connection or the tension that crackled between them. And the memory of his smoky gaze, his thumb sweeping across her lower lip, still sent a shiver down her arms.

So after her discussion with Katie, Avery had made a decision: there was no sense pushing her luck. This week she'd only enjoyed his company in small measures—and definitely not in the privacy of her apartment.

But because of the pouring rain, Wes had been more or less trapped in the small confines of the carriage house day and night. She felt bad about that. From her bedroom window she'd seen the work lights burning late at night. He must be bored silly. He'd never borrowed any of her books, and Avery was hesitant to invite him back upstairs.

Avery ducked under the overhang and knocked. A full minute later Wes opened the door, and the smell of paint fumes wafted out on a cool breeze.

He ushered her in out of the rain. His faded red T-shirt sported dust and splotches of paint. "I'm starting to think I should be building an ark."

She still wasn't used to that clean-shaven face or the defined angles of his jaw. No wonder her staff had begun to take their lunch breaks on the back deck, despite the oppressive heat. "Welcome to Riverbend's wettest month."

"I wasn't expecting this. July is bone dry in the Midwest."

Avery tore her attention from his face and took in the work zone. "The walls are great." The trim still sported blue painter's tape, but the soothing shade of gray contrasted nicely with the white trim. Wes had also torn down the wall between the living room and kitchen, opening up the space. He'd framed the new wall that would separate the bedroom from the living space. "You're making good headway in here."

"I'd love to get the drywall up over that framing, but I'm waiting on an inspection."

"How long will that take?"

"As long as the building department wants it to. And so far, they don't seem to be in any hurry."

"Well, I guess that wall will be Gavin's problem then. As of tonight, your debt is officially paid off."

He blinked at her. "Right. I know we agreed to that. But I don't feel right about leaving you with a tarped roof. And honestly, I don't relish the idea of hiking in the pouring rain—we've apparently got a few more days of this."

"Oh, I didn't realize—" Avery wasn't sure what to say. They were square now, and she couldn't really afford to pay him the going rate.

Wes held up a hand. "I don't expect compensation, except maybe room and board?"

"That's not fair. Maybe the exterior hasn't progressed as you'd hoped, but you've made a lot of progress on the inside."

"I don't mind. Materials are expensive, and I'd like to help you get that second doctor on board."

She felt a pinch in her heart. "That's awfully kind of you."

"It's been rewarding, being productive again after weeks of hiking. Working with tools—that's kind of my sweet spot."

Now she really felt bad about avoiding him the past couple of days. He was living in a small, dusty work zone. And she had no idea what he'd been doing for food—had he walked to the grocery in the rain?

She checked her Fitbit. She had to get going and—She could invite Wes to her parents'. It would get him out of this space, provide a good home-cooked meal, break up the monotony. There was no doubt her parents would welcome him. It was a rule she'd learned early on: everyone was welcome at the Robinson table.

"I'm on my way to my folks' place for supper—you should come along."

A hopeful spark lit his eyes, then extinguished. His gaze drifted around the space. "I should probably finish trimming."

"You can do that tomorrow. Come on, if you're going to be working practically for free, you have to allow me to provide your meals. And since I'm not such a great cook . . ."

His weight shifted on his feet. "I really shouldn't impose."

Avery laughed. "Trust me, that's not a word the Robinsons believe in. My stepmom invites total strangers off the trail for supper. Everyone's used to it, and there's always plenty of food. What's one more?"

"Your whole family will be there?"

Ah, that was the holdup. "I know my brothers can be gigantic pains in the butt, but they're good guys—albeit completely overprotective of me. Don't let them scare you away. And Katie will be there, of course. You know her."

He glanced toward the fridge—thinking of its empty contents? "Well, if you're sure they wouldn't mind."

"I'm positive. And my dad is grilling burgers, so you don't want to miss that."

"I can practically taste them now. Do I have time for a quick shower?"

"You do that while I change and grab the mac and cheese. I'll meet you at my Jeep in fifteen."

———

"We eat outside when the weather allows," Avery said. "But I'm afraid we're stuck in the house today."

Wes followed Avery through her parents' doorway. The boisterous conversation coming from the back of the house made his stomach churn. He didn't know why he was nervous. After being cooped up this week, he welcomed the idea of company. But his previous interactions with Avery's brothers hadn't exactly given him warm and fuzzy vibes.

In the kitchen a woman—presumably Avery's stepmom—was at the sink. Through the sliding door, Cooper and Katie watched Avery's dad grilling out, his gray slicker dripping with rain. Gavin lingered at the island, helping himself to cheese and crackers.

"Hey, everyone!" Avery called.

Her greeting was returned. Gavin noticed Wes first, but his poker face gave no indication of his thoughts.

Cooper did a double take. "Hey there."

Avery took the Crockpot from Wes and set it on the island.

"Oh, how nice." Lisa approached Wes, smiling broadly as she dried her hands on a towel. "You must be Avery's new contractor—or patient, whatever. I'm her stepmom, Lisa."

"I've been a little of both." Wes extended his hand. "Nice to meet you, ma'am."

Lisa chuckled and went straight for the hug. "I'm a hugger. I hope you don't mind. You don't look at all the way I expected."

He rubbed his jaw. "I was probably a fright, coming out of the hills."

"We're certainly used to that around here."

The others greeted him. The brothers were cordial if not overly friendly.

132

Avery put her hand on Wes's arm. "Wes has been stuck in the carriage house all week, so I thought I'd spring him from jail tonight."

"Well, we're happy to have you, honey. Go ahead and grab a seat, everyone. Your dad's plating the burgers as we speak."

By the time Avery set the crock on the table with the other food, Lisa had already set a place for Wes.

Avery's dad entered, dripping rain and carrying a platter of burgers. He seemed a bit older than his wife. But the laugh lines fanning out from his blue eyes gave him a friendly appearance.

The savory smell of the grilled burgers made Wes's empty stomach twist. He couldn't remember the last time he'd had grilled meat.

After introductions were made, Lisa helped her husband shrug from his raincoat, then took the platter while Jeff dried off with a dish towel.

Once they were all settled around the table, Jeff said grace and they began passing the food around the table. Wes intended to take everything offered—it all smelled so good.

Gavin met Wes's gaze. "So I hear you're hitting the trail again tomorrow."

Wes scooped mac 'n' cheese on his plate. He must've gotten that tidbit from the phone conversation he'd overheard Monday. "Actually, I decided to stick around a few more days."

"He didn't want to leave my roof half-done and tarped over," Avery said.

"Well, that's very nice of you," Lisa said. "Avery said you're doing a great job. So I have to ask, what made you decide to hike the AT, Wes? I'm always interested in what drives a person to embark on such a long and difficult journey."

Wes finished chewing a bite of burger. "Actually, I'm doing it in honor of a friend. He passed away a while back."

"Sorry to hear that," Jeff said. "Was the AT on his bucket list?"

"Yes, sir."

Lisa gave him a warm smile. "What a lovely thing to do. Have you experienced any trail magic along the way?"

"I didn't even know what that was when I started out—I was pretty green. But I happened upon a hiker feed in Virginia. I've never been so happy for a home-cooked meal, I can tell you that. And just across the North Carolina border, some friendly folks were passing out energy bars and water."

"We host hikers from time to time," Jeff said. "Sometimes for a meal and sometimes even overnight."

"I'm sure the hospitality is appreciated. You don't really appreciate a mattress until you've spent weeks on the ground. I've hitched a ride or two along the way. People are very supportive along the trail, and the hikers are grateful."

"What's your trail name?" Katie asked.

"I, uh, decided to take my buddy's since I was hiking in his honor—Avocado." His face heated because, of course, they were going to ask.

"I'm guessing there's a story behind the name," Jeff said.

"There is, but it's, uh, not for mixed company, I'm afraid."

Avery arched a brow at him in a way that implied she would pry the story from him later.

"My trail name is Skittles," Katie said. "You can probably guess where that came from."

Cooper gave her an adoring look. "Let's just say she has a sweet tooth that defies logic."

Katie returned the look, giving him a nudge.

"Where are you from, Wes?" Jeff asked. "Certainly not the south by your accent."

Funny how southerners thought *he* had an accent. "The Midwest originally, but I've been working in South America for the past several years."

"He worked for Emergency Shelter International in Colombia, building homes for refugees."

"That's a good organization."

"Yes, ma'am." The back of Wes's neck heated at the attention—at Avery's efforts to boost her family's opinion of him. "Overall, it was a great experience. I met some fine people down there. Sure makes you grateful for all the blessings we Americans take for granted."

"Amen," Jeff said, then addressed Avery. "Any luck in your pursuit of a doctor, honey?"

"I had a résumé come in last week. But when I interviewed him it was obvious he viewed the clinic as a stepping-stone. I need someone willing to stick around for the long haul."

"You might have to take what you can get," Gavin said.

"Maybe, but I'm not giving up just yet."

Over the next several minutes other conversations struck up around the table. Cooper told Gavin about some skirmish that happened on the job, and Lisa complimented her husband on the grilled burgers. The din grew louder as time passed.

What would it have been like, growing up in a big family like this? To sit around the dinner table every night, discussing your day instead of camping in front of the TV alone, waiting for darkness to fall? For your dad to come home? Wes had always done his homework in those long hours between dinner and bed.

It helped pass the time, and once he'd hit high school, his grades had become more important to him. Aunt Cordelia always said education was the key to a bright future—be it formal education or self-education.

"Did you grow up in a big family?"

Katie's question snapped Wes from his thoughts. "No, it was just my dad and me."

"Is he the one who taught you how to build homes?" Katie asked.

"He was, yes. He's since passed away though." He left out the prison part.

"I'm sorry to hear that." Katie gave him a sympathetic smile. "So, you're heading up to Albany after you finish the trail? Putting down roots there?"

He caught Avery frowning at her friend. The other conversations seemed to have died out, and everyone was now tuned in to the one between Katie and him.

"That's the plan."

"You have family there? A job waiting for you?"

"No to both. I plan on searching for work once I arrive."

"All right," Avery said. "Let's let poor Wes get a bite in while you tell us how the wedding invitations are going."

"We got them in the mail Wednesday." Katie whooped and high-fived Cooper.

"Kate did the addresses; I stuffed and stamped."

Katie kissed his cheek. "We make a great team, babe."

Wes was relieved at the change in topic, which carried through the rest of the meal. The next hour passed quickly, the conversation changing abruptly from one topic to another, the siblings hassling each other. When inside jokes crept up, Avery leaned over to fill him in so he wouldn't feel left out.

By the time everyone stood from the table, he was feeling pretty comfortable and most definitely welcome.

Nineteen

It was time to check in with her dad. Avery carried the stack of plates to the kitchen where her dad was running a sink full of dishwater. At almost sixty he was still handsome with dark-blond hair that had receded in recent years. His warm blue eyes only hinted of the wisdom from which she'd benefited all her life. If he hadn't inherited his dad's trail store, Avery had always thought he would've made a great counselor—even though his advice during her teen years had been less than appreciated.

But ever since she and her brothers had grown up, he was careful about weighing in. When he had something to say, he pulled out two pennies from his pocket and set them down. It was up to them whether or not they took his "two cents." These days, she was more inclined to take it.

She thought back to Lisa's frantic phone call in April, and Avery's stomach sank as if weighted with wet sand. Dad's color was good tonight, and his energy level seemed fine. He appeared the picture of health.

But not wanting to worry her over the winter, he'd hidden his symptoms from her. More of that kid-gloves treatment she'd become accustomed to. But when it came to the serious matter of his health, it was not okay.

She glanced into the living room where Wes and the rest of her family gathered around the Braves' game. He seemed to be faring well on his own—currently engaged in conversation with Katie.

Avery set the plates in the sink. "How'd you get stuck with the dishes? You did most of the cooking."

"I don't mind. It gives Lisa more time to visit with you kids."

Avery grabbed a towel and took the plate he'd just washed. "How's the store been this week?"

"Pretty busy—all the hikers came in because of the weather."

"Buying up all the rain gear?"

"You know it."

"And how've you been feeling, Dad? Are you taking the Plavix and Lopressor?"

"Every single day."

"And the aspirin?"

"Of course, honey."

"No more fatigue or pain or tightness anywhere?"

He gave her a reassuring smile. "You've never been one to beat around the bush. I'm doing great. In fact, I had an appointment with my cardiologist Wednesday and got a clean bill of health."

The muscles in her shoulders loosened a bit. Dr. Graber was the best cardiologist in the region. "That's great, Dad. But you know it's important to pay attention to your body even if you've gotten the all clear. And the tightness can present in the neck or even the back or arms."

"I'm all over it, honey. And even if I wasn't, you can bet Lisa is. You don't have to worry about me. I know all the symptoms, and I'm taking every precaution."

She dried another plate. No matter how diligent she was now or how many times she'd apologized, she'd never get over the guilt of not being here. Of letting him down when he'd needed her most.

"I'm so sorry I wasn't here for you in April, Dad."

"Honey . . . it wasn't your fault. You're allowed to have time off. You're working so many hours, and we couldn't be prouder of the work you're doing. But you have got to stop blaming yourself."

"I should've been here," she whispered.

He took the towel from her, dried his hands, and pulled her into a hug. "You can't possibly be available twenty-four seven, 365 days a year. It's not realistic. Anyway, my situation called for a full-fledged hospital. And you did find me the best cardiologist a guy could ask for."

All that was true—but somehow it didn't alleviate her guilt. That night Dad had thought he was suffering from indigestion. If she'd been in town, he might've come into the clinic and she would've known what was happening, would've given him an aspirin. She would've gotten him to the hospital ASAP. That might've been all he needed to keep the situation from escalating. Instead he'd ended up in the ICU for days.

"I just wish—"

He took her face in his hands. "Honey. Let it go. I'm fine now and that's all that matters." His eyes sharpened on her for a long moment. "Did my emergency trigger trauma from child-hood? Your mom's death . . . ?"

They hadn't openly discussed it in years. But he'd hit the nail right on the head—it was uncanny the way he did that. She gave a nod, her eyes burning.

"You're a doctor now—you know how the disease works. You know what happened to her wasn't your fault. It was mine. I shouldn't have left you alone with her, not even long enough to run next door."

"You couldn't have known—she'd never choked before."

"But I knew it was a possibility. You were just a child. Surely you can see it wasn't your fault."

She nodded again. Logically, she knew he was right—even if she couldn't quite make her heart believe it.

"But I wasn't a child in the spring." She'd gone to Asheville to help Katie shop for a wedding gown. She'd so wanted to be there for her friend's big moment, but it had been an ir-responsible decision—one that could've cost Dad's life.

His eyes bore into hers, and his brows pulled into a frown. "It's killing me to know this is eating you alive."

The muscles of her left eyelid twitched. The last thing she'd meant to do was add to his stress. She had to let this go—for her dad's sake if not for her own.

She forced a smile. Willed her spasming eyelid to relax. "All right. I'll let it go. I promise."

He set a kiss on her forehead. "That's my girl."

The din rose as the Braves scored a run, and Avery sent her dad to watch the game while she finished the dishes. A few minutes later she turned to peek in on her family. Wes leaned forward in the armchair, elbows braced on his knees, watching the action. It was nice to see him relaxing with her family. And even though the Braves weren't his team, he was cheering right along with the rest of them.

As if sensing her scrutiny, he turned and fixed his gaze on her. The corners of his lips kicked up.

Good grief he was an attractive man. She returned his smile. What was he thinking? That familiar thread of tension stretched between them, thrumming with energy. She'd missed him this week. Had missed conversing with him, flirting with him. Maybe she'd overreacted to Katie's warning. He'd be gone soon and then she'd be alone again. She'd probably kick herself for not taking advantage of his company while she had it.

A cheer broke out and Wes's attention snapped to the game.

Avery went back to the dirty grilling tools. They had chemistry, that was all. It wasn't anything approaching love that, in her experience, took months to develop.

She set the clean spatula in the drainer as Gavin wandered into the kitchen for a refill.

"Braves winning?" she asked.

"Up by two. Their offense looks great. I think they have a real chance at the World Series this year."

"You say that every year."

"Well, eventually I'll be right then." He filled his glass at the refrigerator dispenser and lowered his voice. "Hey . . . I stopped over at your place on Monday and checked out the work in your backyard."

"Wes mentioned it." She couldn't resist adding in a snarky

tone. "And does his work meet with your approval, O mighty contractor?"

Gavin gave her a mock scowl. "He seems adequate enough."

"High praise coming from you. Does that mean you're done checking up on him?"

"You can't fault me for looking out for you."

"Sure about that?" Maybe she should be grateful he cared. But after having been handled with care all her life, it only annoyed her. Everyone outside her family viewed her as a strong woman—intimidating even. Why could her family only see her through the lens of that wretched disease?

Gavin turned from the fridge and took a sip of water. "I guess I feel a little guilty for not doing the work myself. I should've made time."

"It worked out. I know you're busy with the cabin right now. And have no fear, there'll be plenty of work left when he leaves."

He wandered over to the island and leaned on it. He obviously had something to say. Avery dried the grilling tools and put them in a drawer. She wiped her hands on the towel and leaned back against the sink, facing Gavin.

It didn't take him long to spit it out. "From what I hear, you two are getting pretty cozy over there."

Avery held back a sigh. "We're just friends. He's fun to hang out with."

He studied her for a long minute. Her brother made her feel he could see right down to her bone marrow. Right down to her stem cells. Her left eye twitched again.

"I only mention it because I came up on him while he was on the phone with someone—obviously a woman."

"And?"

"And he sounded kind of, I don't know . . . tender."

She blinked at him, keeping her expression purposefully blank because Gavin was well aware she wasn't in the market for a man. And even though that was true, her mind spun with the question: Who had Wes had been talking to? He didn't have a sister. As far as she knew he had no living family at all. Was it possible he actually had a girlfriend in Albany? Was that why he was planning to put down roots there?

Gavin scowled at her. "Like he was sweet on her or something. Don't be obtuse. You know what I mean—stop making me sound like a teenaged girl."

Unbelievable. Avery shook her head. "Does no one around here listen to me? Were you not present last week when I announced I was permanently opting out of the whole dating scene? Why do I have to keep explaining that Wes and I are just friends? He's going to be on his way in a matter of days, for heaven's sake."

"I just wanted to make sure you weren't getting in over your head with a guy who sounded very much taken."

The words soured in her ears. And her stupid eyelid wouldn't stop twitching. She straightened, crossing her arms. "Believe it or not I can take care of myself, Gavin."

He held up his hands, lowering his tone again. "I didn't mean to butt in—just wanted to make sure he wasn't trying to pull the wool over your eyes or something."

She gave him a withering look. "As I said, he's a *friend*. He can talk to whomever he wants, in whatever tone he pleases."

"All right, all right. Sheesh. Try to do a person a favor. I seem to recall you withholding information last year that might've given me a heads-up. I wouldn't have minded you butting in at that point."

Her bluster faded at the memory. Avery had noticed the sparks between Cooper and Katie long before Gavin caught on. "You know I regret that—and I already apologized for it."

"And I've forgiven you. But I also learned that sometimes butting in can save a person a little heartache."

"Point taken. Sorry I got a little snappy."

"It's all right."

Groans rose from the other room, drawing their attention. They went to see what was happening with the game. Gavin took a seat on the end of the sofa, and Avery leaned against the wall next to Wes, her gaze trained on the TV.

But her mind was back on the conversation in the kitchen. Who was the mysterious woman Wes had been talking to? Why hadn't he mentioned her to Avery? And why did the thought of her hollow Avery's chest?

––––––––

Wes glanced back at the Robinson house as he stowed Avery's empty crock in the back of the Jeep. It had been an interesting gathering. They were a fun bunch. He'd mostly felt like he fit in. It was comfortable, if a little foreign, to be in the middle of a family setting.

But in the time it had taken Avery to wash dishes, every member of her family had had a one-on-one conversation with him. Each discussion touched on one main point: *Be careful with Avery—she's fragile.*

Each person conveyed that message a little differently. Lisa's came with warmth and kindness. Jeff's with such subtlety Wes almost missed the point entirely. The brothers' messages held a warning. Big surprise.

It would've been humorous if it wasn't so perplexing. Wes gave his head a shake as he slid into the passenger seat. Avery was one of the strongest women he'd ever known. She'd moved away from home at seventeen, putting herself through college and medical school in record time. Now she lived independently and ran a thriving clinic. She cared for the entire town's health needs—almost single-handedly it seemed at times.

Maybe he sensed a certain vulnerability where Avery was concerned. But fragile? He all but scoffed at the idea. The two things weren't at all the same. Vulnerability was a cracked foundation; fragility was a foundation built on poor soil.

Now, Lillian . . . sure, he might say she was fragile, especially since her brother had died. She needed someone to be there for her, and now Wes was that person. But Avery was fiercely independent. And yet this was her family. Did they know something he didn't? Or did they simply underestimate her?

Avery turned as she backed from the drive. "I hope my family wasn't too much tonight."

"They're a lot of fun. They sure do take their baseball seriously."

"They're just as bad with football." She spared him a glance. "Did my brothers behave?"

"Don't worry about me. I can handle your brothers."

"I'll take that as a no." She pulled out onto the street and gave the Jeep some gas. "So I have to ask—what's the deal behind the Avocado name? Surely you can tell me."

He rubbed the back of his neck. "Right. Well, you're a doctor so I guess I can."

"Now you've really got me curious."

"Landon was born with one testicle—he was always joking around about it. He chose the name because the avocado, you know, has only one nut."

Avery snorted. "I think it's actually a pit."

Wes gave her a wry look.

"But, yeah, point taken. What did you say on the trail when people asked you about it?"

"Told 'em it was my favorite fruit."

"But is it really a fruit?"

"They're actually considered to be a large berry. They grow on trees, which can take up to ten years to produce fruit."

She raised her eyebrows at him.

"What? I couldn't bear the name Avocado for weeks on end without knowing something about my namesake."

"You're making me hungry for some good guacamole."

"That happens to be one of my few culinary accomplishments. If you want to stop at the store, I'd be happy to make you some."

Avery let out a laugh. "You haven't lived here long if you think our little store actually stays open till nine o'clock—or carries avocados."

"Point taken. Well, the offer stands. I could run into Walnut tomorrow and get the ingredients if you'd spare me your ride."

Avery seemed to consider, then flashed him a smile. "I'll provide the chicken tacos . . ."

His own lips turned up of their own volition. "Deal."

Twenty

Wes set down the roller and stretched his shoulder muscles. Sunday had been another rainy day, but he'd gotten a fair amount of interior work done. He was almost finished painting. He frowned at the incomplete wall he'd framed.

He would call the building department again tomorrow and try to rush them a bit. He only needed one day of good weather to finish the roof, and tomorrow seemed promising. It would be nice if the county got that inspection done tomorrow, then he could hang the drywall before he left Riverbend.

He glanced out the window through the driving rain toward Avery's apartment. He had mixed feelings about leaving her. He would assuage them by leaving her carriage house in good shape.

The flooring had arrived last week, but the tub had to be installed before the flooring, and Stewie couldn't do that until later this week. Avery's brother would have to install it and probably finish the wall as well. Hopefully Gavin wouldn't put her off. Couldn't he see how badly she needed that doctor? It seemed like every other night she was up with some emergency. Strong or no, she was going to wear herself out if she didn't get help soon.

Even last night an emergency call had ended their Mexican fiesta. Avery assessed the woman and ended up calling an ambulance. He only knew this because a while after the call came in, the strobing lights cut across his living room walls.

He checked the progress he'd made on the trimming today. Might as well call it quits for the night. He wrapped the brush with plastic, his mind going back to Saturday night. He and Avery had chatted and laughed over chicken tacos and chips—his guacamole was a hit.

Somehow they got on the subject of Latin American dance styles and the salsa in particular. He smiled at the memory. Giving her a dance lesson was fun. She had good rhythm, caught on fast, and her height made her an excellent partner. He could still envision her swiveling hips and flirty eyes. He had fun, watching her let go and enjoy herself. He hated the way all of it evaporated the instant the emergency call came.

He gave his head a shake. He spent an awful lot of time thinking about Avery. After checking his watch, he decided to call Lillian. He hadn't talked to her in a couple of days.

She picked up on the second ring. "Hey there. How's it going?"

"It's going. Sounds like you had a good day."

"Church always improves my mood. I got to see my friends, and the message was just what I needed. Plus, I got the scoop on a new job opening from one of those friends. I'm going to apply for it tomorrow."

He frowned at the sudden shift. "What about your day care?"

"I hate to let it go, but I can't make it with only two kids. And this other job is for a preschool teacher at a reputable church. It's a year-round position, and I'd have good benefits, including PTO."

"Well, that does sound promising. It would be a big change from working at home though." Maybe it would be good for her to get out. She'd always seemed a little too isolated.

"It would be but maybe not a bad one. Pray I get it. I hate the thought of bailing on my families, but I have to make ends meet. I'm really excited about this position."

"I'll pray you get it then. Maybe it'll be less stress since you wouldn't have to run it all by yourself."

"That's what I'm thinking. So, what's up with you? Still raining down there?"

"It's finally supposed to clear up tomorrow. I'm hoping to get the roof finished."

"Then you'll hit the trail again?"

He'd leave Tuesday if the inspection didn't come through tomorrow. The thought opened a pit in his gut. "That's the plan."

"Have you been searching online for a job?"

"A little but I haven't found anything of interest yet." Honestly, he'd been looking less and less. But it would be easier once he arrived and could apply in person.

"I keep checking the newspaper but I'm not finding much." She paused a moment. "I had a conversation with a man at church this morning that wasn't very encouraging—he works for a local builder."

"What'd he say?"

"I was hoping he might have a lead for you or that his employer had an opening. But he said new construction has been slow this year and that contractor positions were hard to come by."

"Don't worry about me. I'll figure it out. I can always install windows or something until the local economy picks up."

"I'd hate for you to do that. You're overqualified for that." There was a long pause and he knew what was coming next. "Are you sure this is where you want to settle, Wes?"

His mouth curved at her predictability. "Now, Lillian. We've been over this before, haven't we?"

"I just want to make sure you know that you don't have to move here for me. I don't want you to feel obligated."

"I don't." But that wasn't entirely true. "I mean who wouldn't want to live in the great metropolis of Albany, New York?"

She chuckled. "You might want to work on those expectations, pal."

"Don't you worry. They're properly managed." He'd actually done quite a bit of research on the area. And Landon had told him so many stories about his life there, Wes felt like he'd grown up there himself.

"I just want you to know I do have people here I can count on. I'm not alone, if that's what you're worried about."

"I know that. But it's settled, all right? This is what I want." He lightened his tone. "And if you don't stop pushing me away, you'll make me feel unwanted."

"I'm not pushing you away! I'd love for you to move here, and Albany would be lucky to have you."

"That's more like it."

They talked awhile, until she yawned, then he let her off the phone. After a quick shower, he turned in. For a long time he lay in bed thinking of Landon. Thought of the silly pranks he used to play on his friends, of the way he gave out candy to the refugee kids, and the way he pushed himself and the whole crew to excellence.

Thoughts of Avery crowded in. That contagious laugh, her sparkling green eyes, those faint freckles. When he was with her, they rarely ran out of things to say. And when they did, the silence was comfortable.

He heaved a sigh and rolled over in bed. "Don't worry, buddy," he whispered into the darkness. "I haven't forgotten my promise."

Twenty-One

It was Wes's last day in Riverbend. From the riverbank he finished the turkey sandwich as he watched the water ripple past. The afternoon sun on Monday dappled its muddy surface, and he was grateful for the shady shoreline after working on the hot roof all morning. He was almost finished.

He'd finally gotten through to the right person at the county department only to be told the inspection wouldn't happen until Friday at the earliest. He'd have to leave the wall—and the floor—in Gavin's capable hands.

Tonight Wes would finish painting. He'd hoped to talk Avery into letting him refinish the cabinets. They seemed kind of tired now that the walls were freshened up. But there would be no time for that.

His phone vibrated with an incoming text and he checked the screen. Lillian.

I got the job!!!

Pleasure bloomed inside at her obvious excitement. Well, that was great news. She deserved good things. Unable to resist, he found her contact and tapped her number.

"Can you believe it?" she said in lieu of greeting. "They hired me on the spot!"

"Of course they did. They're lucky to have you."

"My new boss, Tricia, is so nice. They're letting me have two weeks so my families have time to find caregivers. I'll be working with three-year-olds. There are twelve kiddos to a teacher, and I'll just be an assistant until I'm trained and have a little more experience at their facility. But after six months, if all goes well, I'll get promoted to teacher, which also means a raise."

He couldn't wipe the smile off his face. That had to be more words than he'd ever heard her utter at once. "That sounds great, Lillian. Congratulations. I'm happy for you."

"What's that sound? Are you running the water?"

"I'm sitting by the river. It's right in my backyard." His gaze climbed the mountain in the background to the startling blue sky behind it. "It's so beautiful. I'll have to bring you down here sometime."

She chuckled. "I've hardly even left the state of New York."

Landon had mentioned Lillian was a bit of a homebody. But she seemed excited about working outside the home, so maybe that was changing.

A child cried in the background, and Lillian soothed him in muffled tones.

"I should let you go," he said. "I just wanted to hear about this new job. And also let you know I'll definitely be hitting the trail in the morning."

"Oh, that's great. How much longer do you have to go?"

"It's two weeks to Springer Mountain—the end of the trail."

"I can't believe that by the time this is over you'll have walked from Pennsylvania to Georgia. Have I told you how much it means to me that you're finishing the trail for Landon?"

"It's been a great experience. I'm glad I was able to do it. So, let's see . . ." He put the phone on speaker, then opened his calendar. "If all goes as planned with the hike, I should finish no later than August first and be able to fly there the second. I'll go ahead and book a flight tonight."

"Wait, did you say August second?"

"Yeah, why?"

"Oh no. That's the week of my training. They're sending me to Rochester for the week. What terrible timing."

He deflated a little. He'd waited all this time to meet her in person. "When will you be back?"

"Not until Friday the fifth."

He injected some enthusiasm into his voice. "All right, that's okay. It's only a few days. And it'll give me a chance to settle in and start searching for a job."

"I feel bad I won't be here."

Last thing he wanted to do was spoil her happy moment. "Well, don't. I'm so proud of you for getting this job. Maybe by the time you get back from your training, I'll have one to tell you about."

Wes wrapped up the phone call and bagged his trash. Despite his words, he couldn't help but feel disappointed. All these months of waiting to reach Albany and Lillian and all the delays . . . and she wasn't even going to be there when he arrived.

Suck it up, Wes. It wasn't her fault. He was the one who'd gotten sick and decided to stay and pay off his bill—and he couldn't find it in himself to regret the decision.

He stood from the log and headed back through the woods toward the waiting roof. He still had a job to finish and laundry to do—not to mention a flight to book.

"All right, Mrs. Warner," Avery said loudly for the hard-of-hearing woman. She'd somehow managed to get a poison ivy rash all over her shoulder and back. "Here are some samples for you: antihistamine tablets and cortisone cream to help with the inflammation. If your daughter's not home, feel free to stop by the clinic and one of us will help you with the cream, all right?"

Mrs. Warner's pale, round face creased as she beamed. "Thank you, honey. That's so kind of you."

"And no more scratching. You can get some Calamine lotion to help with that. Some people find a cool baking-soda bath helpful."

"Thank you for your help." Mrs. Warner followed her out the exam room door. "You have a good day, honey, and tell your mama and daddy I said hello."

"Yes, ma'am. Let me know if you have any questions. You have my number." Avery dropped the woman's chart off with Patti. "I'll be in the office on a call for the next little while, Patti."

"All right, Boss. I'll make sure you're not disturbed."

By the time Avery made it to her office she had only two minutes to spare. She pulled the paperwork from the file and got comfortable behind her desk.

When she'd received Lucy Chan's résumé on Saturday afternoon, Avery nearly jumped for joy. Dr. Chan had graduated from Stanford in the top ten of her class. She'd gone on to Johns Hopkins University, where she specialized in emergency medicine. She'd completed her residency at Johns Hopkins, and now she worked at Sinai in Baltimore. Her referrals were nothing short of glowing. In short, Dr. Chan was the ideal candidate for the clinic.

Well, technically they could use a little testosterone around here—sometimes boys preferred a male physician. But Avery wouldn't reject the ideal candidate based solely on sex. Especially when she'd had difficulty attracting anyone at all.

Avery opened the video app on her laptop, trying to temper her enthusiasm. She'd been hopeful about the last applicant too, until it became clear he had bigger things in mind for his career than a rinky-dink clinic set in the middle of a Podunk town.

A chime sounded as the doctor joined the call and appeared on the screen in a box next to Avery's image. The woman wore her dark hair in a professional knot, a few loose tendrils highlighting her high cheekbones.

Her eyes brightened as she smiled. "Hello, Dr. Robinson."

"Hi, Dr. Chan. It's nice to put a face with a name. Is it all right if we dispense with formalities? You can call me Avery."

"Of course. Feel free to call me Lucy."

"Thank you for meeting up on such short notice."

"Not at all. I'm happy to answer any questions you might have."

"Your résumé speaks for itself. As I said in my email, it's quite impressive."

"I've been blessed with some wonderful opportunities. I've had a chance to research your clinic and town, and I like what I've seen so far."

Avery suppressed a whoop. "Glad to hear it. I thought, since you covered your career highlights so thoroughly in your résumé, that we might just chat about your goals and ambitions and how you see that going so far. Can you tell me how you're enjoying emergency medicine?"

Lucy chuckled. "Well, as with any position, there are some parts I enjoy and other parts I find more challenging. I love helping people in need, and I don't mind the fast pace. But drugs are a pervasive problem here in Baltimore—an incessant problem, I'm afraid. At any rate, I never saw myself in a big city long term. I really miss the small-town atmosphere."

Avery liked that, despite the doctor's obvious intellect, she didn't seem pretentious. That wouldn't go over well here. "Well, Riverbend has that in spades. What exactly draws you to a small-town setting?"

"I actually grew up in a small town—Nashville, Indiana. I like a place where everyone knows everyone, but I'm also used to towns that draw tourists. And Riverbend is particularly appealing because I love to hike."

"We've got you covered there. And the town is very welcoming. It's a wonderful place to call home."

"It sounds perfect." Lucy went on to explain that her hometown was too small to support a clinic, and she had no desire to run one anyway. She strictly wanted to be a doctor.

All that suited Avery just fine. They talked awhile longer,

Avery trying to get a feel for Lucy as a person and as a doctor. So far she liked what she was hearing. Lucy seemed approachable, optimistic, and compassionate. She didn't seem like someone who would cause drama or alienate team members.

Avery told Lucy a little about Katie, Sharise, and Patti and explained her philosophy on the way she ran her clinic. When she'd exhausted that topic, she knew she couldn't delay the inevitable bad news. With knots in her stomach Avery quoted the position's salary, trying to keep her tone and expression confident.

Either Lucy had a poker face or the low salary didn't come as a surprise. She nodded as Avery continued explaining.

"Of course, we intend to increase the salary with time and growth, and as stated in the ad, housing is included as part of the package. There's a lovely en suite carriage-house apartment right behind the clinic with beautiful river views—and, might I add, a very short commute to work."

Lucy's cheeks bunched as she smiled.

"If all that sounds agreeable, I guess the next big question is, when do you think you want to make a move?"

"Fairly soon, actually. Currently, I'm filling in for a doctor who's out on maternity leave, and she's returning in two weeks. My lease also expires then, so I'm hoping to line something up. If you should decide you're interested in moving forward with me, I'd love to visit the clinic sooner than later. I'd like to scope out the town a bit too."

Avery thought of the unfinished house and tried not to wince. "I'm definitely interested in moving forward. But yes, this is a big decision and it needs to be a good fit for both of us. I'd love for you to meet the staff as well."

"Absolutely. I'm off this coming weekend and could schedule a flight for Friday night if that works for you. I noticed you have clinic hours on Saturday mornings, and I'd love to see the place in action."

But the interior of the carriage house was a mess with the old, ratty carpet and the furniture stacked and covered with drop cloths. The bathroom was still unsightly. Her eye twitched as she grinned through her inner turmoil. "That's perfect. Go ahead and make arrangements, and please keep me apprised of your plans. I'd be happy to pick you up from the airport and show you around a bit."

"That sounds great. And in the interest of fairness, I should tell you I'm also considering a practice in Ohio. I'll be visiting them soon."

Avery's stomach shrank two sizes at the mention of competition. "I understand and I appreciate your honesty. If you think of any more questions before your arrival, feel free to shoot me an email or give me a call."

"Absolutely. And you do the same."

They said their good-byes and Avery closed out the program as her empty stomach clenched hard. She was more convinced than ever that the clinic needed this doctor. *She* needed this doctor. Not only for her short-term mental health, but also for the long-term plans for this clinic—if her own health eventually failed, she needed someone to carry this clinic without her. Someone who could take care of this town in her absence. Lucy Chan, with her empathic demeanor, excellent communication skills, and background in emergency medicine could very well be that person.

Maybe it was the adrenaline draining away, but exhaustion

settled over her like a lead blanket. How long had it been since she'd enjoyed a good night's sleep? Since she'd had a true day off? Doctors were supposed to know better.

Her thoughts returned to the promising candidate and her upcoming visit.

Lucy must assume she would be staying in the carriage house. Avery would just have to clean it up best she could and explain that the rest would be completed—somehow—before she started the job. Why hadn't she just admitted the place was in the middle of renovations?

Because you didn't want to scare her away.

Lucy was hoping to make a move soon, and with Wes leaving tomorrow morning, Avery had no hopes of finishing the place in two weeks, much less four days.

Add to her worries, the woman was considering another offer—probably a more promising one than Avery ever could compete with.

She pressed a finger to her twitching eye and prayed for a solution.

Twenty-Two

Avery's emotions had been on a teeter-totter since the video call with Lucy. What were the chances a doctor of her caliber would be interested in settling in a small-town clinic and not be put off by the dismal salary?

She had to figure out this housing situation and soon. She'd already called Gavin, but that had been hugely deflating. The plumbing in the cabin he was building was due for inspection next Monday, and he was behind the gun to get it finished. He obviously felt bad for turning her down, so she underplayed her desperation.

Pushing aside her worries, she slipped into a pair of jeans and a T-shirt and headed out back. Regardless of her dilemma, she owed the man in her backyard a nice supper and a mountain of gratitude. If he hadn't come along, the house would still be sitting in a dilapidated state, and Lucy Chan would probably have passed on the position altogether.

The thought of Wes leaving in the morning made her heart squeeze tight. Handyman skills aside, she didn't want him to go. She already missed him and his easy laugh. Already missed the way she could simply relax around him and forget the pressures of the clinic for two minutes.

Avery made her way through the backyard. The sun had sunk behind the hills, offering a reprieve from the relentless heat of the day. In the distance a lawn mower droned. The sweet scent of flowers teased her nostrils.

From the exterior the carriage house really did look like a storybook cottage now. The roof was complete—the three-dimensional shingles giving the building new life. She took a minute to walk around the building and admire Wes's excellent work before she knocked on the door. She would put her worries aside for tonight and simply enjoy his company.

He pulled opened the door, and there he was in all his masculine glory, smiling sweetly at her. He wore a clean black T-shirt, and his damp hair was slicked back, one stubborn strand falling forward at his temple. He was so handsome she forgot what she'd been about to say.

The corners of his blue eyes crinkled as he smiled. "How was your day, Doc?"

She blinked away the stupor. "It was, uh, good—very good actually. And hey, the roof looks sensational. It really changed the appearance of the place."

He opened the door wider. "Thanks. Come on in. I've been doing a little prep work in here so Gavin will be ready to lay the flooring when he finds time."

As she stepped inside a terrible smell assaulted her senses. She stared at the floor and her stomach bottomed out: The carpet had been stripped down to the concrete slab. The place looked like a construction zone. Her smile wilted.

She covered her nose. "What is that smell?"

"Apparently the previous resident had untrained pets."

"Urine?"

"At least. The carpet and padding were nasty."

There would be no uncovering the furniture and cleaning up the place for Lucy now. Avery would have to put her up at the hotel and promise the renovation would be complete—somehow—by the time she started the position.

It isn't the end of the world. She repeated the thought to herself twice more. But the young doctor was already overqualified for this position. She had the credentials to make big money someplace else. Even some small-town practice might be able to pay her more competitively—probably even the one in Ohio.

"What's wrong?" Wes's brows pulled together as he studied her. "Don't worry, I'm airing it out. Just make sure Gavin rolls on some Kilz before he lays the flooring. It'll knock that smell right out."

"Kilz. Right. I'll tell him. Thank you for getting the carpet up. It'll make Gavin's job much easier."

His gaze sharpened on her. "You sure you're okay?"

"I'm just hungry." She forced a bright smile. "I thought we'd go out tonight and celebrate. Well, honestly, I'm out of groceries and haven't had time to restock."

"What'd you have in mind?"

"It's your last night in town. Why don't you pick—from the five whole restaurants that are open for supper."

"I've been meaning to get back over to the Trailhead. Their brisket's really good."

"Sounds perfect. Are you ready to go?"

"I'll meet you out at the Jeep."

Avery settled into the last empty booth at the restaurant and took a deep whiff of the savory smells emanating from the kitchen. The sounds of conversation and clinking silverware filled the space, and a loud country tune flowed through the speakers.

"I didn't expect it to be this busy on a weeknight," Wes said over the cacophony.

"Taco Tuesday is pretty popular around here. They even make guacamole for the occasion—though it can't compete with yours."

"Thank you kindly, ma'am," he said in an exaggerated southern drawl.

She made a face. "Is that how we sound to you?"

"Forgive my bad impression. I find your southern drawl very charming. It was one of the first things I noticed about you."

"You mean when you were spiking a fever and delirious with dehydration?" she deadpanned.

"I was not delirious."

"Debatable." She couldn't help grinning as she thought of their first hours together. "You were actually quite obstinate for someone who could barely make it to the exam room on his own two feet."

"I don't care to feel like that again anytime soon."

"It's amazing to think you hiked fourteen miles in that condition."

"And collapsed in a heap on your porch. On your birthday, no less."

"Illness waits for no man—or woman."

"Speaking of your obscene work hours—any reply from that doctor who sent her résumé Saturday?"

Avery had told him about Dr. Chan at Saturday night's fiesta-for-two. "Actually, she responded on Sunday, and we had a video call today. I'm happy to say it seems very promising."

He beamed. "Hey, that's great news."

The server stopped by for their orders. Rae Anne was still in her teens, but that didn't stop the girl from sneaking peeks at Wes or blushing while he gave his order. She couldn't blame the poor girl. He was probably the best-looking man she'd ever seen in the restaurant.

As the teenager walked away, Wes leaned onto his elbows, fully focused on Avery. "Now, tell me about your candidate. Where's she from?"

Avery filled him in on the basics, trying to temper her own expectations. He responded with all the right questions, digging for more information where she skimped.

"Sounds like the ideal candidate," Wes said when she finished. "And even with the other offer on the table, she must be seriously interested if she's flying here on her own dime."

"That's what I thought. She's qualified—overqualified, really—has stellar recommendations, and she actually hopes to work in a small-town setting. Only in my dreams did I imagine I'd find someone so perfect for the position and so quickly."

"Then why do I get the sense something's bothering you?"

She should've known she couldn't get anything past him. He paid close attention and read her well. "The fly in the ointment is the timing. Dr. Chan needs to make a move pretty quickly."

He tipped his head back. "And the apartment isn't ready yet."

"It probably won't be a deal breaker."

"But you're concerned it will be. How quickly are we talking about?"

"Her lease and job end in two weeks, and she'd like to start right away."

He gave a slow nod. "All right, that's not unreasonable as far as the construction is concerned. Really, it's just the flooring, plumbing, and the unfinished wall. Stewie will have you plumbed in this Friday, then he'll schedule an inspection. The framing inspection is also happening Friday. Your brother could get the flooring done in a couple of days—the unfinished wall over a weekend. Setting the new toilet, sink, and shower enclosure will only take a day. Two weeks is pushing it but manageable."

She flashed a smile. "Right, it totally is. I'm probably blowing this out of proportion."

———

Wes studied Avery's bright expression. She took a sip of water, then her attention drifted aimlessly around the room.

He didn't see the problem. Surely her brother would step up to the plate once Wes was gone. But Avery wasn't one to make a mountain out of a molehill. "What is it you're not telling me?"

She blinked at him. "What? Nothing."

He waited her out.

"Well . . . ," she said a long moment later, "not much of anything. It's just that Dr. Chan is visiting sooner than later. She's scheduling a flight for this weekend to look the place over.

167

I couldn't put her off since she's on a deadline to find a new position but . . ." She left off with a shrug.

"And since the salary you're offering is on the low side, it would be nice if you could tempt her with attractive housing."

She gave a sheepish smile. "It really would be. But I'll just build a vision for the finished product and promise the house will be perfect by the time she starts—if she takes the job. Did I mention she has another offer on the table? Don't mind me. I'm just overthinking it."

The server returned with their drinks and scuttled off.

Avery was downplaying her concerns. But he knew what another doctor would mean for her mental health. She worked six days a week and was on call twenty-four/seven. That wasn't healthy for anyone.

And according to her, attracting a doctor to a small town for an even smaller salary was a tall order. This Lucy Chan sounded, well, like just what the doctor ordered. It was too bad he couldn't—

Wait a minute. Technically he had a few days to spare. Ever since this afternoon when he'd learned Lillian would be gone when he arrived, he hadn't been eager to get back on the trail. And he hadn't booked that flight yet.

Avery watched a lone couple two-step across the dance floor.

He took in her beautiful mahogany hair, her wide-set green eyes that hinted of both intelligence and vulnerability. Those slim, strong shoulders that seemed to carry the weight of the world. And as he absorbed her essence, he knew . . ,

He wasn't ready to leave her just yet.

The realization was a sucker punch. The relationship could

never go anywhere. But there was something inside, a knowing, that his purpose here hadn't been completed.

He sensed she needed him somehow—and for more than a reno on an old carriage house. That realization prompted him to speak up.

"You know what? Why don't I just stay a few more days? I could start on the—"

"No." Her expression closed up tight. "No way. You are not delaying your hike again."

"Just hear me out. I could easily get the flooring done before she arrives, then there would only be an old bathroom to contend with. And maybe I could get Stewie out a little earlier to—"

Avery shook her head. "I'm not asking that of you."

He leaned forward, holding her gaze. "You didn't ask; I offered. Seriously, I have a few days to spare, and I don't mind hanging around awhile longer."

She seemed to weigh his assertion, her eyes turning down at the corners, her lips pursing.

"It's supposed to rain later this week anyway—you know how I hate hiking in the rain."

"Don't act as if you'd be doing this for yourself."

He pinned her with an unswerving look. "I don't mind, Doc. Really. I hate leaving a job undone, and I really do have time to kill. It would be a win-win for both of us."

"Then why do I feel as though I'm taking advantage of you?"

His eyes lit with humor and his lips twitched. "Sounds like a personal problem to me."

"You're impossible." She held eye contact for a long moment. "Do you promise it wouldn't set you back in some way?"

He lifted his right hand. "Scout's honor—and yes, I actually was a Scout. For about five minutes, between moves." He waited, silently urging her to acquiesce. Convincing her it was what he wanted—and it really was. "Come on. Just say yes. It's that easy."

Avery tilted her chin. "Fine. But I'm going to pay you for your time."

"I'd rather have the meals." *And your company.*

"You'll have both—those are my conditions, take it or leave it."

He pretended to weigh her demands, but there wasn't even a flicker of indecision in his heart. He was staying until he finished the reno or until Dr. Chan arrived—whichever came first.

"All right. It's a deal." He stuck out his hand and they shook on it. He couldn't stop the grin that curled his lips. And even though she probably didn't want him to, he could see the immense relief behind her mock scowl.

Twenty-Three

The load of bricks on Avery's shoulders fell away. She cut a glance at Wes, who seemed to be enjoying his beef brisket, and hoped she wasn't taking advantage of this kind soul. But he didn't seem to mind staying. And she really did need his help.

She wiped her mouth and set the napkin in her plate. The relief at having the renovation completed—or almost completed—by the time Dr. Chan arrived loosened the tense muscles in her neck and shoulders.

But searching deeper, she couldn't deny a secondary reason for her relief: She didn't have to say good-bye to Wes yet. She had at least a few more days with him.

She took in the now-familiar angles and planes of his face. He was pretty to look at, no doubt, but he was even more attractive on the inside. A man who put aside his plans to help another was a man who could be counted on. A man who spent months on the trail to honor a friend was a man to be admired.

He finished his last bite and leaned back in the booth. "How could you let me eat that much?"

"I wasn't the one who ordered double meat. Besides"—her gaze drifted over his torso—"something tells me you'll work it off."

"That doesn't make my stomach any less full." He glanced at the poolroom. "I wonder if Stewie's here. I could try and get him to come a couple days early so we could get the plumbing *and* the framing inspected Friday. That would expedite things."

"We need the plumbing inspected before the tub and stuff are installed?"

"Exactly. I don't see Stewie back there, but I'll call him in the morning." As he tossed his napkin on his plate his focus caught on something behind her. "Your brother's here."

"Which one?" She glanced over her shoulder. "Oh, Coop comes in all the time. He likes to hang out with the townsfolk—I guess it helps in his line of work."

"How long's he been sheriff? Seems kind of young for the position." He lifted a brow at her. "Then again that appears to be a family trait."

"It was something he'd always wanted. I'm really proud of him for working so hard to get there." She thought of the scandal that almost stole the election. "It wasn't an easy campaign."

"I'll bet. But he seems to be well liked."

"He's a great guy. I'm definitely blessed in the family department."

"They seem very supportive. Though I admit Gavin's a bit of an enigma, at least to me."

"He's been through a lot. He was divorced a couple years ago and—" She should leave out the part where he'd lost his son. He was so private about that. "Well, he's been a little adrift ever since."

"Then he lost his girl to his brother? Ouch. I guess that's how a general contractor ends up running a campground."

"He wasn't just any old contractor either—he was the head GC for the biggest residential builder in Asheville. Very successful. He moved back home after the divorce and took the first job he was offered."

"Quite a step down."

"He needed to decompress. He needed his family and friends." They'd circled the tents around Gavin—the Robinsons and his best friend Mike—but it was Katie who'd finally pulled him from his depression. Then he'd lost her too. He seemed to have rebounded from that pretty well though.

"Does he have any plans to build homes again?"

"I hope so. Nothing would make the family happier." But that job might also call him back to Asheville or another town that offered more opportunity.

"How about a game of pool?" Wes asked.

She made a face. "You don't know what you're asking. I'm really bad at pool."

His lips lifted into a smile and he winked. "Maybe you just haven't had the right teacher."

Five minutes later Wes had shown her how to choose a straight stick by looking down the cue from butt to tip. Once she had a good cue, he broke the balls and sank a solid.

He missed the next shot. "Let's see whatcha got, Doc."

Avery bent over the pool table, positioning her hand on the table the way Cooper had instructed her way back when. She aimed the pool stick at a stripe near the corner pocket. "Is this right? It's been a while."

"Let's talk about your stance." Wes approached from behind. He tapped her back foot with his toe. "Move this foot back a bit. Good. Now, when you bend over, keep your knees nice and relaxed. That's it. Move your bridge a little closer to the cue ball—you'll have more control. Lower it a little. You want to hit the ball right in the center. Perfect. Now move the cue back and forth for a little practice."

"Like this?"

"Here." He stepped up behind her and braced his weight on the table beside her. His hand closed over the one holding the pool stick. "Lower this hand a bit. You want a nice, straight slide. Like this." He guided her through the movement.

His breath stirred the hair at her nape, sending a shiver down her spine. She tried to focus on his instruction, her technique, but the low bass of his voice so close to her ear and the feel of his body against hers served as a major distraction. Her skin flushed with heat.

On the table he placed his hand over hers. "Spread your fingers a little more. Yeah, like that. All right, I think you're ready."

When he eased away she immediately missed the contact. She focused on the cue ball. Lowered her bridge.

"Nice steady stroke," he said. "Follow through."

She struck the cue ball.

"Nice."

The ball struck the stripe and it rolled forward, hitting just to the side of corner pocket and bouncing off. "Shoot."

"Don't be discouraged. That was close and your stance and

technique looked really good. You're a fast learner." He rounded the table, searching for his own shot. When he found one he bent over and lined it up.

This time Avery took note of his position over the cue, of the hand that held the stick in a relaxed grip. There was a lot more to pool than she'd realized.

Her phone vibrated in her pocket and she pulled it out. Unknown caller. Not wanting to break his concentration she waited.

"It's my business line," she said after he sank the shot. She answered the call. Maggie Walden was calling about her teenage daughter, Brooke, who'd hurt her ankle at soccer practice. It was swollen and bruised and giving her quite a bit of pain.

"Why don't you meet me at the clinic in, say, twenty minutes? I can take a look and see what's going on."

"Oh, thank you so much. I'm worried it's more than just a sprain."

"Well, we'll know soon enough. See you shortly."

After she disconnected the call, she grimaced at Wes. "Sorry."

"To be continued." His eyes crinkled as he took her cue and set it in the wall-mounted rack. "Let's get you home."

An hour later Avery had treated and released Brooke. The girl had sustained a grade-two lateral ankle sprain. She wasn't elated to hear she'd be sidelined for at least three to six weeks.

By the time Avery replaced Brooke's file in the cabinet, it was going on nine o'clock. She should get some much-needed sleep, but she was too keyed up for bed. She glanced out her office door and saw the work lights burning brightly inside the cottage. Wes had mentioned getting the tack strips up tonight so he'd be ready to apply that odor-stopping product in the morning.

Without thought she slipped through the door and made her way across the lawn. She'd just check in and see how the work was coming along. Plus, she'd forgotten to give him her keys—he'd need the Jeep in the morning to pick up that sealer. Maybe she could even help with the tack strips. It might be fun to work together.

The half-moon was high in the sky, casting a glow over the landscape. The grass swooshed as her feet cut through it, and the scent of freshly mown grass floated over on a mild breeze.

As she neared the carriage house, the low rumble of Wes's voice carried through the open windows. She stopped on the stoop, not wanting to interrupt.

"I'm sure you'll be fine," he said. "You've got a lot of experience. It's not like you're a beginner." He chuckled. "You can say that again."

Avery's stomach wobbled at the gentle sound of his voice. He must be talking to the woman Gavin had mentioned. Who was she? And why hadn't Wes mentioned her? She must be someone important if he was keeping close tabs on her.

He was quiet for a while, and Avery shifted on the porch. She shouldn't be standing here listening. She turned to go.

But his voice halted her steps. "It's coming along really good. I'm hoping to get it finished before I leave, but that's partly out of my hands. You know how I feel about leaving things unfinished . . . Yeah, I know." He let out a low laugh. "I'm glad you had a good day. I worry about you."

Avery pressed a hand to her throat. She didn't like the

feelings roiling just now. Or the notion that she didn't really know Wes at all.

She gave her head a shake. She'd met him less than three weeks ago. Was it even possible to know someone in such a short span of time?

He was silent now, apparently listening to whoever was on the line.

Avery really had stood here too long. She quietly stepped off the porch and made her way across the yard. Maybe the woman was just a close friend. Or a cousin he hadn't yet mentioned. But wasn't it also possible he had a girlfriend waiting for him in Albany?

Avery recalled the way he gazed at her sometimes, with affection and maybe something more. The connection between them couldn't be denied. Their conversation was friendly, sometimes flirtatious, but it wasn't as if he'd ever hit on her. Even when they'd danced in so closely on Saturday, he'd done nothing suggestive.

And yet . . . hearing him talk so softly to another woman made her chest ache. She didn't like the idea of him having a girlfriend—even though nothing could ever come of a relationship with him.

She rolled her eyes. "You are being ridiculous." But the verbal acknowledgment did nothing to diminish her conflicting feelings.

———

It took Wes a while to pull up the tack strips and once he had, he was too wired to sleep. Unfortunate since he needed to get an early start in the morning. He needed to get the Kilz as soon as the hardware store opened. Once that dried, he'd start putting down the vinyl planking. That would take two days. He'd already called Stewie and left a message, asking if he could get the bathroom plumbed in before Friday.

Wes settled on the bed with his phone and started a *Mission Impossible* movie. He'd watch until he was tired, then turn in. The film moved quickly and held his interest as the protagonist found himself facing one trial after another, fighting for survival. The female protagonist reminded him a bit of Lillian with her curly brown hair and olive complexion.

He thought back to their recent phone conversations. When she was down, he somehow felt responsible. After all, if it hadn't been for him, Landon might've survived the attack. How could he ever pay his friend back? Looking out for his sister seemed like such a small price to pay.

At least Lillian had been in good spirits tonight. Excited about her new job. Her current clients had taken the news well. And she'd seemed fine with him staying in Riverbend a few extra days. He got the feeling it eased her conscience—she'd felt bad about being gone when he arrived.

An explosion sounded. Wes dropped his phone. His heart thundered in his chest. He gasped for breath.

His eyes fixed on the violent scene playing out on his phone. His hands shook as he stopped the movie. It was only a stupid film.

But he could still hear the sharp crack of the explosion. Feel the force of Landon's body knocking him to the ground. He still saw the white dots speckling his vision as he opened his eyes. Tasted the dust coating his mouth.

As soon as he'd gotten his bearings, he rolled Landon off his back and saw death in his dazed vision.

Blood.

It was everywhere. Splattered on Landon's Yankees shirt, on the bandana around his head, dribbling from his mouth. Wes searched for a place to press to stanch the flow, but he couldn't find its source.

"I got you, buddy. I got you." Wes looked up to chaos. People running, screaming. Rubble. Bodies on the ground.

"Help!" he screamed. "I need help over here!"

Landon clutched Wes's arm. His breaths came in gasps. A trickle of blood dripped from his mouth. "Take care . . . of Lillian."

A fist tightened in Wes's gut. "You're gonna be fine. Come on. Hang in there."

Landon closed his eyes.

"*Landon*. Help's on the way, buddy. Look at me. Come on. Stay with me."

Landon's eyes fluttered open. He focused on Wes, more lucid now. "Promise . . . me."

Wes's eyes stung. His vision blurred. "Of course I will. But you'll be here to do that yourself. You're going to be just fine. Help is on the—"

Landon's eyes drifted shut. His chest sank. It didn't rise again.

"Landon!" Wes shook him. "Landon!"

A siren screamed somewhere in the distance.

Wes blinked. Became aware of the room. The faint acidic smell from the soiled floor. The weight of the blanket. He pushed it off, his breaths heaving, heat prickling under his arms.

He wasn't in Colombia anymore. He was safe in Riverbend. He was fine.

But Landon wasn't.

Wes closed his eyes against the unrelenting pain and guilt. *Help me, God.* It was just a flashback, a little PTSD. It wasn't the first time, but it was the first in a while. The guilt remained.

He should've gone straight to Lillian when he'd returned to the States. The trail could've waited. Between Lillian's grief and job struggles she'd been in a tailspin since her brother's death. He'd told himself he needed some therapeutic time alone before he was in any shape to support her. But he should've been there for her like he'd promised. When Landon had made that deathbed plea, he hadn't had phone calls in mind.

And now Wes had let his growing feelings for Avery overshadow the promise he'd made to his buddy. He just had to get this place finished, and then he'd be on his way. He would come through for his friend, the same way Landon had come through for him. The thought brought a measure of peace.

Wes lay back against his pillow, not bothering to shut off the light. But it was a long time before he found rest.

Twenty-Four

"You can come look now."

Avery jumped from her seat at the kitchen island and headed toward the door. Finally, Wes was letting her see what he'd accomplished this week—he'd wanted to finish the floor and trim first.

She stopped at her apartment door and tracked back to the living room, grabbed the W-4 form for Wes, then headed out the door. Hard to believe the cottage was almost finished. She owed him a lot more than the measly payment he'd be getting.

She headed down the steps and into the yard. He'd worked right through suppertime tonight. Maybe she'd offer to take him out to eat one last time.

The thought of his imminent departure planted an ache in the center of her chest. She'd gotten used to spending her evenings with Wes. Every night this week Avery had either cooked or ordered carryout. Then they whiled away the remaining hours with a hike, a game of cards, or a movie. One night they'd simply talked for hours on the back deck.

But tomorrow was Friday, his last day. He would finish up the cottage (hopefully), then hit the trail just in time for Dr. Chan to arrive. Saying good-bye to Wes wouldn't be easy. Avery would be grateful for the distraction of the doctor's arrival.

The sun had set behind the mountains, ushering in twilight. Swathes of periwinkle and gold streaked the darkening sky in a striking palette. Just ahead a light shone through the carriage house windows.

When she reached the building, she knocked on the door.

"Close your eyes!" Wes called through the door.

Avery smiled and did as he instructed. "This is how it's going to be, huh?"

The door clicked open. "Yep."

If possible, her smile stretched wider. "Haven't you made me wait long enough?"

"Patience, Doc." He took the form from her, then guided her forward. "It'll be worth the wait. I promise."

With her eyes closed, other senses prevailed. The low timber of his voice sent shivers down her spine. The familiar woodsy scent of him beckoned her closer. And the solid feel of his arm enticed her.

He placed his hands on her shoulders and drew her to a halt. "All right. Open your eyes."

Avery gasped at the sight. Not only was the plank flooring complete, the furniture was back in place. With the freshly painted gray walls and ash-toned planking, it seemed like a brand-new living space.

"Oh, Wes. It's beautiful. The flooring is perfect—like real wood. And you replaced the chandelier."

"It was on sale for a ridiculous price. You did a great job picking out the colors."

Her gaze drifted over the space, taking it all in. Dr. Chan would be impressed. Who wouldn't want to live here? It was nicer than her own apartment. A laugh bubbled up in her throat. She turned and threw her arms around him. "You're amazing! Thank you so much."

He chuckled and her chest absorbed the vibrations. "Don't get too excited now. The bathroom's still unfinished. Not to mention that wall. But after the inspection clears in the morning, I'll set the tub enclosure, stool, and sink. If there's time I'll hang the drywall before I leave, but no promises."

She pulled back and grasped his forearms. "I can't believe you got all this done. How can I ever thank you?"

His eyes softened. "It was my pleasure. Truly."

The moment lengthened. She became hyperaware of her shallow breaths, of the unyielding muscles under her fingertips, of the warmth in those blue eyes.

His expression fell as the seconds drew out, his gaze homing in on hers.

Avery's fingers itched to brush the sharp curve of his jawline. She wanted to cup the strong column of his neck and feel his pulse thrumming against her palm. The way he looked at her made her legs as wobbly as cooked noodles.

But the memory of his phone conversation flashed in her mind. Somewhere out there was a woman who meant something to him. And even if Avery was somehow mistaken, she'd already chosen not to take this road.

She gave his forearms a squeeze before she released him. Then she strolled the length of the space, surveying it as if taking in the changes. But really, she was steadying her breaths, gathering her thoughts. Trying to keep her stilted legs from collapsing beneath her. She would definitely be taking him out to eat tonight. She no longer trusted herself alone with him.

Wes cleared his throat. "Gavin can finish out that wall. Or maybe you'll have time to do it yourself since you'll have another doctor on staff soon."

"She's still considering that other position, remember?" A safe distance away, Avery turned. "But these living quarters will sure help sweeten my offer."

Twenty-Five

Today was the day.

Once Wes finished the bathroom, he'd officially be hitting the trail again. He'd packed his things last night. It was one o'clock now, but as long as he left by four he'd have enough daylight to reach the first shelter. His work had kept him from dwelling on thoughts of leaving Avery. He'd have plenty of time to sort through his feelings on the trail. He would need that time to realign his loyalties. To remind himself of his goals, of his duty, before he reached Albany and Lillian.

He twisted the toilet valve, turning on the water. Once the tank was full, he flushed and checked the base for leaks. Looked good. He stood and surveyed his work. With the vinyl planking, shower surround, and stool, the bathroom appeared brand new. Now he just had to install the pedestal sink, and he'd be ready to go.

But first, he needed to retrieve his bedding from the dryer.

Avery had insisted he leave it for her, but she was busy getting the clinic ready for her guest. He wanted to leave the carriage house clean and ready for her.

As he pulled the warm bedding from the dryer it snapped with static. The minutes were ticking down. He was inching closer to that good-bye scene and dreading it more with each tick of the clock.

He dropped the bundle of bedding on the dresser and grabbed the fitted sheet. The generous elastic pocket stretched easily over the first corner. He reached over the bed to slip the elastic over another corner, and a sharp stab of pain pierced his spine.

"The lobby is spic-and-span, Doctor," Patti said as Avery approached the front desk. "And my work area is organized and clean. Want me to tidy up the office next?"

"Already done." They were a little short-staffed as Katie had the afternoon off. She was headed to Asheville for her final dress fitting. Avery checked her Fitbit. It was just after one o'clock, and she would pick up Dr. Chan at four. "I think we're in pretty good shape."

"How's Hottie McHandyman coming with the carriage house?"

"I've been too busy to check."

"Speaking of busy, there's a patient in four."

"Thanks." As Avery turned that way, her phone vibrated and she checked the screen, hoping for an update from Wes. But it was only Cooper.

Can Katie borrow your boots? We're hiking to Lover's Leap
tomorrow. I can pick them up after work.
Sure. I'll be gone, but my apartment's unlocked. They're in
my bedroom closet.

Avery pocketed her phone and entered the exam room where she was met by a woman who sported a painful shingles rash. Avery gave her prescriptions for Valacyclovir and a Capsaicin patch and offered additional advice on coping with the pain.

After sending the patient on her way, Avery checked her phone again. Two messages had come in from Wes.

Help! Threw my back out.
Hello? Kind of stuck.

Oh no. Avery pocketed her phone as she rushed down the hall, through her office, and out the back door. If he'd strained his back, he sure wouldn't be hitting the trail tonight. Or even tomorrow. Hope welled up and she grimaced at her selfish response. Poor guy was in pain and likely to be laid up a few days, and she was getting giddy over the potential change in plans.

When she reached the carriage house, she burst through the door. "Wes?"

"Back here."

She dashed through the house and found him in the bedroom, frozen over the bed, hands braced on the mattress. "Can you move?"

"I don't know." Tension laced his voice. "I haven't tried yet."

She lifted the back of his shirt. No physical anomalies. That was good. "What kind of pain are you having?"

He grimaced. "Spasms. Stiffness. Happened a few years ago and feels just the same. It was a strain."

Poor thing. Avery set her hand gently on his shoulder as she surveyed the scene. "You were making the bed?"

He gave a wry laugh. "This couldn't have happened while I was carrying heavy pallets or shingling the roof."

She patted his shoulder. "I promise not to take your man card. What precisely caused your back to go out?"

"I stretched across the bed, twisted a little, and bam."

"Any pain or numbness in your legs?"

"No."

"All right. It does sound like a muscle strain. I don't think you'll need an X-ray. Can you straighten up?"

His jaw set and he eased upright inch by inch, exhaling a steady breath as he straightened. Pain pulled his facial muscles taut. He stopped when he was only slightly hunched over.

She took his arm. "Okay, let's get you into bed, mister. You need ice, rest, and an anti-inflammatory. Think you can sit?"

"Not here. You have a guest coming. And I haven't set the sink yet. Just give me a minute. Maybe it'll pass."

She scowled at him. "A strained muscle will more likely take days, not minutes. You know I'm right; you've been through this before. And don't worry about the sink or my guest. I'll figure out something else."

"I'm not staying here. Maybe I can get Stewie to come and set the sink for you."

"Will you forget about the sink? Get in the bed."

"I'll just crash in an exam room or in your office or something."

Avery tilted her head. "Oh, that'll make a good impression. Dr. Chan, please meet a patient of mine who's camping out in the clinic for tonight. I promise he won't raid the narcotics. Get in the bed, Wes."

A shadow flickered in his jaw as it twitched.

This definitely wasn't ideal. He'd worked so hard to get the carriage house ready for Dr. Chan, but Avery didn't know what else to do. The man needed bed rest, and his health had to come first.

"I can stay at the motel then," he said.

"You're going to fold yourself into my Jeep?"

He grimaced. "What about your apartment?"

She arched her brow. "You mean the one at the top of the staircase? Do you really think you're fit to climb stairs right now?"

"I can do it—if I go slow. It's bending at the waist that kills. The doctor's only coming for one night, right? I can sleep on your sofa, then if my back's not better, I'll move back in here after the doctor leaves."

Her gaze met and clung to his. He was being so stubborn about this. It *was* only one night. But she knew one thing for certain: there was no way she'd put him on her sofa—he'd never fit, for one. And he really needed to stretch out on his back. She would put him in her bed and take the couch herself. However, she'd keep that little detail to herself until he made it up the staircase.

"All right. If you're sure that's the way you want it."

"I am so sorry about this, Avery. First an illness now an injury . . . I never meant to be such a pain your backside."

She told herself her smile wasn't provoked by heartfelt relief that he'd be staying a little longer after all. "You're not a pain. And it's certainly not your fault. Now, let's try and get you up those stairs."

Five minutes later they were still navigating the staircase. Avery's arm curled around Wes's waist. She pressed into his rock-hard side and held the hand he had wrapped around her shoulder. Her legs trembled under the extra weight.

He paused midway up the flight, still hunched over, his breaths coming heavily. "This is so embarrassing."

"You pulled a muscle. It could happen to anyone." Avery didn't exactly mind the proximity. He was so solid and male and—

"I'm too heavy for you."

"I'm stronger than I look and we're almost there."

He glanced up the staircase. "We're only halfway there."

"Same difference. Come on. You can do this."

They proceeded slowly up the remaining stairs. When they finally reached the top, she shoved open the door and helped him inside. He headed toward the couch.

"Nope. This way."

He narrowed his eyes at her. "I'm not taking your bed."

Avery utilized her best doctorly expression and tone. "You need to lie flat on your back, Wes, and you can't do that on a sofa that's a foot too short. You're taking my bed or we're going back down to the carriage house."

He glared at her, his mouth set.

She nailed him with a glare, not giving an inch.

"Fine," he said finally. "Have it your way."

"That's more like it." She snuggled into his side again. "Now, let's go, gimpy."

Twenty-Six

What a day. Avery drew in a deep breath and released it steadily.
Everything would be fine. Wes was settled in her bedroom with
a cold pack, drinking water, and a biography. He had an anti-
inflammatory in his system and a painkiller at the ready. He'd even
managed to get Stewie to set the sink.

Now Avery waited in the airport's cell phone lot for Dr. Chan's
text that her plane had landed. She leaned back against the seat
but didn't dare close her eyes for fear she'd fall asleep. She hadn't
had a late-night emergency all week, but she'd still had trouble
sleeping. Cutting back on caffeine didn't help. She also tried a
couple of milligrams of melatonin—she couldn't risk taking more
since she had to be alert for emergencies.

Sleeplessness was common and had many causes, including
stress, and she had plenty of that. But insomnia was also an early

symptom of Huntington's disease—and she had just hit thirty. Avery gave her head a shake. She couldn't let herself go there.

She stared at the airport's exit. *Please, God, let Dr. Chan take this job.*

A text buzzed in. The doctor had arrived and was waiting outside baggage claim. Avery replied she was on her way and set the Jeep in motion. Moments later she pulled up to the curb, put the car in Park, and got out to greet the woman.

Lucy Chan smiled as she approached, pulling a carry-on bag. She was a good five inches shorter than Avery, but she carried herself with an easy confidence. She sported a dressy top paired with trendy jeans and wedged sandals. Her dark hair fell around her shoulders in waves that moved with each turn of her head. "Hello, Avery. It's nice to meet you in person."

Avery shook her hand. "Nice to meet you too. How was your flight? It ran on time at least?"

"It was perfect. I even managed to catch up on some reading." She held up a paperback copy of *Hillbilly Elegy*.

"That's a good one. Have you seen the movie?"

"I always read the book first."

"I knew I liked you. I've been working my way through Austen's books for the second time. I'm currently on *Northanger Abbey*."

"That's a fun one. Which is your favorite?"

Avery chuckled. "Don't make me choose."

They stowed Lucy's bag in the backseat and headed off, making small talk on the drive to Riverbend. Avery told her more about the town, then the conversation turned toward their families. Lucy's father had immigrated from Vietnam and met Lucy's mother when he settled in Indiana. They've been married for thirty years and have five children who live all over the US. Lucy seemed more relaxed in person, and conversation flowed easily.

After they entered the town proper Avery pointed north. "That's the northbound trailhead for the Appalachian Trail. It runs across this bridge and straight down Main Street. The southbound trailhead is on the other side of town."

"I'll bet hikers are really glad to hit civilization."

"They're definitely ready for a shower and a real bed."

"I love to hike, but I don't think I'll ever take on a two-thousand-mile trail."

"It's not for everyone." Avery thought of Wes and the journey he'd started in honor of his friend. How was he faring in her apartment?

Before Avery knew it, they were pulling in to the clinic's parking lot. There was still enough light to make out the clinic and beautiful property surrounding it. She attempted to view the brick building through fresh eyes and liked what she saw. But there was no denying that it was a converted home. She hoped that didn't turn Lucy off.

"Well, here we are," Avery said.

"It has a nice homey feel."

"As you can see, all the houses through here have been converted into businesses. I bought the property a couple years ago and transformed it into a clinic. My brother's a contractor."

"Very handy. You've been busy since med school. When I finished residency, I felt like I could sleep for a year. I can't imagine taking on this kind of challenge. How far away is the nearest hospital?"

"Forty-five minutes but they'll run an ambulance here when necessary."

"I can see the need for your clinic. You must get a lot of injuries from hikers coming off the trail."

"We do. But a good share of business comes from the town itself. Part of our job is, of course, determining when the patient requires more care than we can give. To assist us with that decision, we've acquired an EKG machine, and eventually we're planning to get X-ray and small lab machines as well."

Avery put the Jeep in Park and shut off the engine. After Lucy collected her bag, Avery led her up the walk. "Would you like to see the apartment first? The clinic's obviously closed, but it might be a good idea to check it out tonight so I can answer all your questions without interruption. Then if you're hungry, I can take you out for supper."

"I could definitely eat. That sounds like a plan."

Avery led her around the back, keeping up a running dialogue about the clinic's hours and practices. Nervous energy filled her as she approached the entrance. "We just completed renovations. There's one wall that's still unfinished—the framing was just inspected and approved today, so I'm hoping my brother can finish it next week."

"Is that the river I hear?"

"Correct, the French Broad River. There's a great spot to take a lunch break back there—though most of the staff prefers the breakroom or back deck. We're a sociable group. Here we are." Breath held, Avery opened the door, flipped on the lights, and ushered Lucy inside. She hoped the woman didn't find the space too provincial.

Lucy entered, letting her gaze drift around the apartment. "Oh, it's very nice. I like how open it is."

"We took a wall down, and it really opened up the space."

"The gray tones are so soothing. I love the floor. Is it real wood?"

Thank you, Wes. "Vinyl planking, but it does look real, doesn't it? And it's easier to care for. The furniture is a bit old, but I can certainly store or sell things to make room for your furniture."

"I have a few basic things, but I've been too busy to collect much in the way of household goods." Lucy wandered through the kitchen, then into the bathroom. "This is very nice."

After Wes had strained his back, Avery asked Lisa if she could drop by and finish making the bed. But Lisa had also left some fluffy towels in the bathroom, set a fresh bouquet of flowers on the table, and added candles and accents here and there to cozy up the place. Avery would have to thank her later.

"This is lovely," Lucy said after she peeked into the bedroom. "It's the same size as my current apartment but a lot nicer."

"I'm glad you like it. It doesn't have central air, but the window units cool it sufficiently. A lot of people around here open their windows at night."

"I'm a big fan of fresh air." Lucy ran her hand over the bedroom windowsill. "And these seem new. The window in my current bedroom is painted shut. My super doesn't seem to be in a big hurry to rectify the problem."

"Well, I don't have the skills to fix anything that might go awry, but my brother's pretty handy, and he usually owes me one."

Lucy beamed at her. "It must be a brother thing."

Avery glanced up at her apartment bedroom, where lamplight shone through the window. She'd really like to check in on Wes. "Would you like a chance to get settled before we head over to the clinic?"

"No, I'm good. I'm excited to take a peek."

"Well, let's get to it then."

Twenty-Seven

First an illness, now an injury. Wes had managed to make a real pain of himself around here. He lay flat on his back atop Avery's bedspread, trying to get into this biography about Churchill. But all he could think about was Avery and the doctor she was pinning all her hopes on. He said a brief prayer that she'd love the apartment. That she'd see all the wonderful things Avery was doing with her clinic and want to be a part of it too.

A while ago he'd heard them enter the clinic downstairs. He hoped Avery would come up and check on him so he could find out how it was going so far. But he hadn't heard any sounds from below in a while, so they must've already left.

He turned his head—basically the only thing he could move without pain—into the pillow and breathed in Avery's coconut-scented shampoo. He felt bad for taking her bed. But it was only one night and she'd been right. Just the thought of trying to squeeze onto that cramped couch made his back spasm. He took a sip of water from the straw of the bottle she'd left for him. He was dreading the moment when he'd have to go to the bathroom. The anti-inflammatory hadn't helped much, but the painkiller she'd left had dulled the pain. It also made him sleepy.

Boots hopped onto the bed and curled up at his side. Wes checked his watch. It was time to call Lillian and let her know what had happened.

She picked up on the second ring. "I didn't expect to hear from you tonight. You must not be far from town if you still have a signal."

"That's why I called. I haven't left town at all. I'm afraid I threw out my back this afternoon."

"Oh no. Are you okay?"

"Only if you consider being stuck flat on my back okay."

"You poor thing. I wish there was something I could do. Did your doctor friend examine it?"

"She said it's just a strain. This happened a few years ago down in Colombia, so unfortunately I'm familiar with the injury."

"I remember Landon mentioning that in a letter. Well, at least it didn't happen on the trail. And it's not going to require surgery or a hospital stay."

"No, just a few days' bedrest. I'm sorry I'm getting delayed again."

She chuckled. "What is it about that town? It just does not want to let you go."

The words tweaked his heart. It did seem like someone was conspiring against his departure. Was there a reason for that? Or was it just dumb luck? And what did it mean that he was relieved to be staying in Riverbend with Avery?

Lillian updated him on her new job—she'd gotten the

formal benefits and salary package and was thrilled with the offer. It was good to hear her sounding optimistic again. She'd even gone out with friends this past weekend.

He was laughing at one of her stories about that outing when he heard the apartment door opening. Avery and Dr. Chan must not have left for supper yet.

He wanted to rush off the phone, but Lillian was just wrapping up her story so he waited her out. Footsteps sounded in the living room and grew louder. But they were heavier and slower than—

A man appeared in the doorway. Cooper froze in place, eyes widening at the sight of Wes lying in his sister's bed.

Wes's stomach rolled. Of course it had to be Avery's sheriff brother. In uniform. And he obviously hadn't heard about Wes's injury. He felt a strong urge to get to his feet—especially when Cooper's gaze pinned him in place—but that wasn't happening without a lot of pain and a heavy dose of humility.

"Wes, you still there?" Lillian voice cut through the tension.

He blinked. "Uh, yeah. Listen, I have to go. I'll call you later, okay?" He didn't digest the words as they signed off. He was too busy enduring the waves of suspicion rolling off Avery's brother.

"What are you doing here?" Cooper asked as Wes disconnected the call. "I thought you were leaving today."

"I wrenched my back when I was finishing the apartment. She's got that doctor staying in the carriage house tonight, so here I am."

Cooper seemed to weigh his explanation with no small measure of distrust. His sharp eyes took in the nightstand with the medication and now-watery ice pack. Then his gaze swept over the scene, no doubt taking in the cat's obvious affection for Wes.

"Yeah . . . here you are."

"Look, man. I have a bad back and I wrenched it good. I'll be out of her hair in a few days."

"Seems I've heard that before."

Wes gritted his teeth. Sucked feeling so helpless while Avery's condescending brother stared down his nose at him. "I extended my stay to help her get the apartment finished. I'm not the bad guy here."

"Well, I don't know you, and it's my job to be skeptical. All I know is you're supposed to be long gone, but instead you're lying in my sister's bed, and she's not here."

Wes scowled. "You think I broke in and helped myself to her first-aid kit just for kicks?"

"I don't know what your game is."

Wes's muscles tensed, sending his back into spasms again. "It's not a game. If I wasn't hurt, you really think I'd still be flat on my back right now? She helped me up here, and she took the doctor out to dinner. Call her yourself."

Cooper narrowed his eyes at him. "Maybe I will."

"Be my guest."

With one last glare, Cooper strutted over to the closet and bent to retrieve something. He straightened with a pair of hiking boots and didn't spare Wes another look as he strode out the door.

Wes smacked his fist on the bed. Now he was all jacked up and his back throbbed. What was it with Avery's stupid brothers and their constant suspicion?

Avery slipped quietly into her apartment. It was only a little after ten, but if Wes had taken the narcotic it might've knocked him out. She set her purse and keys on the island and headed for the bedroom. The pressure of the evening had tied her stomach in knots. Tomorrow would be just as tense.

Please, God, let Lucy accept the job.

She found Wes reading the biography, head propped on her pillow, hair mussed, expression intent. A strange impression hit at the sight of him resting comfortably in her bed. An impression of home and belonging. She could imagine walking in to this sight every night. Could imagine crawling into bed beside him, laying her head on his shoulder. She'd ask what he liked about the book, and it would lead to a long, stimulating discussion.

She gave her head a sharp shake, and the floorboards under her feet squeaked.

He set down the book, his face brightening at the sight of her. "Hey there. I've been going crazy, wondering how it was going with Dr. Chan."

"Really good, I think. We get along well and I think she'd fit in around here. She loved the clinic."

"That's great news."

"She went on and on about the carriage house. I guess her apartment in Boston isn't very nice, so she was truly impressed with the accommodations."

"Do you think she'll accept your offer?"

"It's too early to say. She'll get a real taste of the clinic tomorrow morning. She did mention she hasn't yet visited the other practice she's considering, so I don't think she'll give me an answer this weekend."

"That's too bad."

"It's a big decision. I'd rather she was sure. How's your back feeling?"

"Not bad. I managed to get up once, put the ice pack back in the freezer. And I did take one of those pain pills around six."

"You should take another one plus the anti-inflammatory before bed. Let me grab the ice pack."

She wandered into the kitchen and fished the pack from the freezer. The way she'd felt upon seeing him in her bed hovered in her mind like a spring fog over the valley. It was only because she'd never had another man in her bed. But no, that should make the sight of him there foreign, not familiar.

And it definitely shouldn't feel . . . *right*.

She had to stop thinking like this. There was no point in allowing herself to have hopes and expectations that could never come to fruition. It would only make it more difficult when he left.

She returned to the bedroom, peeled back the covers, and helped him arrange the ice pack under his back. She sensed his perusal as she adjusted the covers. How did it feel for him—being here in her space? Was he experiencing the same *rightness*?

Her face heated at the thought. Of course he wasn't. When had she become so fanciful? Maybe Katie had rubbed off on her. Maybe it was just part of coming to realize she'd never make a home with a husband. Her way of grieving each little thing she would sacrifice along the way.

"Your brother stopped by."

Avery blinked at him. "What?"

"Cooper came by to get a pair of boots, I think. Wasn't too happy to find me in your bed."

Avery winced. "Sorry about that. I told him earlier today to stop by and grab them. I hope he wasn't a jerk."

"He was . . . protective of you."

A giggle bubbled up at the obvious understatement. She imagined Cooper's shock at finding Wes, his intimidating scowl and razor-sharp gaze. The laughter escaped.

Wes hiked a brow, humor glinting in his eyes. "Really? I'm lying here helpless and your intimidating law-enforcement brother comes in here, giving me the evil eye, and you find this funny?"

His description only made her laugh harder. She covered her mouth. "Sorry."

His lips twitched. "You don't seem very sorry."

"Come on, it's a little funny."

"He seemed like he wanted to kill me. And he probably knows all the ways to do it without getting caught."

"Stop it."

"And I wouldn't have even been able to defend myself."

It felt so good to laugh. She'd been under a lot of pressure and this weekend was so important. She didn't realize how much she needed to let go. Wes was so good for her.

The thought was sobering. She caught her breath as her humor faded. She gestured to the medications on the nightstand. "Well, it's obvious why you're here. And he didn't text or call so he couldn't have been too concerned."

He gave a mock scowl. "You didn't see the look in his eyes."

Affection for Wes bloomed, swelling until it overwhelmed her. She bent over and dropped a kiss on his brow, then straightened. "I promise I won't let him hurt you."

The humor slipped from his face. His gaze roved over her

features, landing on her mouth. Awareness crackled between them.

Time to go.

She moved the items on the nightstand closer to him. "Um, you need anything else before I turn in? More water? Another pillow? Anything?"

"No thanks." His voice was as thick as honey. "I'm good."

"Well, just holler if you need something." She turned for the door. "Want me to turn out the light, or are you going to read some more?"

"Think I'll read awhile."

"All right." At the threshold she offered a smile. "Good night, Wes."

"Night."

Avery pulled the door shut. It wasn't until she headed down the hall that she realized her legs wavered beneath her and her heart hammered in her chest. Ten minutes later she settled on the couch with a blanket and pillow, but it would be a long time before sleep found her.

Twenty-Eight

It was a sad state of affairs when a Keurig wasn't fast enough. Between the lumpy sofa, anticipation for today, and her unsettling thoughts about Wes, Avery hadn't gotten nearly enough sleep. The possibility that the insomnia was an early symptom hovered in her mind like a pesky mosquito.

No, she wouldn't think like that. Wouldn't let herself become paranoid—also a symptom of Huntington's, come to think of it. *Argh!*

She glanced down the hall. Not a peep from Wes yet this morning. She'd heard him once in the middle of the night. His footsteps were so slow she nearly got up to help him. But the memory of last night's interaction kept her on the sofa.

While Boots ate her kibble, Avery set out an extra mug and the cream. The clinic didn't open until nine, but she wanted to grab donuts from the bakery and brew a pot of coffee before Lucy arrived. Today, the prospective doctor would meet the rest of the staff—except for Katie, who had the day off. Hopefully Lucy had slept well in the apartment.

Just as the Keurig finished, a knock sounded on her door. Lucy? Avery was still in her pajamas. Not to mention—she glanced down the hall as she approached the front door—she had a male guest in her bedroom.

A quick peek through the peephole revealed her brother. Cooper wore a T-shirt, Braves cap, and a formidable scowl.

Great. Avery pulled open the door before he could knock again and wake up Wes. "Well, good morning, Brother."

"Can we talk a minute?" Cooper's gaze darted over her shoulder before returning to her. "Out here."

Here we go. So much for him not being concerned. Should've known better. She slipped outside and pulled the door shut— she definitely didn't want Wes hearing this. "Is this the part where you stick your nose in my business again?"

"The man's in your bed, Avery. Can you blame me for—"

"He threw out his back, and I have a guest in the—you know what? I don't owe you an explanation."

"Don't you find it a little odd that he keeps extending his stay?"

"You mean when he offered to help me out of a jam? He's the one who got that apartment finished just in the nick of time. And he hurt his back doing it, so forgive me if I offer him a place to recover."

"It just doesn't add up."

"He's a nice guy, Cooper, and he's become a friend. I know it's your job to be skeptical and pessimistic but—"

"I'm not pessimistic—I'm realistic."

She snorted. "Sure, whatever you say."

"I found out something you should know."

She pursed her lips. "You did a background check on him."

"Of course not; that's not lawful. But I checked a public database and—"

"Here we go."

"I found some stuff that raises a red flag. He's been sued by three different corporations for large sums of money."

"What, no speeding tickets?"

"Two, actually. Come on, you don't find that a little fishy—that he's been sued three times? How many times have you been sued? Oh, none? Me either."

"It's really none of your business—or mine for that matter. And how do you even know you have the right Wes Garrett?"

"I do."

"How do you know?"

He shifted his feet. "I used his social security number."

She crossed her arms and narrowed her eyes on her brother. "And how exactly did you come by that, Cooper?"

"I . . . might've seen his W-4 on your island."

"And you just helped yourself to that information? Nice."

"I did it for you. I'm concerned about your safety."

"I can take care of myself. Furthermore, I trust him, Cooper."

He pointed a finger at her. "*That* is exactly what worries me."

She was getting pretty tired of this. Tired of her family treating her as if she couldn't manage her own life. Tired of them thinking she needed them to oversee her affairs, be her guardians, and make her decisions. She was not helpless. She was not incapable. And she was not *ill*.

Avery took a step closer. "I have had enough of this. I don't need you taking care of me, Cooper. I'm perfectly capable of handling my own life. Being a potential carrier for the Huntington's gene does not make me incompetent."

"I never said—"

"You've said it a thousand different ways. And I'm tired of this family treating me like an invalid. My decision-making abilities have not been impaired. If I start having symptoms, you'll be the first to know. Until then, butt out."

"Maybe you should—"

She threw a palm up in his face, her muscles quivering with anger. "Stop. I have an important day ahead of me, and you've already managed to spike my blood pressure twenty points. You've come and had your say. Now I want you to go so I can enjoy one stinking cup of coffee before I get on with my day."

He had the grace to look sheepish. "I realize the timing could've been better. But I'm leaving for the day, and I felt you needed to—right. Never mind. I'll go now."

"Good idea."

He turned halfway down the staircase. "I hope everything goes well with the new doctor."

"Thanks," she gritted out.

Then he trotted down the remaining steps and was gone.

———

Wes put the soggy ice pack into the freezer and checked the time for the umpteenth time today. Avery had left a while ago to take Dr. Chan back to the airport. Through the kitchen window he could see twilight was settling over the valley. The last light of the day cast a golden glow over the carriage house.

It was safe for him to go back there now, but Avery had made him promise to wait for her. Getting around was still difficult, and she didn't want him taking a tumble. But it was getting late, and he was curious to know how things had gone with Dr. Chan. Avery had only checked in with him via text to see if he needed anything.

He hobbled slowly back to the bedroom, breath held against the spasms. He could walk without stooping over now, but his back was still stiff. He'd just reached the bed when the apartment door clicked open.

Avery was home. At least he hoped it was her and not Cooper again—or her other brother for that matter. But the quick, light footsteps gave her away.

She appeared in the doorway, dressed casually in jeans and a purple top. Her mahogany hair was down around her shoulders. In short, she was beautiful.

"Hey there." She rushed over and helped him ease onto the mattress. "You're still hurting quite a lot."

"Much better than yesterday." A slight exaggeration. "Boredom has been the worst symptom. But by the look on your face, things went well with Dr. Chan."

Avery's eyes lit up. "Exceptionally well. I think she liked what she saw, and she was great with the patients today. Hallelujah! Keep praying though. She's heading directly to Ohio to check out the other job offer."

"She'd be crazy to turn you down."

Avery's hand still rested on his shoulder. "She really did love the apartment—and that's all because of you. Have I thanked you properly?"

He thought of a few ways she could show her gratitude. He cleared his throat. "My pleasure, Doc."

"Have you been icing your back?"

"Yes, ma'am. I'm following doctor's orders to a tee. In fact, if you could help me down the steps, I can give you back your bedroom."

"You know what? Why don't you settle in for another night? It's late, I brought home pizza, and I'd rather not risk the stairs just yet."

He frowned. "I am not putting you out of your bed again. You need a good night's sleep."

She rolled her eyes. "Please. I haven't had a good night's sleep in weeks."

"Even more reason to let you have your bed."

"Being on the couch has nothing to do with my insomnia. You're not going to ruin my big Saturday night plans, are you? I was hoping to celebrate a successful visit from the esteemed Dr. Chan—and you're the only one here. You don't want me celebrating alone, do you? How pathetic would that be?"

All plans of refusal died on his tongue. "Are you sure?"

At his acquiescence she beamed. "Pizza followed by popcorn and a movie? I'll even let you pick the movie."

"No rom-coms." And remembering the other night he added, "And nothing with explosions."

"You have a deal."

Twenty-Nine

A wave of happiness washed over Avery. Everything had gone splendidly with Lucy this weekend. She was, hopefully, on the verge of some wonderful changes at the clinic and in her life—and Wes awaited her in the bedroom.

She dumped the paper plates into the kitchen trash and shoved the leftover pizza into the fridge. The popcorn was just starting to pop in the microwave, and Wes was picking out a movie on Netflix. She filled his water glass and grabbed a water bottle for herself.

Boots threaded between her bare legs, meowing, then she pranced back down the hall toward the bedroom. Her cat seemed to be enjoying Wes's company also.

When the microwave stopped, she filled a mixing bowl with the popcorn and headed back to the bedroom. Wes stared at the TV screen, frowning thoughtfully at the choices. Stretched out on top of the covers, he didn't seem like an incapacitated man. The lamplight cast a warm glow over the sharp angles of his face, over the curves of his muscled arms.

Boots jumped onto the bed and snuggled up beside him.

Smiling at the image, Avery set down the food and drinks, pulled out her phone, and snapped a photo.

At the flash of light, he turned to her. "What was that for?"

"You just looked kind of cute, staring so intently at the screen, Boots cuddled up next to you. Besides, everyone knows it's not a celebration without pictures."

"It's also not a celebration without at least two people."

He snapped a photo of her as she sat pretzel-style on the other side of the queen bed. "Hey, I wasn't ready!" She set the popcorn bowl between them.

He checked the screen. "It's blurry. Come closer, let's do a selfie."

She leaned in, Boots snuggled between them, and smiled at the image on the screen while he snapped a few pictures.

"Better," he said a moment later. "Look at the expression on Boots's face."

Avery laughed at the image. "Send me one. Did you pick a movie?"

"How about *Safe Haven*?"

"You said no chick flicks."

"I said no rom-coms. This one has a little suspense for me and a little romance for you. Have you seen it?"

"Of course I've seen it. But it's been a long time and it's really good. Let's do it."

As she started the film he dug into the popcorn. "What was that you said about insomnia? Why aren't you sleeping?"

"I don't know. Lately, when I go to bed I just lie awake for hours. It's probably stress. I'm sure things will settle down once I get another doctor on board. I'll have a little more balance in my life."

"That would be good for you. I understand the compulsion to work though."

"Are you a workaholic when you're not hiking the AT?"

"I guess I could be accused of that. But it's not . . . I'm not driven by a need to get rich or prove myself. Or even by altruistic reasons, like you."

"What drives you then?"

He studied her for so long Avery wondered if he was going to answer. "I mentioned I had some debt hanging over my head when I went to Colombia. But it was actually my dad's debt. He stole my identity before he went to prison and ran up some credit cards."

The lawsuits Cooper had found on his record. Her heart broke for him. "Oh, Wes."

"Yeah, he wasn't exactly father of the year. But I've almost paid them off. I'll always be a hard worker—I enjoy what I do. But I don't think I'll be so single-minded once I'm out of hock."

"That's a good thing. It'll feel good to be out from under the debt."

"You have no idea."

The movie got underway and their attention turned to the story. Fifteen minutes into the film she set the popcorn bowl on Wes's stomach. "It's all yours."

She settled into the pillows. This was nice, getting cozy and watching a movie with him. Her decision to have him stay an extra night might have initially been driven by a passive-aggressive desire to stick it to Cooper. But those feelings had faded before she and Wes even tucked into the pizza. Having him here felt natural, as if they'd done it a hundred times before. The analytical side of her wanted to examine the reasons for this, but the exhausted part of her just wanted to live in the moment.

The bed jerked as the popcorn bowl toppled off Wes's lap. He'd reached for the bowl and winced in pain.

She set her hand on his shoulder. "Lie down. Are you all right?"

He sank against the pillow. "I'm fine but I made a mess. Sorry about that." He started picking up the popped kernels strewn across his stomach and on the bedspread.

She paused the movie. "There wasn't much left."

Boots stood, sniffed the popcorn, then left the scene of the crime.

Avery spotted a kernel that had landed in Wes's hair. She chuckled as she reached for it, then popped it into her mouth and helped him clean up the mess. Leaning so close, his familiar woodsy scent mixed with the buttery smell of popcorn.

Since he was otherwise occupied, she allowed herself to stare at his face, taking in his deep-set eyes, straight nose, and the masculine angles of his face. The five-o'clock shadow that now covered his jawline reminded her of the way he used to look.

"What?" he asked.

He'd caught her staring—probably wearing a dopey smile. They'd recovered the popcorn so she settled back on her own side of the bed. "I was just thinking of how you looked when you arrived."

"Like a mountain man?"

She returned his grin. "I was so shocked that day when I walked in here and saw you'd shaved it all off. You looked so different."

"Different good?"

She quirked a brow. "Fishing for compliments, Garrett?"

"I'm temporarily disabled over here—I need something to keep me going."

"You know you're handsome. You don't need to hear it from me."

"Well, it's awfully nice hearing it from you." He held eye contact and his expression sobered a little.

The air seemed to thicken with tension. Avery's blood buzzed through her veins. What was going on in that head of his? Did she even want to know? "What are you thinking over there?"

"I'm wondering if I should tell you why I shaved it off."

"Well, you can't leave me hanging now."

He paused for a long moment, his gaze piercing hers. He waited so long she wondered if he would drop the subject altogether. "You'd gone out with that guy the night before. I saw you dancing with him at the Trailhead—I didn't like it."

Her breath caught. He'd been jealous. A million butterflies danced in her stomach. So she hadn't misinterpreted the subtle signals or the tangible tension that ran between them like an electric current.

But what of the woman on the phone? Who was she? What did it all mean?

He tore his gaze away. "Sorry. I shouldn't have said that. I didn't mean to make you uncomfortable."

She actually wanted him to say so much more. But she was

also afraid of what he might reveal and where it might lead. She had plans for her life that definitely didn't involve a man.

"It's okay. You didn't." She grabbed the remote and started the movie again.

The tension that hung in the room slowly lifted as Avery lost herself in the story of a woman who wanted nothing but a fresh start. As the romance between the main characters blossomed, the past week or so of sleepless nights began catching up with Avery. Her eyelids grew heavier, her body sank, weightless, into the pillows, drawing her to a place of rest and oblivion.

When Avery fluttered open her eyelids, dawn's early light greeted her. Something was different. For starters, she was on top of the covers. She turned and found Wes, still sleeping soundly beside her.

Last night came rushing back—the pizza, popcorn, and the movie. The last scene she recalled was when the hero found the heroine's wanted poster. Avery had drifted off—and apparently slept through the night. Maybe her insomnia wasn't a Huntington's symptom after all. Maybe stress had been keeping her awake, and now that she had a potential doctor, the insomnia would subside.

Or maybe having Wes beside her gave her peace. She turned her head on the pillow and watched him doze. His dark lashes fanned the tops of his cheeks. His lips were slightly parted, and his chest slowly rose and fell. One hand rested on his stomach, and the other curled beside his face. His fingers bore tiny scars— part and parcel for his trade or remnants of the explosion he'd survived?

She considered all he'd been through. His difficult childhood, the loss of a dear friend. And yet he'd somehow flourished as a human being. Emerged from his trials a good and caring man.

She was thankful God had brought him to Riverbend just when she'd needed him. And now here he was, a man she'd known only three weeks, lying in bed beside her—and waking up next to him felt like the most natural thing in the world. How was that even possible? She thought of what Katie had said a couple of weeks ago, about love creeping up on you when you least expected it.

Is that what's happening here?

His eyes opened, immediately alert, and locked on hers. They said nothing for a long moment. Just drank each other in as the morning outside awakened with them: a mourning dove cooing outside the window, a ray of sunshine pushing back the night's shadows.

"You drifted off during the movie," he said.

The deep sound of his sleep-roughened voice sent a shiver down her arms. "You should've woken me up."

"You looked so peaceful. And you said you were having trouble sleeping."

She stretched, feeling quite delicious.

Boots, curled up between them, stirred and stretched as well.

"I had the best night's sleep."

"Glad to hear it." He carefully pushed to a sit and stroked the cat. "Boots tried to smother me in the middle of the night. Didn't you, girl?"

"She likes to sleep on your head."

"When I pushed her off she came right back." He slowly stood and made his way toward the bathroom.

"You should've put her on my side. I'm used to it."

"You needed your sleep."

When he disappeared into the bathroom Avery sat up in bed and checked her phone. It was too late to make the early church service, but there was plenty of time to make the late one.

A few minutes later, when Wes emerged from the restroom, she noted his fluid stride and straight posture. "You're moving a lot better today."

"My back was a little stiff at first, but it feels pretty good now. I definitely feel up to navigating the steps."

"Do you feel up to going to church this morning?" When he hesitated, she added, "My family won't be there—they go to the early service."

He tipped a smile at her. "In that case . . . maybe. Let me get down to my apartment, take a shower, and see how my back feels."

"Sounds good."

Thirty

Avery's phone rang, pulling her from a deep sleep. She blinked, trying to orient herself. The ring tone for her work line sounded again. She grabbed the phone, sat up in the dark, and cleared her throat. "Riverbend Medical Clinic."

The sound of heavy breathing came over the line.

"Hello?" Avery said. "Can I help you?"

"I-I'm outside your clinic." The woman groaned. "I'm in labor. I-I think the baby's coming." Panic laced her voice.

"I'll be right down. I'm Dr. Robinson, and you are . . . ?" Avery jumped from bed and threw a lab coat over her leggings and cami.

"Nadine Reynolds."

The name was vaguely familiar. "Has your water broken yet, Nadine?"

"Yes. I think I feel the baby. I'm afraid it's going to drop out!"

"I'm almost there. How far along are you?"

"I'm due in two weeks." She gave a long grunt. "I thought it was just back pain."

Avery slipped on her shoes and headed out her apartment door. "Listen to me Nadine, I don't want you to push. Next time you feel the urge, just pant through the contraction. You can do this."

"It hurts . . . ," she cried.

"I know, honey. You're doing great." Avery had a full battery of questions she wanted to ask but that could wait. "I'll be there in a minute."

She disconnected the call as she flew down the steps. On her way through the darkened lobby, she grabbed disposable gloves, then unlocked the front door. The porchlight beamed down on a twentysomething woman Avery recognized from high school. She'd been a few years behind her.

Nadine bent forward at the waist, hand braced against the building, panting like mad. She wore only a long pink T-shirt and socks.

"You're doing great, Nadine. When the contraction passes, we'll get you inside."

"I can feel the heeaaad!" Nadine bore down, grunting with the effort. Her face turned strawberry red.

Oh boy. Too late to move the woman. "Okay, plan B. Let's see where things are at, huh? Have you done this before?"

Still in the grips of the contraction, Nadine just shook her head.

When the contraction eased up, Avery said, "Let's ease you down to a sit and check your progress, all right?"

Once Nadine was sitting, back supported by the building, Avery turned on her phone's flashlight. Nadine had already shed her underwear, and a quick peek proved Avery right. The baby was already crowning, a good three inches of the head visible. At least it wasn't breech.

Seemed like Avery would be delivering this baby. Thank God she'd had plenty of practice during residency. "You're making great progress, Nadine. And your baby's in good position."

She could really use an extra set of hands and quick. But Katie and Sharise lived on the other side of town, and this baby wouldn't wait. She grabbed her phone and tapped on Wes's contact. Thank God his back was better.

He answered on the second ring, his voice groggy.

"I need a hand, quickly. Could you come to the clinic's front porch? And bring a few clean towels."

"Uh, sure. Be right there."

Avery disconnected and positioned herself between the woman's legs. The contraction had eased up but Nadine looked beat. "You're doing great. Just another contraction or two and the head will be out. Do you have any health conditions I should know about? Any problems with the pregnancy?"

"No."

"How old are you?"

"Twenty-six."

"Do you know if it's a boy or girl?"

"Girl. My husband's going to kill me . . . all those birthing classes."

"Well, it's hardly your fault. Should we call him?"

"He's on his way but he's coming from Georgia so—" Nadine's face tensed up, her eyes tightening at the corners. She sucked in a breath. "It stings down there!"

They should slow this down to avoid a serious tear. "All

right, Nadine, we're going to pant through the contraction again, like before, okay?"

The contraction intensified but Nadine did as she requested.

"That's it. You've got this. I can see a good four inches now." She smiled up at Nadine. "Your baby has a headful of hair. Keep panting now. You're doing great."

Footsteps sounded behind her as Wes bounded up the steps, then scuffled to a halt. "Holy . . ."

Fortunately, Nadine was positioned in a way that provided a modicum of privacy. Nadine sagged into the brick wall, out of breath as the contraction passed. Sweat dampened her dark hair.

"You're doing amazing, Nadine."

Avery took the towels from Wes. "Thank you. Grab my phone and call 911, then put it on speaker. Then could you run inside and grab a couple pillows and a blanket from the supply closet at the end of the hall? Oh, can you turn on the flashlight and set me up with some light please?"

"Sure thing."

After Wes left, Nadine started bearing down. "Pant with me, Nadine. Come on, like this." Avery joined the woman in blowing out short puffs of air.

The dispatcher's voice came over the line. "911. What's your emergency?"

Avery began spreading one of the towels beneath Nadine's legs. "This is Dr. Robinson from the Riverbend Medical Clinic. I need an ambulance here ASAP. I have a twenty-six-year-old woman in stage-two labor, thirty-eight weeks gestation."

"Thank you, Doctor. I'm sending one out now. What's your address?"

"946 Mulberry Hollow Lane, Riverbend Gap."

"Help is on the way. ETA is forty minutes, Doctor."

"Thank you."

She suspected the baby's head would emerge with the next contraction, and the perineum had had sufficient time to thin and stretch a bit.

"On the next contraction I want you to bear down again, all right? We're going to birth this baby."

Wes burst through the door, laden with bedding.

"Help me situate her. We need to get her into a reclining position. Let's be quick. Careful of your back."

"I'm Wes, by the way," he told the woman as he squatted down.

"Nadine."

Wes grasped the woman's shoulders and whispered, "I didn't see a thing."

Nadine breathed a tired laugh. "My dignity's long gone."

Wes and Avery shifted the woman, and finally Nadine settled back against the pillows.

Avery slipped on the gloves. "Wes, can you cover her with the blanket? Nadine, your baby will need skin-to-skin contact to warm up. So, while you're covered up, let Wes help you out of your shirt."

Nadine started taking it off. "I usually require . . . at least a nice dinner out first."

"I promise not to tell." Wes helped her with the shirt, then tossed it aside.

"Perfect," Avery said just as Nadine's face tensed up again. "Wes, prop her shoulders up through this last contraction. That's it. All right, here we go. Whenever you're ready, Nadine."

Frown lines creased Nadine's forehead as her brows pulled taut. Her eyes were closed, her breaths coming in ragged puffs. The contractions were coming fast and hard now.

"All right, Nadine, when you feel ready, it's time to push."

"I can't . . . I can't."

"You've totally got this. Let's push for ten. Take a breath and go! One . . . two . . . three . . ."

Avery continued the count as Nadine gave it her all. More and more of the baby's head showed. "Eight . . . nine . . ."

As she supported the head, it glided out. Anterior position. Perfect. "Good job, Nadine. Her head's out. "

The sight of the umbilical cord around the neck stole the saliva from Avery's mouth. This wasn't uncommon. But the question was, how long had the nuchal cord been in place, and had blood flow to the baby been impeded? She grasped the cord and gently looped it over the head. But since the baby was face-down it was impossible to see her skin tone. And the light wasn't exactly conducive to—

"What's wrong? Is there something wrong with my baby?" Nadine's words quivered with fear.

Avery flashed Nadine an encouraging smile. "Not at all. In fact, it's time to bring her into the world." The sooner the better. A vise tightened around Avery's heart. *Please, God, let this baby be all right.* "Okay, Nadine. Take a deep breath, then we're going to push for ten."

The woman sucked in a lungful of oxygen and grabbed Wes's hand as she bore down.

Avery counted for her, guiding the shoulder out. "Four . . . five . . . six . . . You're doing great . . . eight . . . nine . . ."

The baby slid out in a rush of flesh and liquid.

Avery's hands filled with the slight, slippery weight of the child. She flipped the baby over. Her face was lax, her pallor ghostly white in the glare of the light. *Please, God.*

"Is she okay?" Nadine asked.

Avery placed the baby facedown against Nadine's bare chest, covered her with a clean towel, then stimulated her by rubbing her back, her arms and legs, her feet.

Come on, little one. Please, God.

"Why isn't she crying?" Nadine asked. "Is something wrong?"

Just then the baby let out a tiny screech that quickly turned into a warbling wail.

Avery's breath released in a rush. She couldn't hold back the beaming smile. "Congratulations, Mama. You did a great job."

"Is she okay?"

"She seems perfect to me. And listen to those lungs." Avery checked her Fitbit. "Time of birth 2:18."

When Avery finished drying the baby, she covered her with the blanket and put the last clean towel on top for added warmth. It might feel like a balmy summer night to them, but the baby was accustomed to a ninety-eight-degree womb. "If you're planning to nurse, it's not too early to get her on the breast."

Nadine chuckled, gazing down at the baby. "I think she already figured that out."

Sure enough, the baby had attached.

"You've got a real pro there, Mama. What's her name?"

"We haven't been able to agree on one yet." Nadine's expression was a study in love and joy. "Look at you! Wait till your daddy sees you. You're so beautiful. Isn't she beautiful?"

"She's absolutely gorgeous." Avery shifted her gaze to Wes, who was staring back with a shell-shocked expression. "Not bad for a contractor. Stick around much longer and I'll have to hire you as my assistant.

Thirty-One

Avery removed her gloves and washed up in the clinic's restroom sink. She'd left mother and baby in exam room two, encapsulated in a haze of maternal love.

The baby had checked out fine. Avery clamped and cut the umbilical cord and delivered the placenta, which she put into a plastic bag for the OB to examine later. Nadine had some minor tearing, but Avery would let her OB handle the sutures.

Even though it was the middle of the night, she was wide awake, high on adrenaline. She smiled at her reflection. Tonight had been a pretty amazing experience. A great reminder of why she did what she did. If she hadn't been here, who knows what would've happened? But because her clinic existed, a woman and her newborn baby were safely ensconced in the other room.

Wes appeared in the doorway, and she shifted her gaze to his in the mirror. "Hey there, delivery partner."

"Everything okay with the baby?"

"Perfect. Would you mind going out to the street and flagging down the ambulance? The clinic's a little hard to find in the dark, and they should be here in about . . . eight minutes."

"Sure thing." He started to leave, then turned back. "Have you ever done that before—delivered a baby?"

She chuckled as she shut off the water and dried her hands. "Quite a few times as a resident—but that was my first solo flight here."

He shook his head, wonder gleaming in his eyes. "You were . . . you were amazing, Avery. So calm and collected. I saw what was happening on that porch and froze."

"You were a real trooper. I couldn't have done it without you."

"Well, color me impressed." With one last smile he was gone.

Avery strode back to the exam room to check on Nadine.

The woman was FaceTiming with her husband. Nadine caught Avery's eye and turned the phone around. "Oh, honey, this is Dr. Robinson. This is my husband, Brendan."

The handsome young man was inside a car, but it wasn't moving. "Thank God you were there, Dr. Robinson. I don't know how to thank you for what you did."

"Your wife did all the hard work."

"And everything's fine? With Nadine and the baby?"

"They're the picture of health. The ambulance should be here any moment. Do you have the address for Mission Hospital?"

"It's already in my GPS. I'm about thirty minutes away."

"You might beat them there. Travel safely. We don't need any more excitement tonight."

"I will. Nadine, you want to tell the doctor what we decided?"

Avery lifted her brows at the woman.

Nadine's eyes sparkled. "We want to name our baby after you, Dr. Robinson: Avery Elizabeth Reynolds. What do you think?"

Avery's breath caught. She stared at the little one, whose translucent eyelids had closed. They wanted to name their precious first child after her?

"I think she's speechless," Nadine teased.

Avery blinked against the sting behind her eyes. "I-I don't know what to say. I'm so honored."

"I could not have done this without you." Nadine winked. "But we're really glad your name isn't Helga."

Avery expelled a wispy laugh.

The couple finished their call and disconnected.

A siren wailed in the distance. "I think that's your ride, Mama."

The ambulance arrived, siren pealing, lights whirling, in an organized flurry of motion. "Can you hold the baby, Dr. Robinson?" One of the paramedics lifted the baby from Nadine's arms and placed her in Avery's.

She took the sleeping bundle and left the room to give the paramedics space to lift Nadine onto the gurney. Once Avery delivered all the pertinent patient information their demeanors relaxed. All was under control. It was just a matter of transporting the patients now.

In the lobby Wes hung back, ready to assist if needed. Avery strolled over to wait with him.

He peeled back the baby's blanket, his face softening as he peered at the infant. "How can she sleep through all this ruckus?"

"Ever heard the phrase 'sleeping like a baby'?"

He touched her little hand. "She's so tiny. Look at those fingernails."

Avery stared down at her. "Seven pounds, twelve ounces, and twenty inches long."

"Amazing, this job you get to do."

She chuckled. "Broken ulnas and strep cultures don't exactly leave you with the same feelings of awe."

"Point taken." He grinned at her. "I'm going to go clean the porch while the paramedics finish up."

"You don't have to do that."

"I'm way too jacked up to go to sleep at this point."

"I know the feeling. Careful of your back."

"It's feeling pretty good."

He was on the mend—and planning to leave tomorrow. Avery watched as he headed outside. She didn't want to think about that.

Avery turned her attention to the sleeping baby and tucked the blanket around her head to help maintain her body temperature. She had delicate brows and pale eyelashes that swept over her flushed cheeks. The bridge of her nose was wide and flat above the little button tip. Her bottom lip buckled in the center, tucking into the upper one.

She was perfect.

And she was something Avery would never have. She would never know the joy of carrying her baby beneath her heart. Never know the exhilaration of bringing her child into the world. Or holding the precious weight in her arms. She would never gaze down on her baby's face and assess whose eyes, nose, and lips she had.

Something heavy and terrible swelled inside. She was vaguely aware of the paramedics pushing the gurney through the lobby and lifting it down the porch steps. But she couldn't tear her attention from the infant in her arms. Her breath felt stuffed in her lungs.

Think about something else. The patient form she needed to fill out. The good possibility of acquiring an additional doctor.

The baby's eyes fluttered open and locked on Avery. They were as blue as the summer sky and studied Avery's face with startling alertness.

"Hello, little one." Her voice quivered. Did the baby think Avery was her mama?

The infant turned her head and began rooting.

The raw yearning to be a mother clawed at her insides. What would it feel like to hold a piece of yourself in your arms? To nurture her and protect her and love her with all your being? She would never know. She cradled the infant against her chest, against her empty womb, against the breasts that would never nurture a baby.

She tore her gaze from the child and swallowed against the achy lump in her throat.

Think about something else.

The ambulance lights that strobed around the lobby. The jovial chatter of the paramedics outside her door. The pungent smell of antiseptic hanging in the air.

A paramedic stuck his head in the doorway. "Ready for the baby, Dr. Robinson." He tapped the door frame and was gone.

Avery's arms tightened around the infant, fighting the ridiculous urge to run. To take the baby away somewhere. It was a crazy thought. Completely irrational. Something she would never do. What was wrong with her? She held babies all the time. She did well-checks and gave vaccinations and treated ear infections and colic.

Moreover, the decision not to have children had been her choice. She stared down at the baby's sweet face, the extraordinary night flooding back and making her feel emptier somehow. Before this moment she'd never really digested all she was giving up. And right now, the immense weight of that sacrifice was crushing.

"Dr. Robinson?" someone called from outside.

Avery forced her feet to move toward the door. Tried to prepare her heart for the imminent parting. Time seemed to disintegrate and then she was letting the paramedic take the baby from arms that felt suddenly empty and weightless. She lifted the corners of her mouth as Nadine said good-bye. She heard the doors slam shut and the engine rev as the vehicle pulled from her parking lot.

She turned to the clinic. Wes stood under the porchlight, watching her as she approached. Wes. She couldn't even think about him leaving tomorrow. She was losing him too.

"I'll put these in the washer." He followed her inside.

She beat back the emotion welling up inside. *Not now. Not yet.* "Thanks."

She made her way across the lobby and down the hall. Paperwork. She would distract herself with details. She needed to hold it together for just a few more minutes. Once Wes left, she could release this well of emotions she hadn't even known was on the verge of overflowing.

As she entered the office, she straightened her spine. Tried to breathe in the familiar scents of lemon polish and stale coffee. But she couldn't pull in a full breath—her lungs seemed to be filled with cement.

Before she could gather herself, Wes entered and lamplight flooded the room.

He studied her, a frown crouched between his brows. "I locked up and shut off all the lights."

"Thanks." Distraction. She needed a distraction. She went for the folder on the desk—the one she'd started for Nadine. The woman had provided her insurance information, but Avery needed to fill in the details of the delivery.

Wes studied her with keen eyes. "Are you okay?"

She was so air-hungry. She struggled to draw in a full breath. It didn't help. *Pull it together, Avery.* She forced her lips into a smile. "Of course. I have some paperwork I need to do before I head up to bed." Amazing how she could sound so natural when she felt completely gutted.

"All right." He headed toward the door that led out back. "I'm going to turn in then."

Her face was frozen in that plastic smile. *Almost there.* "Good night."

"Good night. Lock up behind me, okay?"

"I will."

She should thank him again for tonight, but if she opened her mouth, it would all come spilling out. All the emptiness. All the grief. All the agony. And she couldn't let him see her like that.

The door closed behind him.

She placed her hands on the desk and sagged into it as pain unfurled in her chest. It spread like an insidious weed, roots sprouting and stretching, slithering around every organ, squeezing and strangling.

A sob burst forth. Another followed, and another. The force of them racked her body. She thought of the baby she would never have. Of her empty womb and empty arms and empty life.

Why does it have to be me, God?

Why did she have to deal with the ramifications of this wretched disease? Why had God allowed it in her family? Why had He taken her mother? Why had she, a helpless child, been there when it happened? It was all so unfair.

The door opened and there was Wes. He froze in the doorway, eyes widening on her. "Avery?"

But there was no stopping it now—the pain was not finished ravaging her.

Thirty-Two

Wes had known something was wrong with Avery—she hadn't been herself since the ambulance left. But this . . . The gut-wrenching sound of her sobs eviscerated him.

"Hey . . ." He took her in his arms. "Hey, what's wrong?"

She sank into his weight, sobbing, a quivering mass of despair. Her legs gave way, and he eased her down to the sofa. She turned into his chest, and he wrapped her up in his arms. Their bodies shook with the force of her sobs.

A terrible ache pressed into the space where his heart resided. "I'm here, honey. It's going to be okay. Let it all out."

Had the baby's birth triggered some painful event? Had she lost a child of her own? It didn't matter right now. All that mattered was being here for her, giving her comfort.

God, I don't know what's wrong, but please help her.

For a long time he stroked her back. Murmured meaningless

words. He buried his face in the softness of her hair, completely helpless in the wake of her pain.

He wasn't sure how much time had passed when her sobs finally subsided. He only knew that his T-shirt was damp with her tears, that he ached for her, and that he never wanted to let her go.

The aftermath of her grief came as recurring shudders. Her hand clutched repeatedly at his shirt.

He had to know what had brought his strong, stoic Avery to her knees. He recalled the vulnerability he'd sensed in her from the beginning. Was it related to this pain she now experienced?

He pressed a kiss to the top of her head. "What's wrong, honey? Talk to me."

Another tremor passed through her.

He tightened his arms around her, and she pressed farther into his chest as if she wanted to climb inside him.

It was killing him, this helplessness. He wanted to fix whatever grieved her. Wanted to replace her heartache with joy. He'd do anything. "Can you talk to me?"

"I-I can't have children." Her words crumbled away on another sob.

His heart squeezed tight. "Aw, honey." He couldn't even pretend to know what that would feel like. But he could imagine how difficult it must've been watching another woman give birth, bond with her newborn baby, when she would never experience that for herself. "I'm so sorry."

"It's not that I *can't* have children. I just—"

When she didn't finish the thought, he tipped her chin up. Her face was damp and blotchy. Her lashes clumped together. She stared back, her eyes dull and lifeless despite the sparkle of tears.

The ravages of pain on her face wrecked him. He swept his thumb across her cheek, wishing he could wipe away her pain so easily. "Just what?"

She closed her eyes for a long moment. Her chest rose and fell against his.

He waited.

Then she opened her eyes and met his gaze. "I told you my mom died of a progressive disease, but I didn't tell you . . . I might have it too. There's a 50 percent chance that I do. And if I do have the disease and I had kids, there'd be a 50 percent chance they'd have it too."

He couldn't even fathom that Avery could have some terrible disease. She seemed so healthy. He digested what she'd said. "You said you *could* have it. Surely there's some kind of test to see if—"

"There is. There is a test. But it's Huntington's disease. You don't know how awful it is, Wes. It struck my mom in her thirties, and I watched her become a different person. She became delusional and paranoid. She suffered from tremors and loss of muscle control and it all just got worse and worse. And then I watched her *die.*"

She lifted her head from his chest. "I could literally become symptomatic any day, and if I found out I carried the gene, I don't know what I would do. I don't know how I would cope."

This was about so much more than infertility—he saw that now. The woman was living with the very real possibility that she might suffer and die the way her mother did. Her future was so uncertain. She didn't have the luxury of planning out her life—not really.

What a terrible thing to have hanging over her head. He swept away another tear. "I'm sorry you have to deal with this.

But you don't give yourself enough credit—you're stronger than you think."

She shook her head. "I'm not strong."

"Look at all you've accomplished. You got through medical school—which is no small feat all on its own—and now you run your own clinic. You've single-handedly taken on the health care of this entire community." It struck him that hiring another doctor was about so much more than giving her a well-deserved break. She was providing for this town . . . just in case.

Aw, God, she's such a caring, selfless person. And her grief is tearing me up.

He cupped her face. "Avery . . . you're the strongest woman I know."

"I'm scared to death."

His insides went soft and mushy even as a smile curved his lips. "Don't you see? That only makes you braver."

She wanted to believe him—it was right there in her eyes. He wished she could see herself the way he did.

Another tear tracked a trail down her face.

He pressed a kiss to her forehead, wanting nothing more than to offer comfort. "If anyone can handle this, Avery Robinson, it's you."

Another tear. Another kiss. This one to her temple. Another to her wet cheek. He brushed his thumb across her impossibly soft skin. And set his forehead against hers.

With each touch, each brush of his nose against hers, he willed her to absorb his comfort, his strength, his belief in her. One moment bled into another. One second he was breathing in her warm breath, and the next his lips were on hers. Offering comfort, tasting the salt of her tears.

And then she turned more fully into him and pressed her palm to his jaw. The subtle shift in position took things to a different level. It was no longer about the giving and receiving of comfort. It was about hunger and need.

He tightened his arms around her and drank her in. She responded with equal fervor, and his heart kicked like a jackhammer. He couldn't get enough of this, of her. How had he gone all this time without her in his arms, in his life?

The question startled him. He couldn't think of Avery in terms of forever—could he? Not with Lillian waiting in Albany. The thought crashed over him like a cold wave.

————

Avery sank into the warm cocoon of Wes's arms. She yielded to his soft exploration. Couldn't get close enough to him. She wanted more of his comfort, more of his love, more of him. The pain piercing her heart only moments before faded in the wake of his magnificent kiss. Nothing had ever felt so good. So right.

She felt him pulling away full seconds before he physically did so. When they parted, their breaths crashed between them, their chests heaving against each other.

He put a few inches between them, his half-lidded gaze sending mixed messages. "I'm sorry," he said finally. "I shouldn't have . . . I'm not . . ."

She waited for him to continue, her mind filling in the sentence a dozen different ways. "You're not . . ."

His focus dropped to their fingers, which had woven together at some point, then he looked back up at her. "I'm not exactly available."

She pulled her hand from his. Her left eye twitched. The memory of the phone conversation she'd overheard sprang into her mind. She remembered the softness of his tone. She'd known it was a woman, hadn't she? She'd told herself it didn't matter.

But now it mattered a lot because Wes might be . . . "Are you *married*?"

"*No.* No, of course not."

"But you're not . . . single."

"No. I mean yes. It's complicated." He closed his eyes in a slow blink. "There is sort of someone else—Landon's sister, Lillian. I promised him I'd take care of her."

Avery's head tipped back. It was starting to make sense now. "She's waiting for you in Albany."

"I haven't promised her anything but—"

She waved him off. What was the point in hearing an explanation that was only going to hurt her? She wasn't exactly in the market for a relationship herself. "It's okay, Wes. I mean, you're leaving tomorrow—today. There's no reason this has to . . ."

"I should've mentioned her earlier. But I didn't think anything would happen between us. I didn't expect—"

"You don't owe me anything, least of all an explanation."

"Listen, it's late. We're both tired and you've had an emotionally draining night—and I complicated things by . . . I shouldn't have kissed you." A smile glinted in his eyes an instant before his lips twitched. "But man, it was a good kiss."

Laughter bubbled out of her. He could always make her laugh. Even in the midst of pain. "For a minute there I forgot how to breathe."

"Who needs air?"

"Well, technically . . ."

"Technically, those lips of yours taste like heaven." He touched her face, still smiling. "Why don't we table this for now? We both need some rest and clearer heads."

The weight of exhaustion hit her like a boulder. "You're right. I'm wiped out."

He took her hand and pulled her to her feet, then he pressed a kiss to her forehead. "Get some rest."

Thirty-Three

As dawn's light slipped through the slit in Wes's curtains, the truth seeped into his heart: he was in love with Avery. He hadn't meant for it to happen. He'd told himself she was just a friend. That she was just pleasant company, someone to while away the evening hours with.

But the woman had slipped past his guard and conquered his heart. He'd been in love before but never like this. He couldn't tolerate the thought of leaving her—especially after what she'd disclosed last night. She was facing a difficult and uncertain future. She needed him and he wanted to be here for her. Needed to be here for her.

An image of Lillian flashed in his mind and guilt pricked hard. Landon had counted on him to take care of his sister, and Wes had given his solemn word. How could he go back on a deathbed promise? He was torn between duty and love.

Yet as the morning light pushed back the shadows, he toyed

with the idea of staying. Of pursuing a relationship with Avery. Did she love him too? His heart quickened with hope.

He could continue to check in on Lillian, couldn't he? He could even visit her periodically. He'd made her no promises regarding marriage. He'd promised only his friendship, and surely he could carry out that pledge from afar. How many times had she assured him he wasn't obligated to move to Albany?

What would it look like for him to stay in Riverbend Gap? Would Avery welcome him into her life on a permanent basis? She seemed to enjoy his company, and she'd been receptive to his kiss. But that didn't necessarily mean she wanted a long-term relationship with him.

Could he accept her uncertain future? A life without children? He shifted to his back, lacing his hands behind his head. As he stared at the ceiling, he let the questions simmer, rejecting the easy answer. There was nothing easy about Avery's situation. It was a difficult reality, and she'd been carrying the weight of it for years. She'd fashioned her life, her career and goals, around this reality. But she still grieved all she would sacrifice.

The longer he lay here, the more he knew. He could not only deal with the uncertainty of Avery's future, he needed to be with her through it. When she wavered, he would remind her of her strength. He could be strong for her. They could be strong for each other.

This love was an all-consuming thing. And he could hardly wait to see her again. He smiled as he sat up in bed and checked the time. It was going on seven. He'd had only two hours of sleep, but he felt high on life. High on love.

He gave his head a shake as he headed for the shower. He'd never been much of a romantic, but Avery seemed to bring out that side of him. He turned on the shower and stretched, letting his back muscles slowly loosen. It had healed enough that he could hit the trail. He could do it today—get these two weeks of hiking under his belt and return to Avery. Or maybe he would stay another day and take her out to dinner tonight, someplace quiet where they could talk. He had so much he wanted to say. Yes, the trail could wait another day.

Wes could hardly keep the goofy grin from his face as he combed his damp hair in place. Despite the lack of sleep, he felt like a new man. Part of him wanted to dash up the stairs to Avery's apartment, burst inside, and tell her how he felt.

But after last night, she had a lot to process and a full day's work ahead. He could be patient. It would be worth the wait—he hoped.

Since he had time today, he'd finish that wall. He'd taped and mudded it yesterday, despite Avery's concern about his back. Today he'd sand and paint, then the carriage house would be finished and waiting for Dr. Chan, should she choose to accept the position.

Wes would have to find another place to stay once he returned—and more importantly, he'd have to find a job. Was there a need in Riverbend for a building contractor or even a handyman? He'd have to figure it out.

His phone buzzed an incoming call, and he dashed to the bedroom and snatched it off the nightstand, hoping it was Avery. But the name on the screen wilted his spirits.

He drew in a deep breath and accepted the call. "Hey, Lillian."

"Sorry to call so early." Either she had a nasty cold or she'd been crying.

"That's okay. What's wrong? Are you sick?"

"Oh, Wes," she cried. "I've messed everything up."

Dread slithered up his spine. "Aw, it can't be that bad. Did something happen with your new job?"

"It's not that." She paused a beat. Sniffled. "I don't want to tell you. You're going to think less of me."

"Don't be silly. Nothing you could say would change the way I feel about you."

"That's what you say now but—I've been so *stupid*."

"You're not stupid. Just tell me, whatever it is, and we'll sort it out together, all right?"

"I'm *pregnant*."

His thoughts ground to a halt. His jaw dropped. He stared, unseeing, at the bedroom wall.

"See? You do think less of me."

"That's not true. I'm just—processing. I'm confused. You never said anything about having a man in your life."

"Remember that guy, Jordan, I mentioned a few months ago?"

He vaguely recalled her going to a festival or something with the guy. "You said he was just a friend."

"He was . . . until he wasn't." Her words broke off as she dissolved into tears. "But we had an argument weeks ago, and I haven't spoken to him since, and now I'm *pregnant*." She sniffed, obviously trying to get herself under control. "I have to keep the baby, Wes. I could never . . . How am I going to hold down a job and be a mother too? I don't earn enough to pay for childcare on top of everything else. Why did I get myself into this mess?"

He faltered for the right words. "Have you told Jordan yet?"

"No, and he won't be happy about it. I don't think he was wanting anything permanent. He didn't even want to commit to me, much less a child."

Wes scrubbed a hand over his face as he searched for the right words. But all he could think was that this call changed everything. He could never desert Lillian now. He could never leave her alone and pregnant. Landon would expect Wes to be there for her. He'd given his word.

A vise tightened around his heart at the thought of losing Avery. But he had to put his own feelings aside for now. "Okay, Lil, listen to me. It's going to be all right. I'll catch a flight tomorrow, and we'll figure this out together."

"No, you have to finish your hike. I want you to finish it. I'll be fine. I'm just—I just took the test, and I have a lot of things to figure out. I needed to talk to someone, that's all. Promise me you'll finish the hike."

"If that's what you want."

"It is." She sniffled. "I have to get ready for work or I'm going to be late. I'm sorry to dump all this on you so early in the morning. When I bought the test, I never really believed—but I am. I'm going to have a baby."

"It's going to be okay, I promise. I'm always here for you. You know that."

"Thanks, Wes. You don't know how much that means to me."

After they said good-bye Wes exhaled slowly, feeling his lungs deflate like balloons. Everything inside felt hollow and dead.

Thirty-Four

Avery was running on three hours' sleep and caffeine. Between patients, last night's events crowded into her thoughts. The exhilarating birth of the baby, Avery's emotional breakdown, the glorious kiss she'd shared with Wes . . . There was a lot to process. She just had to get through today, and then she and Wes could have a long conversation.

The only question was, what was she going to say? Everything inside her wanted to be with him. But she couldn't entertain that notion. Could she? Would it even matter? Surely her disclosure had scared him away just as it had Sam. And what about his devotion to Lillian?

Her phone buzzed with an incoming text, and she whipped it out, smiling when she saw Wes's name. Can you meet me on the porch at noon?

She frowned. Sounded as though he was also eager to have

that conversation, but her stomach twisted at his directness. He was probably in a hurry to leave now that he knew what kind of future she faced. Even she didn't want to deal with her reality—why would he?

She raised the phone and thumbed in Sure. Then she sent the message and slipped into the exam room to see her last patient before lunch. The middle-aged woman was suffering from a urinary tract infection. Avery advised her to drink plenty of water, avoid coffee and alcohol, and use a heating pad for discomfort. Then she gave her a prescription for an antibiotic and sent her on her way.

The clinic closed from noon to one for lunch, and by the time Avery emerged from the appointment, the rest of the staff had already retired to the breakroom. Their chatter and laughter carried down the hall.

Avery headed to the front door, steeling herself for the coming conversation. The stifling heat smacked her in the face as she exited the clinic.

"Hey." Wes was leaning on the porch rail, wearing a T-shirt, shorts, and a somber expression that did nothing to dispel her dread.

"Hi." Her attention dropped to the backpack slouching at his feet. The sight of it gutted her. He was leaving *now*.

A wave of despair engulfed her. She should've known. Of course he'd run after what she'd revealed. Had she really expected him to stay? She crossed her arms, a flimsy barrier against the impending pain. "I thought—" *you might stay here with me.* She pushed the pathetic words from her mind. "I thought you might stick around a day or two."

A muscle flickered in his jaw and his gaze darted away.

"There's been a . . . development in Albany. I need to finish the trail and head that way."

She swallowed hard and dredged up a professional smile. "Of course. How's your back feeling today? Do you need any meds to take with you?"

"I have ibuprofen." He gave a nod toward the clinic. "Will you tell your staff good-bye for me?"

"Of course."

A beat of silence ushered in tension. It tightened between them with each passing second, vibrating like a wire pulled taut. "Avery, about last night . . ."

She gave a wry chuckle. "Which part?"

He took her hands in his, those callused fingers that had touched her so gently the night before. She could still feel the sweep of his thumb across her tearstained cheek.

His gaze sharpened on her. "Thank you for opening up to me last night. I know it was hard for you, and I just want you to know . . . I believe in you. You are the most amazing woman I've ever known and I—"

The pause that followed was so long she wondered if he'd continue.

"I'm so glad we met," he said finally.

Her eyes stung with tears. "Thank you. I-I'm glad we met too."

"I wish I could stay. I hate leaving so quickly after—"

"It's okay. I understand."

She took in those beautiful eyes, the expanse of his forehead, tanned from hours in the sun, the sharp turn of his jaw. She committed it all to memory because soon, that's all he would be. Her chest constricted at the thought.

His gaze roved over her face, settling on her lips. A little smile played around his mouth. "Maybe we should talk about that other thing that happened last night."

The kiss. Her heart crumpled up in her chest like yesterday's newspaper. She squeezed his hands. "Why don't we just let that one go?" She would never be able to let it go. That kiss, the best one she'd ever had, would also be her last. It was fitting somehow.

"If that's what you want." His eyes twinkled. "But I still stand by last night's assessment."

"I'm inclined to agree." She lifted her lips as they stared at one another, sharing the memory of that one beautiful kiss. The moment lingered as a nattering squirrel filled the silence, and a humid breeze stirred the loose hairs at her nape.

He cleared his throat and the moment was gone. "I, uh, washed the bedding and towels. I'm sorry I wasn't able to finish the wall. It still needs to be sanded and painted."

She shrugged. "I think even I can handle that much." She'd already given him his check. She had his W-4. There was no business left to discuss. Nothing left to say.

His gaze grew intense as the silence lengthened. Then he held out his arms. "Come here."

She stepped between his legs, into his embrace, encircling his broad shoulders. Leaning on the rail as he was, they were the same height. She laid her head on his shoulder, breathing in the woodsy smell of him. Committing it to memory. Her fingers found the soft hair at his neck.

His warm breath hit the tender flesh between her neck and shoulder, sending a shiver down her spine. Her heart thumped against the hard wall of his chest, and his arms cocooned her in safety. She never wanted to let him go.

"I'll miss you." His voice was gruff.

She swallowed against the lump in her throat. "I'll miss you too. Take it easy out there. You don't want to aggravate those muscles while you're miles from civilization."

"I'll be careful, Doc." He pulled back and set a soft kiss on her forehead.

She stepped back and the space between them seemed as broad as Linville Gorge.

He stood and stooped to retrieve his pack.

This was it. Wes was leaving her, just like Sam had. He'd hike down the road and onto the trail, and she'd never see him again. He was going to this other woman—this Lillian.

"Do you love her?" She hadn't meant to say the words aloud. Wished she could call them back, especially when pain flickered in his eyes.

———

Wes halted in his efforts to shoulder his pack. Avery's direct question gave him pause, and denial clawed for release in his throat. He didn't want to talk to her about Lillian. Instead, he wanted to tell her how much he loved her. That he would always love her. That every cell in his body longed to stay here with her.

But duty demanded otherwise.

He forced himself to make eye contact as he grated out, "Yes." He did love Lillian—just not the same way he loved Avery. He tried to convey with his eyes what he couldn't say with words. It would serve no purpose to say them aloud when he couldn't act on them.

She gave a wobbly smile. "Then I hope you'll be very happy. You deserve that, Wes."

Her kindness tore him in two. He opened his mouth to say . . . something. But he couldn't think of anything that would ease her suffering—or his own. "I guess I should go."

She cleared her throat. "You should have plenty of time to make it to the shelter before dark."

"That's the hope."

"Let me know when you finish the trail?"

"Of course." He couldn't help but feel he was deserting her to an uncertain future. But she had a good family who would support and encourage her. He couldn't resist touching her one last time. He cupped her chin and drank in her features. "I'm so glad I got sick. I'll never forget you, Avery Robinson."

She opened her mouth but nothing came out. When she closed it again, he gave her one last smile. Then he turned and took the porch steps.

Grief compressed his chest until his lungs struggled to draw a full breath. Walking away from her was the hardest thing he'd ever done. He stared straight ahead, down the road that led to the trail. If he glanced back, he might not have the strength to go.

He was leaving a woman he was madly in love with to be with a woman he merely loved. He'd never been so aware of the enormous gap between the two. But what he felt for Lillian would have to be enough.

———

Avery deep-breathed all the way to the office. The smell of Chinese food wafted from the breakroom, making her stomach turn. She just needed a few minutes to collect herself, and then she'd join the others. She could process Wes's sudden departure from her life after work.

She closed the door and walked to her desk. Was it reluctance that had slowed his movements as he shouldered his pack? His last sad smile ripped her heart in two.

But no. She couldn't think about any of that right now. She blinked back the tears and forced herself to think about cellular structure instead. *Contents of the cytoplasm: cytosol, cytoskeleton, centrioles, endoplasmic reticulum, golgi complex, mitochondria, ribosomes, lysosomes, vacuoles—*

A knock sounded. Avery's gaze darted to the door, hope rushing into the empty cavity of her chest. Had Wes returned?

The door swept open and Katie appeared on the threshold. "Hey. Can I come in?"

The disappointment was crushing. Fifty-pound weights pressed on her shoulders. She sagged onto the sofa.

Katie frowned as she stepped inside and closed the door. "All right, that's it. Something's wrong. You've been quiet all morning, and now I find you alone in your office when we both know gossiping in the breakroom is your favorite part of the day."

Avery couldn't even pretend to be okay. "Wes just left. He said to tell you good-bye."

She sank down beside Avery. "I'm sorry."

"I thought he might stay another day or two." Or forever. "But something happened in Albany—it's complicated, I think. There's a woman there—the sister of that friend who died." She tried unsuccessfully to keep the jealousy from her voice.

"Oh, honey."

Avery released a wry laugh. "You were right. You warned me,

but did I listen? Nope, I just went merrily on my way, spending time with him, getting attached to him, falling in—" No. She wouldn't say it. "And now he's officially gone and I'll never see him again."

Katie put her arm around Avery. "I'm so sorry, sweetie. I know how quickly it can happen—how it can just crash over you like a wave and knock you to your knees. How it can twist you up inside until you think you're going to die."

"I can't do this right now. I can't think about this." Avery knuckled the tears from her eyes.

"Why don't you take the afternoon off? You could catch up on your sleep. The rest of us can handle things around here."

"I'd rather stay busy. I don't do naps and it won't do any good to sit around stewing on my feelings." Avery took a cleansing breath, stood, and straightened her lab coat. "Anyway, this was my strategy all along, right? Concentrate on the clinic and care for the community. Nothing has changed really."

She forced her mouth into a smile and ignored the pitying look on Katie's face as she swept out of the office. But they both knew that everything had changed.

Thirty-Five

If only the hands digging into Avery's back muscles could reach deep enough to soothe her aching heart. She breathed in the calming aroma of lavender and eucalyptus as the table beneath her creaked under the masseuse's pressure. The bachelorette day at the Riverview Bed-and-Breakfast was well underway. She and Katie had already received manicures and pedicures. Now they were being massaged within an inch of their lives. Avery would take all the pampering she could get.

A heat wave had ushered in August. It had been eleven grueling days since Wes's departure, and the pain of his absence sat like a heavy brick in the center of her chest. She'd thought he might text her when he had reception, but she hadn't heard a word from him. That only sharpened the sting of loss. Not an hour passed that she didn't think about him. Wonder where he was and how his back was holding up. She'd begun to text him a dozen different times. Had written out complete messages—everything from a simple *How are you?* to entire paragraphs about how she felt. She'd deleted them all.

A moan sounded from the table beside her. "Oh my gosh," Katie said on a sigh. "That feels like heaven. Gretchen, you're amazing. Can you come home with me?"

"You just relax and let me massage away all that wedding stress."

Avery needed to get her head in the wedding game. "Only four weeks now. I can't wait to see Cooper's face when he sees you in that gown." The dress featured a fitted bodice and spaghetti straps that set off Katie's delicate collarbones and long, graceful neck. The gown's soft, full skirt transformed her into a modern-day Cinderella.

"Ooh, that spot right there," Katie said. "It's where I'm holding all my wedding stress. This is bliss. Ave, I'm so glad you finally have a day off to enjoy this with me."

"Me too. It's been fun."

Dr. Chan had accepted the position on Sunday and wasted no time moving to Riverbend. Avery's mind still spun with how quickly it had all come together. It was such a relief to have another doctor on board. To have that piece of the puzzle in place. She could hardly believe she'd found someone so perfect for the clinic, for the town.

The entire staff was thrilled to have Lucy on board, and she'd jumped right in with both feet. She was just what Avery and the clinic needed. Today was her first time as the solo doctor at the clinic, but Sharise was there to answer any questions that might arise. All Avery had to do was lie here and enjoy the bliss of having nothing to do.

She suppressed a yawn. The dim lights and soothing instrumental melody made her sleepy. That and the fact that she was still experiencing insomnia. Her last good night's sleep was when Wes—

No. She would not think about him anymore. It was Katie's day. "Are you nervous about the wedding?"

"I'm really not. I'm just eager to become Mrs. Cooper Robinson. I know our engagement was quick, but it seems like I've waited forever to be his."

"Maybe because you were in denial about your feelings for months on end?"

"Oh, hush, you. What was I supposed to do? I took one look at Cooper and lost my heart."

The words ushered in a cloud of tension because something similar had happened to Avery and they both knew it. But she wasn't about to open that subject today. Time for a change of topic. "Any wedding details I can help with?"

"I don't think so. The cake and flowers are ordered, invitations out, and we've made final arrangements with the caterer. It's all under control."

"It's sweet that your mom's walking you down the aisle." Katie had been raised in foster care after her mother's addiction had cost her her children. But Beth was in recovery now, and the two had reunited last year. They seemed to be on a good path.

"It was the right choice. She's my only family, after all, and even though she wasn't there for me as a child, she's trying to make up for that."

"I think it's amazing that you're giving her another chance. Not just anyone could do that."

"Everyone makes mistakes—and she's deserving of a second chance."

Avery groaned as the masseuse began work on her hip flexors. "So, when's Cooper moving his things to your place?"

"The boys are handling that the week before the wedding. You think Coop might ditch that ugly recliner of his somewhere between his place and mine?"

Avery laughed. "Yeah, I think you'll be stuck with that for a while. But it'll be good to have him all moved in when you return from your honeymoon." Katie and ~~Gavin~~ Cooper had rented a cabin in Gatlinburg.

"That's the plan." Katie shifted on the table. "Lucy's really working out well, don't you think? She even got little Simon Reeves to take his vaccine without that ear-piercing scream."

"She's a gem. I don't know how we got so lucky. And so far she seems to love the town."

"Well, what's not to love? It's a great place to live. But I get it. A lot of doctors would prefer a more exciting locale and a more lucrative position."

"I think she got enough excitement in Boston."

The masseuse wiped the oil from Avery's back and lifted the silky sheet into place. "All right, ladies. How are you feeling?"

"Marvelous," Katie said.

"I think my bones have melted."

"Then our jobs here are done." The women said their good-byes and left.

Katie's phone buzzed an incoming call. She wrapped her sheet around her and grabbed her phone. "Hi, honey." She flashed a grin at Avery, then headed for the attached bathroom.

Avery got up slowly, stretching. Her muscles felt gloriously loose and limber. After she dressed she sat in the wingback chair and pulled out her phone to kill time while she waited for Katie.

A message from Wes appeared as a notification on her screen. Her pulse quickened as she clicked on it. He'd sent a photo of himself, standing in front of the stone archway at Springer Mountain. His text simply said, Made it!

The sight of him made her heart buckle. She zoomed in on his face. His beard was growing back once again, reminding her so much of those first days together. She pressed a palm to her chest. His big smile was testament to his joy and relief that the long, arduous journey was complete.

His message had come in seventeen minutes ago. He'd made what was normally a fourteen-day hike in only twelve days.

Must be in a big hurry to reach Lillian.

The thought soured her stomach as she contemplated her response.

What was taking her so long to reply? Wes took a sip of the delicious coffee and settled back in his chair, staring at his phone as if he could will Avery to respond. After completing the trail at long last, he'd hitched a ride to the nearest town. Tonight, he'd enjoy creature comforts once again before boarding a plane for Albany and Lillian.

He stretched his back, which felt pretty good, all things considered. Other muscles complained, sore from the arduous hike and nights on the hard ground. He wasn't nineteen anymore.

His phone vibrated and a text appeared on the screen. Congratulations, Wes! I'm so happy for you.

He sagged from sheer relief that she'd responded. He reread the text, then stared at the words for a while. He hadn't considered what he'd do after she replied. But his thumbs hovered over the phone, at the ready. He wanted to ask how the clinic was going. Wanted to ask if Dr. Chan had accepted the position.

But was continued correspondence a good idea?

He'd pushed himself hard on the trail, trying to drive thoughts of Avery from his mind. But it hadn't worked. He kept reviewing their time together—playing cards, chatting, and laughing. That amazing kiss, so fiery. Their last embrace, so bittersweet. Then he envisioned her going on another date, swaying with that slick guy she'd danced with at the Trailhead. The thought of another man's hands on her made him want to—

He gave a low growl.

From the next table a middle-aged man glanced up from his laptop, eyeing Wes. Probably thought he was losing his mind. Maybe he was.

But if anything was clear from his long hours on the trail and all the headspace he'd given Avery, it was this: he needed to make a clean break from her. Tomorrow he'd arrive in Albany, and he needed to focus on Lillian—and the baby. He couldn't do that with thoughts of Avery swimming in his head, much less texts flying back and forth between them.

With one last wistful glance at Avery's text, he pocketed his phone, grabbed his coffee, and left the shop.

Thirty-Six

Even though he'd never seen Lillian in person, he would've known her anywhere. She stepped from the blue Corolla, parked at the curb by baggage claim, and ran to him, her wispy white top floating out behind her slender frame. "Wes!"

"Hey, Lillian." They embraced, holding each other.

In his arms she gave a soft sniffle.

Wes couldn't help but think of Landon. His friend should be here right now greeting his sister. He should be ruffling her hair and teasing her about her tears. But he'd forfeited all that when he'd thrown his body on top of Wes.

"It's so good to see you finally," she said. "I was starting to think you'd never get here."

"Me too." He pulled himself from the past and focused on the here and now: the coarse feel of her brown curls, the sharp curve of her shoulder blade, the sweet floral scent teasing his nose. The sensations warred with memories of Avery: silky hair, soft curves, the subtle tropical scent of her shampoo.

Stop it. It wasn't fair to compare. He was only just meeting Lillian. They needed a chance to make memories of their own beyond letters and phone conversations. His feelings would deepen with time.

She pulled back and gave him a once-over, grinning. "I'm not used to seeing you with a beard, but it suits you."

"I'm not used to seeing you at all."

They shared a laugh.

"I'd better get my car going before security comes around again."

While she hopped into the driver's seat, he stowed his pack in the trunk and got into the passenger side. He pushed the seat back as far as it would go and made room for feet among the empty fast-food bags and coffee cups.

"Whoops, sorry. Just throw those behind you. I just got back from training last night and haven't cleaned out the car yet."

He set the trash in the backseat with the rest of the empty food containers. "How'd that go, by the way?"

"It was really good. I learned so much about early-childhood education, my head's still spinning. I can't wait to put the information to good use. If college classes were that practical, I might've actually gone."

"It's good they're investing in you like this. They must want you to stick around awhile."

She spared him a glance. "I don't have much choice now, with a baby on the way. I can't take risks with my future anymore."

He covertly took her in, noting her chewed fingernails and

flushed cheeks. "How are you doing with all that? Are you feeling better about the pregnancy?"

"Honestly, I've hardly had time to think about it this week. But it's starting to soak in—the reality of it all. At least I have good insurance now and a steady job. It's nice not to have the stress of running my own business. I can show up and play with the kiddos and go home."

"That's a blessing." He wanted to ask her about the baby's father. Did he live in Albany? Was she planning to tell him about the child? Was she ready to move on? So many questions . . . but he didn't want to overstep.

"The good news is I haven't felt too bad except for some nausea in the morning. Also—a little warning—I cry at the drop of a hat. And I'm prone to falling asleep in front of the TV."

"All part of the process, I'm sure."

"I assume you want to head to your new apartment?"

"Sure. I'm eager to check it out." A friend of hers from church had an inexpensive apartment for rent above their garage. That would allow Wes to settle in and find a job before seeking someplace more permanent. He'd have to buy a used truck and tools on credit. He'd sold his own before he left for Colombia. He hated to rack up debt, but it couldn't be helped.

As the strains of TobyMac's "Help Is on the Way" flowed through the speakers, Lillian worked her way through the airport into traffic.

Wes let her focus on the task, taking in the sights of Albany. As she drove, his mind turned toward her pregnancy. This time next year she'd have a baby to care for. Was Wes ready to be a father? He'd wanted to have children someday, but he certainly hadn't been in any kind of hurry.

Thoughts of babies led to the memory of Avery on the night of the emergency labor and delivery. It didn't seem fair that the woman who wanted a child so badly couldn't have one, and the woman who didn't want a baby was unexpectedly gifted with one. He whispered a little prayer for Avery.

He really had to stop thinking about her. It wasn't helpful. "I have a couple leads on jobs. There's a home-improvement company looking for window and door installers."

"That's great. I think you'll find the cost of living here really good."

He'd hoped to find a position as a contractor. It paid better and he found it more fulfilling. But he'd take whatever he could get and keep an eye out for something better. The town seemed nice. Much bigger than Riverbend Gap, of course. There were several concrete high-rises in the distance and the typical Saturday afternoon congestion on the highway.

He scanned the landscape surrounding the town and found himself missing the towering mountains he'd been hiking for months. A silence had settled between them. "I'm ready to get back to a steady job and a bed I'm not carrying on my back."

"I'll bet. I thought I'd cook something tonight. Figured you'd probably be ready for a home-cooked meal by now."

"That sounds great. Landon always said you were a great cook. He raved about your lasagna."

"He was such a mooch. He'd invite himself over for dinner all the time."

"Well, he was a terrible cook so . . ."

She laughed. "He really was. He wasn't even allowed in my kitchen. Once he set off the smoke alarm reheating pizza."

"He told me about that. He also told me if you don't want

to be tasked with a job, just do it badly. So I'm not entirely sure that pizza incident was an accident."

"You're probably right. He was an expert at weaseling out of what he didn't want to do. All that charm . . . the women went nuts for him. He could've been married three times over before he ever went to Colombia."

"Oh, believe me, his charms weren't overlooked there either."

She cut him a sideways look. "I'm sure the two of you got plenty of female attention."

"Aw, not me."

"Ha! You're as bad as he was—completely oblivious to your charisma. That's part of your charm, I guess."

Wes didn't think he was in possession of said charisma but he let it go. He changed the topic back to her job as they drove toward the place he'd call home for at least a few months. The weight in his stomach was only fatigue from his long journey. He just needed some good sleep and a day or two to recover. Then he'd feel more like himself.

Thirty-Seven

Wes moved the stack of *People* magazines and settled on Lillian's sofa. She'd lived in the lower-level apartment for a while. In fact, Landon had lived here with her before he took the job in Colombia.

Wes had accomplished a lot in the two weeks since he'd arrived in Albany. He'd bought a beater truck and all the tools he needed for his new job installing windows. The work was okay and the people in the office were pleasant, but he'd be glad when the stifling August heat gave way to cooler autumn temperatures.

However, once winter set in, window installs would come to a grinding halt. He'd already started setting back money to prepare for leaner months. Maybe there'd be opportunity for promotion within the company later when residential building picked up again.

Since he was a subcontractor, the company didn't offer health insurance, and he couldn't afford his own just yet. He hoped his back held up—the only doctor who'd offer free care was eight hundred miles away.

Wes scanned the lived-in space, taking in the piles of newspapers and socks and shoes, discarded right where they'd been removed. The kitchen seemed to have a perpetual pile of dirty dishes—he'd loaded them in the dishwasher the three times he'd been invited over for dinner. Landon had never mentioned Lillian was a bit of a clutter bug. Then again, Landon hadn't exactly been a neat freak himself.

Wes wasn't compulsive by any means—he'd been known to go weeks without dusting or vacuuming—but the clutter bothered him. When he built homes, he expected subcontractors to leave the work space tidy. And as a window installer, he left no traces of the job behind. He even touched up the landscaping to make sure he left it as he'd found it.

But to each his own.

He'd attended Lillian's church twice and met a few of her friends. They seemed like nice people. The pastor was a solid preacher, and the worship was refreshing. It was good to know she had a support system.

The smell of popcorn wafted his way. He was supposed to be selecting a movie. He surfed through the Netflix guide, searching for something that might appeal to them both. *Safe Haven* showed up among the selections, taking him back to the night Avery and he had watched the movie in her bedroom. He recalled the easy banter, the light teasing, the delicious tension. The sultry way she looked at him, making awareness crackle between them. The way he admitted to being jealous of that man she'd danced with—what had he hoped to gain by admitting that?

Unable to resist, he pulled out his phone and opened the photo of Avery and him on the bed. She seemed so happy, so relaxed. For that matter, so did he. He missed the comforting way she'd rested her hand on his shoulder when he was hurt or upset. He missed their engaging conversations about politics and religion and books. Had it really only been four weeks since he'd seen her? It seemed like an eternity since he'd last set eyes on her pretty face, heard her melodious laughter, smelled that tempting tropical scent that hovered about her like a cloud.

He remembered how peaceful she'd appeared after she drifted off to sleep, the light from the movie flickering over her delicate features.

"Whatcha looking at?"

Wes jumped and darkened the phone screen. He smiled at Lillian. "Nothing. Forgot to ask what kind of movies you like."

"This might surprise you, but give me a good horror flick any day."

"Like . . . Stephen King horror or *A Nightmare on Elm Street* horror?"

She settled on the couch with a microwave popcorn bag between them. "Anything that scares me to death. Is it weird that I like being scared?"

"Little bit. But I'm flexible." He pulled up the horror genre and they settled on one. It opened in the typical fashion—teenagers partying in some remote stretch of woods. This wouldn't end well.

A while later, finished with the popcorn, he dusted off his hands and let them rest in his lap. Lillian had settled on the end of the sofa a couple of feet away. They were much more comfortable with each now than they'd been on their first meeting, and when they fell into silences, it was companionable enough.

His plan had been to further the relationship organically. Subtle touches here and there that progressed to kisses on the cheek and hand-holding. But he hadn't been able to move past the subtle-touch stage.

He observed her from the corner of his eyes. Her leg was right there, encased in a pair of floral leggings. He should ever so casually set his hand there. Would she be surprised by the action? Appalled? She was hard to read. He couldn't tell if she thought of him that way. Sometimes she'd look at him with such fondness . . . and she *had* kissed his cheek once.

But he didn't want to spoil things between them by assuming anything or moving too quickly. Also, he couldn't quite bring himself to touch her in that way yet. He remembered the chemistry he'd had with Avery. The irrepressible magnetism between them—that inevitable passionate kiss. He pushed away the thoughts. He and Lillian just needed more time for those feelings to develop, that was all. He would get there eventually.

"I haven't been out here since the funeral," Lillian said as they walked up the memorial garden's grassy rise a few days later. She carried a small pot of fresh flowers.

"I hated that I couldn't be here for you." The explosion on the work site had set back construction on the hotel they'd been converting, and the need for housing was urgent.

"Landon would've wanted you to stay. He really had a heart for those people."

"He did." The refugees had been pushed from Venezuela by a crumbling economy that left them homeless, much the same way Landon and Lillian had been pushed from their childhood home. He'd worked tirelessly for the underserved, displaced people group.

"It's right up there," she said.

He followed her up the rise, past grave sites, some well tended, others not. She stopped in front of a simple granite marker with his name and the dates denoting his life span. Below that, the marker read *Beloved Brother and Friend.*

Wes took in the simple burial plot. It didn't seem like enough for a man who'd given so much to others. So much to him. He deserved a big marble monument declaring him a hero. But there hadn't been money for that. Wes had sent Lillian two thousand dollars to help with burial expenses, and she'd run a fund-raiser on social media to cover the rest.

"Happy birthday, Brother." A hot breeze pulled at her curls as she set down the pot of flowers, then she glanced at Wes. "I know the marker doesn't look like much, but he wouldn't have wanted anything fussy."

"You're right. He would've hated having some big shrine."

"Would've called it a waste of money." Her words trembled with emotion.

Wes took her hand. He was glad to be here for Lillian on Landon's first birthday since his death. This was right where his buddy would've wanted him to be.

"Sometimes I still can't believe he's gone," she said. "The other day I picked up my phone to take a picture of a Ferrari I saw downtown. I was going to send it to him."

"I know what you mean. It doesn't feel real sometimes."

She squeezed his hand. "Thanks for coming with me today. I've been dreading it a little. My emotions have been all over the map."

"I've been wanting to visit him. And you're doing great. He'd be really proud of you."

Her gaze fell to the dry ground. "I'm afraid he'd be disappointed in me. I got pregnant out of wedlock just like our mom did with him."

"This is different. You're not marrying some loser who's not cut out to be a father—then having a second child with him just for kicks. You're putting your baby first. And for what's it's worth, you'll always be able to count on me."

She took hold of his arm, pressing close. "It's been really nice having you here, Wes. Thank you."

"You don't have to thank me." It was the least he could do. He put his arm around Lillian's shoulders, and she laid her head on his shoulder.

Wes's gaze lifted to the hazy blue sky where billowy clouds drifted past. *Don't worry, buddy. I got her.*

As had become his Saturday habit, Wes went home to shower and change after work, then headed over to Lillian's. He was in the mood to venture out tonight. Maybe he'd take her out to eat—there was a Mexican restaurant nearby that his coworkers raved about. Maybe they could go dancing afterward. It would let them cut loose a little, and holding her in his arms for a slow dance might be a natural way to advance their relationship.

He'd been in Albany three weeks, and so far Lillian's idea of showing him around the city was driving the streets and pointing out landmarks. He enjoyed the broader perspective of the community, but he also wanted to dive in and see what this town was all about.

When he arrived at Lillian's apartment, she answered the door on the third knock. The curls alongside her face were frizzed, and a pink stain flushed her cheeks. "Come in, come in. I've gotta stir the roux or it'll be ruined. Make yourself at home."

Looked like they were staying in again. The cool air-conditioning was a welcome relief from the late-August heat. "Need some help?"

"No, I think it's going to be okay," she called from the kitchen. "I've never made Cajun food, so I hope it turns out. Also, I hope you like chicken and sausage gumbo because it's kind of a pain to make. I've been on my feet for two hours and dirtied every pot and pan in the place."

"I love gumbo and it smells great." He stepped around newspapers that had fallen to the floor and a sweater that hadn't quite hit the coatrack and headed to the kitchen to keep her company. "I can set the table if you want."

"Sure." Lillian whisked the contents of a skillet, and the steam rose like a dissipating spring fog. "The plates are up there, and you know where the silverware is. Oh, wait, everything's actually in the dishwasher. I think they're clean though."

He retrieved the settings from the dishwasher and cleared a space on the table for them to eat. "Looks like you're opening a yarn factory over here."

She chuckled. "Oh, just shove all that aside. I'm teaching myself to knit. I got it in my head that I need to make a baby blanket, and all the yarns were so pretty I couldn't decide. I thought I could teach myself, but now I'm not so sure. My friend from church—Honor, you met her—she offered to help me. She makes the prettiest sweaters and scarves."

"Can't she just make you a baby blanket?"

She spared him a *duh* look. "Well, of course she could, but then it wouldn't be as special."

"Oh, right."

"Plus, it'll give me something to do in the evenings. I need something to keep my hands busy—I can't seem to stop eating."

She was so thin—surely she wasn't worried she'd gain too much weight with the pregnancy. "Well, you're supposed to be eating for two, right?"

"Sure, but I don't want to have too much to lose afterward." She poured the brown sauce from the skillet into a big pot. "I hope this turns out okay. I don't think I burnt it."

"I'm sure it'll be terrific. You're a great cook." After he finished setting the table he wandered into the kitchen.

She added a few ingredients to the pot, then put a lid on. "There. Now it just needs to simmer awhile. Did I tell you what little Corbin said at work yesterday? He said his mama had to stay home from work because she had a high temper. Isn't that cute? I couldn't even bring myself to correct him."

While the stew simmered Lillian regaled him with stories of the kiddos she'd already bonded with. He knew she was scared about the future, but there was no doubt she would make a wonderful mom.

Last week she'd finally gotten up the nerve to tell the father about the baby. Jordan had apparently been upset she was keeping it and unwilling to commit to any kind of parenting role. Lillian seemed to accept the news with resignation.

Wes didn't understand how a man could turn his back on his child. On his responsibility. It was unthinkable.

But he was more than willing to fill the gap. The question

was, what kind of father would he make? He hadn't exactly had the best example. His dad met his physical needs, but that was about it. Wes wasn't even sure what a good father looked like. But then he'd managed to rise above his upbringing in other ways. Surely he could do the same for Lillian and the baby.

"How've you been feeling today?" The nausea seemed to have subsided as she approached the three-month mark.

"Pretty good." She glanced at the messy kitchen, giving him a wry look. "Obviously I thought I was up for a challenge."

"I'll handle cleanup. It's the least I can do. How about after that we go do something fun? I was thinking it might be nice to check out some of Albany's hot spots. Is there a place around here with a dance floor and a live band on Saturday nights?"

She wrinkled her nose. "Oh, trust me, you don't want that—I'm a terrible dancer. The last time I danced was at my prom, and I'm pretty sure I left bruises on the poor guy's toes."

"Okay, well, let's see. How about pool? Or darts?"

She chuckled. "You'd really be risking life and limb then. I'm not coordinated *at all*, Wes. I always end up spraining something or hurting someone else. I'm sure Landon must've told you. He was forever teasing me about it."

He didn't remember his friend mentioning that. "All right, well, what sounds good to you?"

"Honestly? I'd just love an evening at home with you. There's a new movie on Netflix that looks good—and it's not a horror flick. It's got Denzel Washington in it. I know you like him."

Wes pushed back the disappointment and tried not to think about the way Avery had always been up for something new: card games, salsa, pool lessons. She threw herself into whatever it was and had fun with it.

But Lillian wasn't Avery. "Yeah, of course. That's fine. A movie it is."

She tilted her head. "You sure? I don't want to be a wet blanket, but I'm a little tired after taking on this recipe."

He'd thought he knew Lillian pretty well from all the letters and phone calls. But he was starting to see they were things you couldn't know about a person until you met them face-to-face.

He attempted to dredge up a modicum of excitement about another evening in front of the TV. "Whatever you want. The movie sounds good, and I'm sure dinner will be delicious."

Thirty-Eight

Avery grabbed the empty burger platter and carried it inside her parents' house. The cool waft of air was a welcome relief from the August heat. For the life of her she couldn't figure out why they'd eaten outside tonight.

Laughter carried through the screen door. Sounded as if the rest of her family was having a great time. She wasn't sure why that left her with an exaggerated sense of loneliness.

In the kitchen she found Lisa doing dishes. Her stepmom sported a short blonde ponytail and yellow sleeveless top that exposed her freckled shoulders.

Avery set the platter beside her on the counter. "That's the last of it." She picked up the dish towel and started drying the stack of plates in the drainer.

"I got this," Lisa said. "You should go outside and play cornhole with the others. You've been working too hard."

"I'm fine. I have fewer hours than ever before now that Lucy's on board."

"I'm sure that's true but"—she spared Avery a glance—"you still look tired. And you don't seem yourself lately. You could probably use a little fun in your life. You should go out more."

Avery ignored the pinch of irritation as she reached for the next plate. "I'll play a game after I finish here."

"Do you and Katie still go out? Just because she's with Cooper now doesn't mean she doesn't have time for you—and yes, I know you work with her every day. But sometimes it's good to let loose and just relax with your friends."

"I know that. We still go out sometimes."

A beat of silence passed. "Are you getting enough sleep, honey? As I get older I'm finding melatonin is my new best friend."

"I'm fine, really." How many times did she have to say it? Time for a change of subject. "How are the plans going for Trail Days? Katie said you have plenty of volunteers this year."

"We're right on schedule. It's a lot easier now that we have the first year under our belts. We've just tweaked a few things that could've gone better last year. But all the vendors are enthusiastic, and after last year's crowd, the bands are eager to perform again."

"That's great." Avery thought back to last year—Cooper's run for sheriff and the scandal that plagued him. God had brought them through all that. He'd also bring Avery through this . . . desert in her life.

The designation made her feel ungrateful. At the relatively young age of thirty, she'd already achieved her career goals. But that knowledge did nothing to fill the cavity in her chest. Something was missing in her life. In her heart.

Wes.

She hadn't heard from him since that one text three weeks ago. Even so, she jumped to check her phone every time a message arrived. The cycle of hope and despair left her worn and exhausted. Was he settled in Albany? How were things with Lillian? Had he kissed her yet? Of course he had. He'd said he loved the woman. He'd probably scooped her into his arms the second he saw her. The thought of his lips pressed against another woman's ripped her heart in two. Her chest actually ached with grief.

She scowled at the plate in her hands. She had to stop thinking about the man. Had to put him behind her. He'd moved on and she needed to also.

"How *is* the new doctor doing?" Lisa asked. "She fitting in okay at the clinic?"

"She's been great. She's fantastic with the patients, and she blended right into the staff. Today was my first Saturday off since I opened the clinic." Avery didn't mention she'd spent it catching up on paperwork. Somehow all that extra time she had now only worsened her mood. Gave her the feeling she'd been hiding behind her work all this time. "She's assumed half the on-call hours so I can finally get a good night's sleep."

"What a blessing."

Not that Avery was actually getting a good night's sleep. The insomnia continued, some nights worse than others. But even though her workload had been greatly relieved, dealing with the possibility of an illness was its own kind of stressor—and the insomnia only perpetuated the anxiety as she continually worried the first symptom had struck.

Time to think about something else. "How's Dad doing?

He says he feels good, but I'm not sure he'd tell me if he felt otherwise."

"He really is doing well. He's taking his meds and not having any symptoms. You don't have to worry about him, honey."

It was hard to feel reassured when she wasn't sure Lisa would tell her if something *were* wrong. With the back of her hand, Avery wiped the sweat from her brow. She was just irritable from the heat and from the . . . emptiness she'd been feeling. The heartache.

Heartache. What a stupid word. The heart was the center of the circulatory system, pumping blood throughout the body. The organ had nothing to do with love or feelings. And yet she couldn't deny that spot where it resided in her chest ached every time she thought of Wes.

Lisa pulled the drain and the soapy water gurgled down the pipes. "Let's go see who's winning."

Avery dried the last of the silverware and followed Lisa outside. But what she really wanted to do was retreat to her apartment and lose herself in a tub of chocolate fudge brownie ice cream.

"Good job, honey!" Katie called to Cooper when he sank his second sandbag in a row.

The brothers were playing Dad and Lisa, and it was a tight game.

Katie had joined Avery at the picnic table. They'd mostly been talking about wedding plans and all the trails she and Cooper planned to hike when they went to Gatlinburg for their honeymoon. Personally, Avery thought they might find better things to do. But being Cooper's sister, she didn't want to think about, much less talk about, that subject.

She couldn't help but think of Wes, though, and that scorching kiss they'd exchanged the night of the emergency birth. The gentle way he'd touched her face, the commanding way he had with his lips. They'd both lost control that night.

Well, if it had to be your last kiss, at least it was smoking hot.

The wry thought did nothing to ease the ache in her chest. Or the longing for another kiss just like it. How long would it take her to heal from this loss? Her only real experience with heartbreak had been with Sam, and she'd moved on from him in a matter of weeks, throwing herself into academics. It had been thirty-three days since she'd last seen Wes, and not an hour passed that she didn't think of him.

She was even having trouble losing herself in books. Several days ago she'd finally finished *Persuasion*—the last in her marathon. She wasn't sure if it was the book's melancholy mood or the romantic narrative, but it had taken her three weeks to get through it, and she hadn't picked up another book since.

Katie touched her hand. "Avery . . . ?"

She'd obviously missed something. "Sorry, what? You caught me daydreaming."

"I was just asking how you're doing with everything. You've seemed a little distracted lately, and I know you must have a lot on your mind."

Avery gave a strained smile. One more time. "I'm fine. The heat just makes me irritable, that's all. I'll be glad for fall." For good measure she swept her hair from her neck.

"I know you must miss him. The two of you seemed to have gotten pretty close."

"Who?"

Katie tilted her head and gave Avery a *Really?* look.

"All right, fine. I miss him. There. Happy?"

"Not really. I care about you and you're obviously hurting. You can talk to me about it, you know. And just because I'm about to marry your brother doesn't mean I'll go blab everything to him."

"It's not that. It's just—why talk about it at all? He's gone and obviously he's moved on. I'm trying to do the same."

"Love really isn't that tidy, hon."

"Who said I—" Avery blinked. Who was she kidding? If she didn't love Wes, she wouldn't still be aching over his departure like this. Or checking her phone compulsively. Or torturing herself with thoughts of him and *Lillian*. How could she hold such dislike for someone she'd never even met?

"Have you talked to him since he left?"

"Just once. He let me know when he finished the trail." And only because he'd promised he would. There was that honor coming through once again.

"Maybe you should reach out to him. Let him know how you feel."

"There's someone else in his life, remember?"

"Are you sure about that? I saw the way he looked at you."

Avery shook her head. "I think they have some kind of special bond. He seems devoted to her, and I can't really compete with that. Anyway . . . I already made a decision about my future, and I plan to stick with it."

Katie studied her for moment. "Decisions can always be unmade, you know."

"Just because they *can* doesn't mean they should." Why

would she put someone she loved through, at best, an uncertain future and, at worse, a lingering, progressive illness that robbed her of dignity and life?

"Booooo." Gavin jeered from the picnic table beside Avery. "Coop can't hit the broadside of a barn tonight."

"He's too distracted by his girl." Lisa's dimple flashed as she took her turn, and the sandbag hit the board a few inches shy of the hole.

"He must be in love," Dad said.

"I should hope so." Cooper wrapped his arms around Katie as he whispered something into her ear. When she pressed into his side, he gazed down at her like a besotted fool.

Avery's stomach bottomed out as realization sunk in: she would never have a man look at her that way.

Cooper and Katie made it seem so easy. But that wasn't fair. They'd had a long and winding journey to love. And Avery was glad for them. Really, she was. They deserved a happily ever after.

It was just that she couldn't help but juxtapose their obvious contentment and joy with her current lack of the same. In just a week Cooper and Katie would get married, and eventually Gavin would find a nice woman to settle down with. Avery would be surrounded by a family of loving couples. She'd be the pathetic spinster auntie who collected cats for company.

"You feeling okay, Ave?" Gavin asked.

She rolled her eyes. "I'm just hot. Can't anyone else tell it's a million degrees out here?"

Gavin studied her. "You've seemed a little out of sorts lately."

"Really, Gavin? Have I seemed out of sorts? Maybe I have some things going on in my life, huh? You ever think about that?"

"Jeez. Just asking. Don't have to jump down my throat."

Avery drew in a long breath and blew it out slowly. What was wrong with her? She wasn't fit for company tonight.

She was about to apologize when the game ended and Gavin took Cooper's spot. Cooper grabbed a broom and started sweeping off the patio. Avery pretended to be invested in the game. She wouldn't stay much longer, but she didn't want to be rude and leave the second supper was over. She checked her Fitbit. Another ten minutes or so, then she could go home and stop trying to pretend she was all right.

The sun had set behind the mountains, ushering in twilight. She gave a deep yawn and covered her mouth. All that lack of sleep was catching up with her. She might even forgo the ice cream and just retire early. Then she thought of the dreaded hours tossing and turning and changed her mind.

"You getting enough sleep, Sis?" Cooper asked quietly from the patio, wearing that stupid, pitying look.

Avery pressed a finger to her twitching eyelid. "Yes."

"Are you sure because—"

"Oh. My. *Gosh.*"

"*What?*"

Katie and Dad turned to stare. Gavin froze midthrow. Lisa's brows furrowed.

Now that Avery had their attention, might as well settle this for the whole family. "For the record, before anyone else asks—I am *fine.* I'm just sick and tired of everybody staring at me sideways every time I sneeze."

"Um, sneezing isn't even a symptom of—"

Avery shot Gavin a glare.

"Okay, I'm just gonna . . . go back to the game."

"Even perfectly normal people sometimes lack focus or feel irritable or suffer from insomnia. I am not a delicate flower. And I don't need you sheltering me from stressful information or checking up on me"—she threw a glare Cooper's way—"or doing background checks on people I care about. Also, I don't need you all constantly reminding me that I might have a disease. I think about it enough all on my own, thank you very much." She snatched her purse from the bench, stood, and addressed Lisa and her dad. "Thank you for having me, but I think I'll be going now." Her voice quivered with emotion.

She took off through the grass, rounded the house, and hightailed it toward her Jeep. Her legs trembled beneath her. Her chest heaved and tears burned the backs of her eyes. When she reached the safety of the vehicle, she got inside and dug through her purse for the keys.

The passenger door opened. Dad quietly slipped inside. He shut the door and stared out the front windshield as silence swelled around them.

Avery forced herself to breathe. She fought the embarrassment clawing inside. She had every reason to be upset with her family. She was tired of them treating her with kid gloves, and it was about time they knew it. Okay, maybe she should've had a calm conversation with them long ago instead of letting it all build up and exploding on them like a shaken can of soda.

"I'm sorry I handled that badly," she said.

He gave her a cautious smile. "I didn't come out here for an apology, honey. You're right. We do all the things you said we do. I'm as guilty as anyone."

"But I didn't have to lose it like that." It was so unlike her. Did her overreaction qualify as a mood change—yet another symptom of Huntington's? All this speculation was driving her mad! She hit the steering wheel. "Arghhh!"

Her dad's eyes flickered with panic. "Honey, what is going on? Talk to me."

Thoughts raged in her head, twisting and curling like a tornado. She attempted to assemble them into some coherent order. "I'm just so tired of living with this disease hanging over my head, Dad. Of questioning every little mood change and symptom. And then there's everything I've given up—and I'm mad about it! I want what *they* have." She flung a hand toward the backyard. "What you and Lisa have. I want a husband and a family, and this stupid disease has stolen all that from me."

Her ragged breaths filled the interior. She probably shouldn't be saying all this. It might make him feel bad about having her. But Avery's mom had been adopted, and she hadn't known her biological family carried the disease until she'd become symptomatic—and by then, of course, they'd already had Avery.

Silence settled around them once again. Movement to her right caught her eye, and when she looked, two pennies sat on the console between them.

She huffed. Oh, why not? What did she have to lose? She reached out and picked them up.

"You're already living your life like you have the disease, honey. You're letting it rob you of everything you want when you don't even know if you have it."

She snorted. "Well, I guess I'll always have my career."

"That's not enough. Not for a warm, loving woman like you. You deserve a man who loves you like I loved your mom. Like I love Lisa."

"I don't want to take the test, Dad."

"Why not?"

She gaped at him. "How can you ask that? You saw what Mom went through. I don't want to live in dread of that happening to me."

"Aren't you already doing that? At the young age of thirty, you've already reached all your career goals—and I couldn't be prouder. But there's more to life than work. And ever since that young man left you've been unhappy."

She hadn't thought her dad had noticed. She'd been trying pretty hard to hide it. "He was just a friend." The words felt stale and bitter on her tongue.

"Really?" He tilted his head, pinning her with an unwavering look. "I think you're in love with him."

She gave a wry laugh. "Fine. I am. And I also want kids, but I guess we can't always have what we want. Even if Wes felt the same way I do—and I don't think he does—I wouldn't want to saddle him with this burden, Dad. I have a 50 percent chance of having that awful disease."

He reached over and took her face in his hands. "Let me explain something to you, Daughter. When a man loves you like I loved your mom, he won't want to be any other place than at your side—disease or no. He'll *want* to be there with you through it. Honey, I never regretted marrying your mom—not for one minute. If you're in love, then you know I'm right." He gave her chin a soft pinch and let go.

His words sank in. She tried to flip things around—what

if Wes were the one with the disease? She didn't have to think twice: She'd want to be there for him. She'd want to take care of him and be his emotional and physical support. She wouldn't have it any other way.

"And Avery," her dad's voice softened. "While it's true you have a 50 percent chance of inheriting the disease, it bears saying . . . you also have a 50 percent chance of having everything you want."

A shiver passed through her. She'd never thought of it quite like that. And he was right. She'd been living as if she had the disease, and the only thing standing in the way of a better future was that test.

Of course, either way, her future wouldn't include Wes—he was in love with someone else. But maybe someday she'd find someone she loved just as much—and he would love her back.

But that familiar dread compressed her chest because there was also the other 50 percent. The dreaded 50 percent. "I'm so afraid, Daddy," she whispered.

He squeezed her hand. "But you're also brave and strong. Honey, God will give you everything you need to get through whatever your future holds. I'm a living example of that sentiment. And I would've trusted Him that much more if I'd been able to see how He would turn my pain into joy."

"In my head, I know you're right . . ."

"When you know it in your *heart*, you'll know what to do."

The fog lifted, bringing a moment of perfect clarity. She had a 50 percent chance of being free from all of that. It was worth pushing through the fear, taking the chance.

As the decision settled over her, her heart drummed out a staccato rhythm that made lungs work overtime. She was strong.

She was brave. She could feel the fear and do it anyway. God would provide all she needed.

Her gaze connected with her father's in the waning light. "Thanks, Dad. I know what I'm going to do now."

Thirty-Nine

Almost a week had passed since Lillian cooked gumbo. Wes had been over to her apartment three times in the past six days, and their relationship still hadn't progressed. When opportunities to make an advance presented themselves, he faltered every time.

Tonight, for instance, they'd ordered pizza and were binge-watching a reality TV show about newly married couples. He kept thinking he should reach over and take her hand. He'd done it that day at the cemetery, hadn't he? But that was different. That could've been construed as affectionate support. Holding hands while watching TV, however, was undeniably a romantic gesture.

He was just getting up the nerve to take her hand—at least that's what he told himself—when the show ended and the credits began rolling. This was getting to be ridiculous. Why was it so hard to do something with Lillian that had been so natural with Avery? And why, when he was finally living up to his promise to Landon, did he feel so . . . unmoored?

"Want to watch another?" He was determined to get up the nerve before the first commercial break.

"To be honest, I'm exhausted, and I'm having breakfast with Honor in the morning."

"You should get your rest then." Kicking himself for another lost opportunity and feeling like an insecure middle schooler, he followed her to the door as had become their habit. "I'll pick up a sample of that paint and put some on the nursery wall tomorrow night so you can see if you like it."

"Silver Shimmer," she reminded him.

He turned at the door. "I've got the swatch."

Her gaze fastened on him, and her doe eyes softened at the corners. "Thank you so much, Wes. I love having you here." She reached out for their standard good-bye hug.

But instead Wes diverted. Heart hammering against his ribs, he leaned in to kiss her. He felt the warmth of her breath on his mouth a moment before their lips met.

She pressed a hand to his chest and shot backward.

Relief swamped him at the close call. But that unfortunate emotion quickly drained away at the sight of Lillian's wide eyes.

"What—what are you doing?"

He let out an awkward laugh. "If it wasn't obvious, I must be out of practice."

"Wes . . . I—" She cupped her throat. "Where did that come from? Did I say or do something to make you think . . . ?"

He ran a hand over his face, finding his skin hot. No surprise there. His armpits prickled with heat, and sweat beaded on the back of his neck. "I thought . . ." He wasn't even sure how to finish the sentence so he just let the last word hang, suspended in the air like a ruptured piñata.

"Wes . . . Come sit down." She took his hand and led him back to the sofa.

They were finally holding hands. He huffed at the irony.

When they were side by side, she gave him a compassionate smile. "Talk to me. What's going on?"

He thought back, his mind rewinding past all the conversations they'd shared over the last few months, past the letters they'd exchanged following Landon's death. Time rewound all the way to that hot summer afternoon when an explosion had stolen his friend. To the moment he'd looked into Landon's knowing eyes and made a promise he was honor bound to keep.

He swallowed past the lump in his throat. "I never told you the last thing Landon said to me."

Lillian shrank back a little, her eyes clouding with wariness. "What—what was it?"

"He asked me to look after you—and I promised him I would."

Understanding flickered in her eyes and she took his hand. "And you have. You've been there for me every step of the way. I couldn't have gotten through this past year without you."

"At first I just planned to come here and put down roots, be like family to you. It's not like I had anywhere else to be. But somewhere along the way I started thinking . . . wouldn't it make sense if . . . well, if we were more than that? You didn't have a man in your life—at least, I didn't think you did. And since I already loved you . . ." *It was the least I could do.*

"Oh, Wes. I love you too, I do. But . . . not like that. And I don't think you love me that way either."

He needed her to understand. "I promised him, Lillian. And

you can't tell me it doesn't make sense. Especially now that . . ." He dropped his gaze to her stomach. "Well, I think I could be a good father for your baby. And I'd be a good husband. I'd treat you the way you deserve to be treated." Not like that idiot who'd gotten her pregnant and ditched her.

"I have no doubt all of that's true. But I can take care of myself—and my baby. Having you here has been wonderful, but I never intended to make you think . . . Why didn't you say anything? All this time . . . ?"

"I was trying to let things progress naturally." He felt a little silly now, admitting where his thoughts had gone. Because if her reaction to his kiss hadn't told him everything he needed to know, her words now did. He must be the world's worst communicator. "I thought it was what Landon would've wanted. I owe him everything, Lillian. Surely you can understand that."

Her lips curved in a soft smile. "He never would've wanted either one of us to settle this way. You love me like a sister, not like a wife. I deserve more than that—and so do you." She squeezed his hand. "What Landon did . . . it's not possible to pay that back. And he didn't sacrifice his life so you'd have some kind of debt hanging over your head. It was a *gift*. He did it so you could *live*. Period."

The words struck like an arrow into the bull's-eye of his heart. Landon's sacrifice had felt like a debt he had to settle—a very heavy debt. Was Lillian right? Would Landon simply want Wes to live his life? How could that ever be enough?

"But he gave his life for me." The wonder of it never ceased to steal his breath.

"So that you could *live*," she repeated.

The words sank a little deeper, familiar somehow though he'd never thought of Landon's sacrifice this way. They sank through his skin and melded into his heart. His friend had given him the gift of life. His eyes stung at the thought.

Thank you, buddy. I'll never know why you did it—why you made that split-second decision to save me but—thank you.

Lillian nudged his shoulder. "Why are you even here, Wes? In Albany? It's become pretty clear to me that you're in love with your doctor friend."

He'd only mentioned Avery in passing. "What?"

"For one thing, ever since you got here you've been mooning around. Every time I bring her up, you get this wistful look on your face, and your voice gets all tender. And then there's this." She opened her phone and showed him a photo. It was the selfie he'd taken of Avery and him the night they'd watched *Safe Haven*. What was Lillian doing with . . . ? "I meant to send that to Avery."

"I figured." She studied the photo, her lips tilting. "But look at you. You're so happy. I haven't seen you smile like this since you arrived in town. Does she feel the same about you?"

"I don't know." He'd been too set on getting here to start a life with Lillian. He'd left her the day after he'd kissed her with such passion. The day after she'd confided in him about her health. He hadn't bothered to ask how she felt.

Stupid.

"Don't you think you owe it to yourself to find out? I mean, I know I'm younger than you, but even I know love like that doesn't come along every day."

"But what about . . . ?" His gaze dropped to her still-flat tummy. He remembered how broken she'd sounded on the phone that day she told him. "What about you? When you told me about the baby you seemed so . . ."

"Upset?" She pursed her lips and gave him that look women everywhere seemed to have down pat. "Of course I was upset. Being pregnant is a huge change, and having a baby is a big responsibility. But I've been taking care of myself—and other people's kids, I might add—for years. Just because I vent to you doesn't mean I need you to fix everything. I'm perfectly capable of handling my own life, Wes."

"I know that." But did he really? Hadn't he started thinking of Lillian as a little bit . . . helpless? Landon had never viewed her that way, and she'd never given that impression in her letters. But maybe Wes had set her up as a project to relieve the guilt he'd felt over Landon's sacrifice. He winced at the thought. "I'm sorry I underestimated you. I should've known any sister of Landon's would be tough as nails."

Her face softened. "I never needed you to be my knight in shining armor—Landon knew I didn't need one of those. I just need you to be my friend."

He'd made this decision about Lillian—*for* Lillian—all on his own. And he'd clung to it like a life preserver. But he was not his father and he was not Landon's proxy. He was his own person, and he could make decisions that were right for *him*.

All the weight he'd carried for months seemed to drain away, leaving his limbs light, buoyant. He didn't have to ransom his own life. He didn't even have to repay Landon. He just had to go out and live. Debt-free.

What did that even look like?

An image of Avery formed in his head. In it she wore her lab coat and that ever-present stethoscope around her neck. She was smiling at him, those wide-set green eyes twinkling with knowledge. *It looks like me,* her expression seemed to say.

Forty

The sanctuary of Riverbend Community Church was aglow with candlelight. Sprays of white peonies and lilies of the valley draped from the pews' ends, their sweet aroma adding to the intimate ambiance. It was a small gathering, family and close friends, just as Katie and Cooper had wished.

Avery faced the guests from the front of the church as the music shifted to the song that would welcome the bride down the aisle. The crowd stood.

The door swept open and Katie appeared, almost angelic in appearance. Her blonde hair was arranged in a half-up, half-down style and adorned with a simple veil. On her mom's arm she glided down the aisle in her beautiful Cinderella gown—but it was her beaming smile that stole the show.

Cooper's gaze fixed on his bride, his love shining like a beacon from his face. And as Katie drew closer, his eyes went glossy.

Katie's smile wobbled with emotion as she reached her place beside Cooper.

Avery's heart tightened and her throat thickened. She was so happy for her brother in that moment. So happy for them both. They'd overcome so many obstacles to be here today, committing their lives to one another.

Avery glanced past the lovebirds to the best man—Gavin. If it was difficult watching his brother marry his ex-girlfriend, he hid it well. Gavin's gaze found Avery's across the way and he winked.

A breath escaped on a deep sigh as Avery faced front. The pastor welcomed the crowd and took a few minutes to express his thoughts on love and marriage. Then Katie and Cooper shared their personal vows. The words were lovely and poignant and funny, each one alluding to their tumultuous journey. When that was over, they exchanged rings, and then the pastor announced the couple husband and wife.

Almost before the words were out of his mouth, Cooper swept Katie into his arms and gave her a kiss that seemed to go on and on. And on. Or maybe that was just her.

"All right, already . . . ," she muttered. But the acoustics carried her words and the crowd chuckled.

Avery stood with Patti and Lucy on the sidelines of the dance floor where the cha-cha slide was in full motion. Katie and Cooper were at the center of it all, laughing and cutting up with friends. The first dance, toasts, and dinner were behind them, as well as the cake cutting.

Avery had been at Katie's side all night, anticipating her

every need. She'd repaired the bride's hair, located a knife with which to cut the cake, and found Band-Aids for Katie's blistered heels. Now it was time to have fun.

You remember how to do that, right?

"We should probably go dance," Avery called to Patti and Lucy over the music.

"I don't know this one." That had been Patti's standard answer tonight.

Avery gave her a mock scowl. "The directions are literally in the lyrics."

"You know I have two left feet. I always end up going the wrong direction, then people trip over me."

Lucy pointed toward the dance floor. "Look at Sharise go."

Avery located the woman, hamming it up in the center of the floor. A minute later the song wound down and a slower melody took its place—"Bless the Broken Road." The crowd thinned out to couples only.

"Oh, I love this song," Patti said. "It's so romantic."

"You should ask Lloyd to dance."

The woman's eyes fixed on a point over Avery's shoulder. "Too late—he's already found the cake line. I won't see him the rest of the night."

Lucy took a sip of her drink, addressing Avery. "Not to bring up work, but when do you think that grant money will be coming our way?"

They'd just gotten the news this week. The grant would easily cover an X-ray and an ultrasound machine. "Just a couple weeks. And I'm still hoping for the one that'll help supplement your salary."

"I'm doing all right. I'm comfy cozy in that apartment—not that I'd turn down a raise."

Avery's gaze caught on Rick Rodriguez, who approached their group, drink in hand. He was handsome tonight in a navy-blue suit and crisp white shirt, his thick black hair styled just so.

Avery gave him a welcoming smile. She hadn't seen much of him since the awkward end to their date back in July.

As he neared, his gaze drifted to Avery's right where Lucy stood sipping her drink. He froze. His mouth opened but no words emerged.

Avery glanced at Lucy, who admittedly looked stunning tonight. Black waves cascaded past her shoulders in a gleaming waterfall. The fitted floral dress clung to every curve, and the halter-style neckline flattered her sculpted shoulders, while the hemline showed off her legs.

Looking back to Rick, Avery grinned. "Rick Rodriguez, meet the clinic's new doctor, Lucy Chan. Lucy, Rick's one of our fine deputies."

Lucy's cherry-red lips turned up at the corners. "Nice to meet you, Rick."

Rick's mouth moved, but the music must've swallowed his words. His dark eyes, still fixed on Lucy, had a deer-in-the-headlights look.

Patti smirked. "Cat got your tongue, Ricky?"

His mouth opened, then closed again.

Avery took pity on him. "Maybe you should ask Lucy to dance."

When he didn't respond, Avery elbowed him hard.

He startled and looked her way.

"Maybe you should ask Lucy to dance."

He blinked and glanced back to the obvious object of his desire. Wet his lips. Shifted. Tried to adjust the hat he wasn't wearing. A flush crawled up his neck. "Um, ma'am? Would you like to dance?"

Lucy's eyes twinkled. "Don't mind if I do."

Patti relieved them of their drinks, then Rick took Lucy's hand. She followed him onto the floor and into his arms.

"Seems like Deputy McDreamy has finally met his match," Patti said.

Rick's hand settled into the small of Lucy's back. She was a few inches shorter than him even in her heels. With their dark hair and coordinated clothing, they seemed like the perfect couple.

"Good grief, they look good together," Patti said. "Their clothes even match."

"Girl, you read my mind."

From the darkened corner of the room, Avery watched Katie and Cooper sway to a Billy Currington ballad. Cooper gazed down at his new bride as if she were the only woman in the room. Something about seeing the two of them together made Avery feel so alone.

Ridiculous. She pushed the thought away. She was surrounded by people.

But she couldn't deny that the alone feeling had been constant since a certain contractor had left town. *You are no more alone than you had been before Wes arrived.* Maybe she'd been a little lonely, but she had her family and friends.

She surveyed the half-empty cups and dessert plates littering the table. Maybe she wouldn't feel so alone if she hadn't put herself in a dark, empty corner. But she was peopled out. Unfit for company. She grabbed a napkin and tore off a corner, then another.

She was just tired and stressed. This had been a big week for her. On Tuesday she'd had blood drawn for the Huntington's disease test. She'd hunched in the lab's vinyl chair, rubber band pinching her arm, and watched as her blood filled the vial. Maybe she'd broken out into a sweat, maybe her heart threatened to jump outside her body, and maybe her eye twitched to the point of distraction. But she'd done it. And it felt good, finding the courage to do what she'd put off her whole adult life. She wasn't hiding from the future anymore but facing it.

And in part she had Wes to thank for that. He'd inspired her. He'd emerged from a difficult childhood and found the courage to be better than the example he'd had. And losing his best friend had been difficult, but he looked to the future with hope.

She could do the same, regardless of the results, which would come in two to three weeks. They were going to be long ones. But then she would know for certain. Then she could face her future—whatever it was—head-on.

She was watching her fingers shred the napkin when a shadow fell over her table. She lifted her gaze, following the muscular male frame all the way up to the handsome, smiling face.

"Come dance with me." Ever since Rick had danced with Lucy earlier, he hadn't been able to wipe that dopey grin off his face.

"Where's Lucy? I didn't think you were ever going to let her go."

He ducked his head. "She had a heel malfunction, and she stepped away for a minute. Come on, I need to do some recon on your new hire."

Avery took his hand. "Oh, that's all I'm good for now, huh?"

"Hey . . ." He shrugged all cocky, seeming much more like his old self. "You had your chance, Robinson."

───────────

Where was she? Wes stood in front of Avery's apartment door. He'd knocked half a dozen times even though the lights were off. The carriage house windows were also dark, and of course the clinic was closed up tight too. Where was everyone tonight?

He hadn't wanted his first connection with her to be over the phone, but it seemed like he'd have no choice. *Think, Garrett. Where could she be?*

It was a Saturday night, past dinnertime. He refused to believe she was on a date. Maybe she'd gone out with the girls. Or maybe she was at her folk's place. It was only nine thirty. He got into his rental and headed that way. The last-minute flight hadn't been cheap, but once he'd realized what a mistake he'd made, he had to act. He couldn't believe he'd been such an idiot. He loved her so much. And love like this didn't come along every day.

Lillian had been so sweet last night. Before he'd hardly admitted his feelings for Avery, she flipped open her laptop and started searching for flights. It seemed like days ago as the hours passed in slow motion. And now that he'd finally reached Riverbend, Avery was nowhere to be found.

When he came to the Robinson's property, he turned into the drive and pulled closer to the house. Not a single light was on—even the porch was dark. It seemed the whole family was missing in—

The whole family . . . *the wedding*.

He fumbled with his phone and checked the date. September third. Cooper and Katie's wedding night. Of course.

The ceremony would be over, and the reception would be in full swing by now. He'd overheard enough to know it was being held at a barn venue near town—how many such places could there be around here? He googled the information and came up with the place, only a seven-minute drive.

Once he set the map, he backed the car from the drive and pulled out onto the street. He needed to think about what he would say. He couldn't leave that to chance as he'd done in the past. What was it Lillian said to her kids? *Use your words.*

This time he wouldn't leave anything up to assumptions. He was going to lay it all on the line. He was going to tell Avery he wanted to be with her no matter what her future held. And then he was going to find out if she felt the same way about him.

That was the scary part of the plan.

She'd never exactly admitted to loving him. And he'd only been in Riverbend for a few weeks. He'd been gone almost twice that long. They'd only kissed the one time, and she hadn't contacted him since he'd left—other than the one time he'd texted her. It really wasn't much to go on.

Was he about to make a royal fool of himself?

The question flashed like a neon sign in his brain a few

minutes later when he pulled in to the venue's lot and parked. As he exited the car, music drifted from the open doors, and that's when it occurred to him: What if she'd come with a date?

He stopped in his tracks, rearing his head back. It was a wedding—of course she would come with a date.

He was an idiot. Why hadn't he thought this through? He stared at the barn, gleaming white in the moonlight. A few children wearing dress clothes scampered around the porch, playing chase under the glow of lanterns.

He thought of Avery, somewhere inside that building. Date or no, he was going to tell her how he felt tonight. He hadn't come this far for nothing.

He pressed on. The steps between the lot and barn stretched ahead like a football field. Still, he kept going. For the first time in months he would follow a path he chose for himself. Whether Avery wanted to walk it with him or not, he didn't know. But he was going to find out.

He marched on, up the pavers and through the open doorway. He stopped at the back of the room, his gaze sweeping the space. A handful of people sat at tables, but most of them gathered on the dance floor, moving to the melody of a slow song.

It didn't take long to spot Avery—swaying in the arms of an all-too-familiar man.

Forty-One

In her beautiful green dress, hair falling over her bare shoulders, Avery looked even more gorgeous than Wes remembered. She spoke animatedly with Rick, then listened as he replied. As she tossed her head back in a laugh, Wes swore he could hear the melodious sound over the music.

He scowled as he raked his gaze over Romeo's white shirt and fitted dress pants. Wes glanced down at his own attire, only now aware that he stood out like a sore thumb in his jeans and button-down.

He watched the chatty couple on the dance floor, his chest tightening, his breath hitching at the sight of them together. Avery seemed so happy. Had he made a terrible mistake in coming here? Had she moved on since he'd left? Was she with this guy now?

But even while his heart ached at the sight of them, at the possibility of losing her . . . he couldn't let this moment pass. He'd come all this way to tell her he loved her and that's what he'd do.

It would be up to her what, if anything, would come of his declaration.

He forced his feet into motion. The dance floor grew closer with alarming speed, his heart measuring the distance in beats. Before he knew it, he was at Avery's side, a trembling mass of terror.

Rick saw him first. The smile slipped from the man's face and his broad shoulders stiffened.

Avery must've noticed too because she glanced over her shoulder, doing a double take at the sight of Wes. She froze in place. Her lips parted and her eyes widened. Those beautiful eyes. Oh, how he'd missed having them trained on him.

"*Wes.*"

The rich melody swelled in the awkward gap between them. Tension flared.

Wes cut his gaze to Rick and he forced an even tone. "May I cut in?"

Rick's gaze darted between the two of them. "Uh, sure."

Now that Wes had her full attention, he was barely aware of the other man slipping away. He took a step closer, trying to figure out what to make of her wide eyes and tentative smile. Was she glad to see him? She was impossible to read.

He took a deep breath and set his hands on her waist. Eons passed before she slid her hands up to his shoulders. Then they began swaying in time to the music.

Avery stared at Wes, her pulse racing. Was he really here in Riverbend? In her arms? With her own future so up in the air, she didn't dare hope . . .

"Sorry to crash your date," he said finally.

"What are you doing here, Wes? Why aren't you in Albany?" *With Lillian.* She managed to suppress the name but not the pang of jealousy.

He opened his mouth. Closed it again. His gaze flittered over her face.

She felt the sweep like a caress, and her skin tingled with want.

"I had it all planned out, what I was going to say, and now that you're standing in front of me I can't remember any of it."

"Just . . . just tell me why you came." She wasn't even sure if the words were audible over the music and laughter floating around them. Unable to help herself, she slipped her hand down his chest and rested her palm over his heart. It had been so long, and she'd missed him so badly. She needed that connection. "Is Lillian all right?" she made herself ask.

"She's fine. She's great."

Her stomach shrank two sizes but she forced a smile. "That's good. You found a job and a place to stay? I thought I might hear from you once you'd settled in." She winced at the needy sound of her words.

"I couldn't . . . I thought it would be best if we—"

Cut ties, cold turkey. "I understand." She couldn't resist adding, "And yet, here you are."

He breathed a laugh. "Yeah. About that . . . A lot has happened in the past five weeks."

Five weeks and five days, but who was counting?

"Sometime after promising Landon I'd take care of Lillian . . . I decided I should marry her."

His words punched her in the heart. She swallowed around the hard knot forming in her throat. "I see."

"I thought that's what he'd want. What he'd expect of me. I owed him so much—how do you repay someone for sacrificing his life for you?"

Her insides twisted hard and her legs trembled beneath her. She just wanted to get this over with. Go to the bathroom and throw up.

He tilted her chin up until she met his gaze. "And then I came here and met you. And you . . ."

Hope sprang to life. She was going to burst if he didn't complete that sentence.

He stopped swaying, giving up all pretense of dancing. He cupped her face and pinned her with an intense look. "You amazed me. You mesmerized me. You captured me. It was impossible to be with you and not want you. And then I gave into temptation that night and kissed you and it was . . ."

Beautiful. Passionate. Soul-stirring. How many times had she relished every memory of that kiss?

"Perfect," he finished. "I didn't want to leave you, Avery. After that night, after everything you confided in me and everything you meant to me, I wasn't going to go to Albany. But the next day . . . Lillian told me she was pregnant."

Avery sucked in a breath.

"I felt so torn. Between what I wanted and what I felt I needed to do. But I wanted to do the honorable thing, and I owed Landon, and Lillian needed me."

She was really starting to hate that name. "Right."

"But like I said before . . . a lot has happened since I left Riverbend."

She lifted her chin. "A lot's happened here too."

He blinked. Uncertainty flickered in his eyes. After a pause he continued. "I want to hear all about that. But first I need to say what I came to say, even if . . . well, even if it doesn't matter to you. The gist of it is, Lillian helped me see . . ."

Avery drank in his tormented eyes as the air crackled between them. Her lungs felt constricted, and she struggled to draw a breath. "Helped you see what?"

"That I don't feel for her what I feel for you." He gave a humorless laugh. "Not even close. I told you I loved her and I do. But I'm not *in* love with her, and she's not in love with me either. I've been a real idiot. I was trying so hard to do the right thing, but it wasn't the right thing at all—she helped me see that.

"I know we haven't known each other very long, and maybe it should be too soon, too quick, for me to say this . . . but somehow it isn't. I love you, Avery. I love you so much my chest aches when we're apart and I don't know if—"

Avery pressed her lips to his. She didn't need to hear any more. He loved her and that was all that mattered. All she needed to hear. Her mouth curved against his lips.

Apparently he didn't feel the need to finish his thoughts, and that was fine by her. He simply drew her closer, deepening the kiss. His lips worked hers with patient precision, each breath, each sweep of his lips making her come undone. Wes was here with her. He loved her. The most wonderful feelings fluttered in her stomach. She'd thought she would never feel this way—this kind of love had been for everyone else, not for her. But it was right at her fingertips now. Hers for the taking.

And she hated to ruin the moment with uncertainty—but there was something of which she had to be sure.

She gathered her courage and ended the kiss. Oh, she could

sink right into those eyes and happily drown in their blue depths. "In case that wasn't clear enough, I love you too."

His eyes softened at her words, and the corner of his lip lifted. He leaned in.

She pressed her palm to his chest. "But . . . I told you a lot has happened since you left."

Worry flickered in his eyes as they drifted over her face. "Tell me."

Fear sucked the moisture from her mouth. It wasn't the first time this disease had struck fear into her heart. But she wouldn't let it immobilize her. Wouldn't let it steal another second of her life. She would counter it with courage this time. Every time.

She swallowed hard and met his gaze. "This week I took the genetic test for Huntington's disease. I don't know the results yet. It'll take another week or two, and until then maybe you'd prefer—"

"Avery." He cupped her face, his eyes sobering. "I am so proud of you for doing that. I know it was hard for you. But you need to know that whatever the results are, it changes nothing for me."

"You don't have to say that. It might make more sense if we—"

"It changes *nothing*. No matter the results, I want to be here with you."

Her eyes stung with tears as his words settled over her like a warm down blanket. "Are you sure you mean that, Wes? I'm not certain you understand the ramifications of that decision. I'm not sure you can fully realize the devastation this disease causes."

"I'm not going into this blindly. I've done some research. And while I know that reading about it can't begin to illustrate the reality of the illness, that doesn't change anything." He set his forehead against hers. "Don't you know, sweetheart? I belong with you. No matter the results . . . I couldn't stand to be any-place else but *with* you."

She blinked at his words—almost verbatim what her dad had said he'd felt about her mother. Avery only had to accept Wes's decision and believe God would give them both the strength to get through whatever the future held. After all, who really knew what the future held?

Her pulse steadied, her muscles loosened, making her limbs go weightless. She pressed a palm to his scruffy jaw and drank him in. "I'd really like that."

His eyes darkened to a stormy blue, and his gaze dropped to her lips. Then he was kissing her again, and in an instant it was just the two of them, cocooned from the world. Protected in a bubble of wonder and joy. Her pulse was no longer so steady as she threaded her fingers into the hair at his nape. She didn't know how, against all odds, she'd fallen for this man so quickly. But she knew they belonged to each other.

The kiss lingered, warming her from the inside out. Until at some point she grew cognizant of the noise surrounding them. The music pounded and someone gave a bark of laughter.

She leaned away, meeting a sleepy-eyed gaze that nearly drew her right back into his embrace. Her gaze dropped to his oh-so-tempting mouth.

It tipped up at the corners. "When did the song change?"

They were more or less slow dancing to "I Like It, I Love It" in a sea of rowdy dancers too wrapped up in their fun to notice a couple of lovebirds making out.

She chuckled. "I have no idea."

Smiling, he set his forehead against hers. "I've never crashed a wedding before."

"You can be my plus one."

He scowled. "Didn't you come with *Romeo*?"

The snap of jealousy in his voice warmed her heart. Didn't he know that no other man could possibly compare to him? Apparently she still had some work to do there—and what fun work that would be. "I actually came alone."

"Good. That'll save me the trouble of getting rid of him."

She began swaying in time to the rhythm, giving him a cheeky smile. "Well, far be it from me to cause trouble. And it just so happens my dance card is wide open the rest of the night."

"Is that a fact."

"It is a fact." She gazed into his eyes, savoring the way he stared at her—as if she were the only woman in the room. In the world. And, oh, she planned to enjoy being the center of his attention. "Welcome home, Wes Garrett."

Epilogue

The savory scent of cooking burgers wafted into the November air, tantalizing Avery's senses. Autumn colors had rippled down into the valley, coloring the town in vibrant shades of red and gold. Fall ushered in cooler temperatures, a welcome relief from summer's heat. Today, with a mild seventy-degree temperature, was likely their last chance for an outdoor meal.

The Robinsons gathered in her parents' backyard. Wes had teamed up with Lisa for a competitive game of cornhole with Cooper and Katie. Gavin watched the match from the sidelines.

Avery set the last Crockpot on the picnic table and turned as Wes tossed his last sandbag. It arced through the air and sank through the hole. Lisa and Wes did a virtual high five.

Wes seemed to be enjoying his job with Valley Cabinet Company. The position didn't fully utilize his skills, but since there were no builders in town, it would have to do. At least, as he said, the work would keep him busy through the winter, unlike the window-installer position he'd left in Albany. That would allow him to make rent on his new apartment in Mulberry Hollow, just two streets from the clinic.

They had supper together most nights, either out or in. Sometimes on the weekend they even went all the way to Asheville for a night out. Lucy covered the on-call hours, and Avery was learning to let go—she was still a work in progress. Having Lucy as backup had not only given Avery extra time, but it had somehow helped her see that the town wasn't her sole responsibility. It took all of them striving together to make the community work. She only had to do her part.

From the grill Dad called encouragement to his wife as she hit the board with a critical shot. Wes cheered her on.

Avery had brought him around several times in the past two months since the wedding. His determination to stick by her side no matter her test results had won over her family. As she watched him now, a smile curved her lips. It had won her over too.

She'd never felt a love like this. She pressed her palm to her heart, which seemed to expand several times over every time she thought of him. Medically impossible, perhaps. But some things defied science.

A week after the wedding she'd gotten her lab results back. It took two days to get up the nerve to check them online. And when she did, Wes was right at her side, holding her hand, loving her through the moment.

An entire mountain of weight fell from her shoulders as she read the hoped-for results—she didn't carry the Huntington's gene. She would never endure the horrible symptoms as her mother had. She would never have to dread putting Wes through the disease. She would never have to worry about passing it along to her children.

She could look toward her future without that dark cloud of dread hanging over her head. She could make plans that didn't revolve around contingencies and uncertainties. She had a freedom and a hope she never thought to possess, and it was a wonderful feeling.

As she had every time the results came to mind, she closed her eyes and thanked God for the outcome—and whispered a prayer for all those who weren't so fortunate. She would never stop praying for them.

She might even do more than that. A few days ago, a seed of an idea sprouted in her head and had since begun growing roots. Maybe when things settled at her clinic, she'd start a foundation that offered financial and therapeutic relief to families who suffered with the disease. There were grants to be had for such causes—she knew all about applying for them, and now that she had Lucy at the clinic, she had more time to devote to another cause.

Speaking of Lucy, she and Rick were officially going out. Avery and Wes had even double-dated with them once. They'd hiked to River Ridge Loop and had a picnic overlooking the river. It amused Avery to see Rick so smitten with the young doctor. And though Lucy seemed adept at playing hard to get, Avery suspected the game had already been won.

A rousing cry arose from the yard as the players disputed the score. The banter was loud and playful and quickly settled, with Cooper and Katie emerging as the victors.

Avery joined her dad at the grill. "How's it going over here, Dad?"

"You're just in time." He plated the last burger and handed her the platter. "Come and get it!" he called.

On her way to the table she glanced at Gavin, and a niggle of worry wormed through her. He'd been awfully quiet tonight. In fact, he'd been quiet lately, period. She could only imagine how hard it was being the only single person in a sea of couples. Especially when he had so much heartache in his past. He seemed to have moved through most of the grief, but he still wasn't himself. Maybe he never would be again. The loss of a child was surely life-changing, and she had a feeling losing Laurel had broken him in a way that could never be fully healed. She said a quick prayer that God would bring the right woman into his life. He deserved to find happiness too.

The family gathered around the table, Wes at her side. He leaned over and whispered in her ear, "Cooper cheats."

She shrugged. "Told you."

Lisa said grace and the family dug in. Conversations carried around the table, getting louder as the meal progressed. Dad caught them up on Trail Conservancy issues, and Lisa told them about the changes they wanted to make for next year's Trail Days. They talked about what a cute couple Lucy and Rick made, and Cooper shared a story about a recent car accident with a miraculous outcome.

Three-quarters of the way through the meal, a rare moment of silence ensued.

Avery was about to remark upon it when Gavin spoke up. "So, I was thinking about opening my own business."

All eyes darted to Gavin. Forks froze midscoop. Drinks stopped en route.

As if he hadn't just made the announcement they'd hoped for since his return to Riverbend Gap two years ago, Gavin shoved a bite of baked beans into his mouth.

"Oh, honey"—Lisa palmed her chest—"I am so happy to hear that."

"We need a residential builder here in town," Jeff said. "I think you'd do real good business."

"I think so too," Gavin said. "I've been collecting data and making a tentative plan. But I'm going to need some help. Anyone know of a competent contractor for hire?"

Avery glanced between Gavin and Wes. Was that a trick question? Was her brother considering hiring Wes? This would be his dream job.

Gavin frowned at Wes. "I'm talking about you, Garrett."

Wes lowered his napkin, the corner of his mouth turning up. "Well . . . you said competent, so I wasn't sure."

Cooper's laugh bellowed in the waning twilight. "I like this guy. You should bring him around more often, Ave." He took a big bite of his burger.

Wes and Gavin held eye contact as the moment stretched like a wire, vibrating with tension.

Finally, Gavin spoke. "What, are you gonna make me beg, Bro?"

Avery raised her hand. "I, for one, would enjoy that."

"Ditto," Cooper said.

Gavin shot his siblings a glare. "I don't need an answer tonight. You can think about it if you want."

Wes took a swig of lemonade, taking his time. "It so happens I might consider a new challenge. Would you be a pain-in-the-butt boss?"

"Probably. But I pay well—and I might be willing to consider a partnership down the road."

"Partnership, huh?"

"*If* you can pull your own weight"—Gavin's gaze shifted to Avery and back—"and if you treat my sister right."

Avery snuggled up to Wes's side, curling her hand around his muscular arm. She placed a kiss on his bristly cheek. "Don't you worry . . . he always treats me right."

Gavin held up a palm. "And I don't have to hear about any of *that* stuff. Ever."

"I'd like two weeks off annually to do volunteer work."

"I'm sure we could work something out."

Wes seemed to consider for a moment. Then he gave a nod. "All right then. It's a deal."

Gavin straightened in his seat. "Seriously?"

"We'll talk salary later, but if you're fair, you've got yourself a deal."

"Should've made him sweat it out a little," Cooper said.

Avery nudged Wes. "At least overnight."

"It's going to take some time to get things up and running," Gavin said. "I haven't even found a good location yet."

"I'm in no hurry. I've got my job at Valley Cabinet to keep me busy."

"Maybe we could meet this week and talk things over."

"Yeah. Sounds good."

The family went back to their meals, the topic going from the new business to the cold spell coming the following week.

Gavin went quiet again. Maybe the start-up was what had her brother so introspective lately.

It was almost dark by the time the family gathered their plates and carried them into the house. Wes and Avery were the last ones at the table, sitting beneath the glow of a thousand emerging stars and the twinkle of white string lights. A cool breeze blew, stirring the canopy of leaves, and somewhere in the distance an owl gave a lonely hoot.

Avery leaned into Wes's side, inhaling the familiar smell of him. "So, that's pretty exciting. But are you sure you want to work for my brother?"

He draped his arm around her shoulders. "Would you mind? I mean, is that too messy for you, mixing business with family?"

She snorted. "You do realize Cooper's new wife is my best friend, and we work together?"

"True. I guess that's worked out okay."

"Minus some very tense moments last year. But we got through it. That's the thing about family—when conflicts occur, we talk things out and try to remember we love each other."

"Well, you know I'm on a learning curve where family is concerned. But I promise I'm working on my communication skills."

She leaned closer, nuzzling his nose. "I like the way you communicate," she whispered.

"Oh yeah?" He brushed her lips with his.

Her pulse sped at the touch. She set her hand on his thigh, relishing the feel of hard muscle beneath her palm.

"So, what did that kiss say to you?" The low timber of his voice sent a shiver down her arms.

"That's easy." She brushed his nose with hers again, the warmth of his breath teasing her lips. "It said, 'I love you.'"

"My skills are improving by the second."

"Hmm." She gave him a saucy smile. "I actually think they could use more work."

"You do, huh?"

"Much, much more work."

"Well, practice does make perfect," he said before he leaned in and went to work.

Acknowledgments

Bringing a book to market takes a lot of effort from many different people. I'm so incredibly blessed to partner with the fabulous team at HarperCollins Christian Fiction, led by publisher Amanda Bostic: Kimberly Carlton, Caitlin Halstead, Jodi Hughes, Margaret Kercher, Becky Monds, Kerri Potts, Savannah Summers, and Laura Wheeler.

Not to mention all the wonderful sales reps and amazing people in the rights department—special shout-out to Robert Downs!

Thanks especially to my editor, Kimberly Carlton. Your incredible insight and inspiration help me take the story deeper, and for that I am so grateful! Thanks also to my line editor, Julee Schwarzburg, whose attention to detail makes me look like a better writer than I really am.

Ronda Wells, MD, was gracious enough to read the manuscript for medical errors. And OB nurse Kimberly Fenstermacher helped me fine-tune the labor and delivery scene. I'm so grateful for their help! Also, my husband, builder extraordinaire Kevin Hunter, answered my many construction questions. Thanks, honey! Any mistakes that made it into print are my own.

Author Colleen Coble is my first reader and sister of my heart. Thank you, friend! This writing journey has been ever so much more fun because of you.

I'm grateful to my agent, Karen Solem, who's able to somehow make sense of the legal garble of contracts and, even more amazing, help me understand it.

To my husband, Kevin, who has supported my dreams in every way possible—I'm so grateful! To all our kiddos: Chad, Trevor and Babette, and Justin and Hannah, who have favored us with two beautiful granddaughters. Every stage of parenthood has been a grand adventure, and I look forward to all the wonderful memories we have yet to make!

A hearty thank-you to all the booksellers who make room on their shelves for my books—I'm deeply indebted! And to all the book bloggers and reviewers, whose passion for fiction is contagious—thank you!

Lastly, thank you, friends, for letting me share this story with you! I wouldn't be doing this without you. Your notes, posts, and reviews keep me going on the days when writing doesn't flow so easily. I appreciate your support more than you know.

I enjoy connecting with friends on my Facebook page, www.facebook.com/authordenisehunter. Please pop over and say hello. Visit my website at www.DeniseHunterBooks.com or just drop me a note at deniseahunter@comcast.net. I'd love to hear from you!

Discussion Questions

1. Which character did you most relate to and why?
2. Despite their plans for the future, Avery and Wes felt a connection that only grew with time. What do you think drew them together? How might their past relationships have played into their connection?
3. Wes grew up with a father who shirked responsibility and made a living duping people. Discuss how this played a role in shaping Wes. Did you have a parent whose behavior may have caused you to go in the complete opposite direction? Discuss.
4. Avery felt guilt and helplessness over the way her mother died, which eventually led her to pursue a career in medicine. What inspired your career?
5. Wes was also dealing with guilt. His friend's sacrifice led him to make an overreaching commitment to Lillian.

How did you feel about that? Has guilt ever led you down a wrong path?

6. Avery's potential genetic condition has been a heavy burden all her life. If you had a fifty-fifty chance of inheriting a deadly disease, would you want to know? Why or why not?

7. Avery's family tended to treat her like a fragile flower because of her potential illness. Do you deal with any kind of disability that causes others to see you or treat you differently? Do you underestimate someone with a disability? What can we learn from Avery and her family?

8. Would you ever take on a major trek like the Appalachian Trail? If yes, what would your trail name be?

9. The last book in the Riverbend Romance series, *Harvest Moon*, will revolve around Gavin, whose love story has been a long time coming. Discuss what you think might be in store for him.

Return for more romance in

Riverbend Gap!

AVAILABLE SEPTEMBER 2022

THOMAS NELSON
Since 1798

A beach wedding. An ex who turns out to be the best man. And a hurricane storming up the coast. What could go wrong?

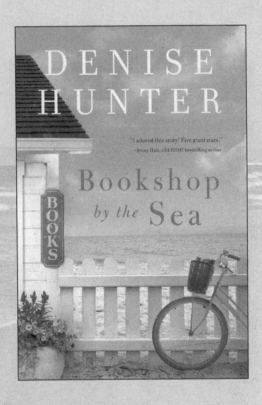

"Sophie and Aiden had me hooked from page one, and I was holding my breath until the very end. Denise nails second-chance romance in *Bookshop by the Sea*. I adored this story! Five giant stars!"

—JENNY HALE, *USA TODAY* BESTSELLING AUTHOR

About the Author

Photo by Amber Zimmerman

Denise Hunter is the internationally published, bestselling author of more than forty books, three of which have been adapted into original Hallmark Channel movies. She has won the Holt Medallion Award, the Reader's Choice Award, the Carol Award, the Foreword Book of the Year Award, and is a RITA finalist. When Denise isn't orchestrating love lives on the written page, she enjoys traveling with her family, drinking chai lattes, and playing drums. Denise makes her home in Indiana where she and her husband raised three boys and are now enjoying an empty nest and two beautiful granddaughters.

DeniseHunterBooks.com
Facebook: @AuthorDeniseHunter
Twitter: @DeniseAHunter
Instagram: @deniseahunter